Into the Mist

Look for these titles by

Maya Banks

Now Available:

Seducing Simon

Colters' Woman

Understood

Overheard

Undenied

Brazen

Love Me, Still

Stay With Me

Reckless

Falcon Mercenary Group Series:

Into the Mist (Book 1)

Into the Lair (Book 2)

Print Anthologies:

The Perfect Gift

Caught by Cupid

Coming Soon:

Amber Eyes

The Cowboys' Mistress

Into the Mist

Maya Banks

A Samhain Publishing, Ltd. publication.

Samhain Publishing, Ltd.
577 Mulberry Street, Suite 1520
Macon, GA 31201
www.samhainpublishing.com

Into the Mist: Falcon Mercenary Group Book 1

Print ISBN: 978-1-60504-015-8
Digital ISBN: 1-59998-069-X

Editing by Jennifer Miller
Cover by Anne Cain

First Samhain Publishing, Ltd. electronic publication: February 2008
First Samhain Publishing, Ltd. print publication: February 2009

Chapter One

She had the look of a woman on a mission. Eli Chance recognized a sexual predator when he saw one. And damn if he didn't want to be her next victim.

He watched from his perch at the bar as she waded through the mass of writhing bodies on the dance floor. Music boomed and swelled, bouncing off the walls and shaking the room. The tight techno beat wielded a frenetic energy, reflected in the wildly rotating laser lights.

The popular Singapore nightclub sheltered a wide variety of people and types, from the very young—too young to be in a nightclub—to the not much older orange-haired, pierced, tattooed throwbacks to the eighties. Mixed in were the deadbeats, those who dealt in prostitution rings, gun running and drug dealing.

And yet, he'd bet his last dollar his mystery woman fell into none of those categories.

She paused on the outer rim of the dance floor, her gaze searching the crowd beyond. Then her eyes settled on him. She moved forward again, her long, dark hair sliding like silk over her shoulders.

Eli raised one brow. Was she looking for him? He held her gaze before allowing his to drop meaningfully down her body. The thin piece of material posing as her shirt was nothing more than a square of satin held together by two strings. One circling her neck and the other tied around her back just below her breasts.

And very nice breasts they were.

She wore jeans tight enough that he guessed it hadn't been an easy task to put them on, but he appreciated the effort, because he simply knew her ass would be to die for. And he would get a glimpse before the night was over.

He moved down her shapely legs until he got to her feet. Lord have mercy, she wore combat boots. *Color me in lust.*

"Like what you see?"

He lifted his gaze back to her face. She was a mere foot away from him now, and he leaned forward, wanting to see the color of her eyes. All the damn flashing lights in this joint were about to make his head bust wide open, not to mention they were interfering with his perusal of the woman he planned to take home for the night.

She stared back at him unflinchingly. She raised one eyebrow in question.

"Yeah, I like," he drawled.

She moved past him to the bar, and he was forced to turn sideways on his barstool. He pulled his head back to let his gaze wander down her backside. The "shirt" she wore had no back. It bared a tantalizing expanse of her skin. And her ass... Oh yeah, he liked very much.

She wasn't all soft woman and curves. She had a lean muscle tone that bespoke of a rigid fitness regimen. Nice. He bet he could bounce a quarter off her abdomen. But her breasts and ass? Just perfect. Just the right amount of soft and swell. He listened as she gave her drink order to the bartender, puzzling over her accent. It wasn't one he could place, and he was an expert at languages. At first, he'd thought it sounded Eastern European, but she had hints of other places mixed in. A little American, a little French and maybe even a little Hispanic. A regular mutt.

He leaned in closer, not wanting to shout over the bellowing music. "Where are you from?"

She cocked her head sideways, her green eyes glowing from the florescent tube of lighting that ran the length of the bar.

"I'm from lots of places."

Vague heifer. Ah well, it didn't really matter. It wasn't as though he was marrying her.

The bartender slid a shot glass toward her, and she curled

her hand around it, raising it and throwing it back in one gulp. Eli liked a woman who could hold her liquor. Unless being sober was an impediment to him getting her into bed.

She turned around, resting her elbows against the bar as she gazed out at the sea of gyrating bodies. Then she slid him a sideways glance from narrowed eyes.

"Want to dance?" she asked.

Eli leaned back on his stool and let his eyes glide suggestively over her. "I've got a better idea. Why don't we ditch the dancing and hit the bed? My bed."

She turned more fully to him, staring coolly.

"I said dance, pretty boy. Not fuck."

He trailed a finger down a strand of hair hanging over her shoulder. "I may be a lot of things, but pretty I ain't. Let me take you to bed, and I'll show you. You look like a woman who likes it rough."

She stared at him for a long moment, her expression indecipherable. Then she laughed.

She pushed away from the bar and walked, if you could call that come-and-get-me strut walking, toward the dance floor. She hooked one finger over her shoulder in a come-hither motion, but she never once looked back at him.

Hell. He didn't dance. Dancing was for fucking pussies, but if she wanted to do some dirty dancing moves on him while he stood there, he certainly wouldn't tell her no.

He followed her onto the floor, dodging hands and hips the entire way. She stopped in the middle and turned to face him. Game on.

He stood, legs apart, his arms folded across his midsection. It was her move.

She closed the distance between them, her hips swaying and those delectable breasts straining at the thin material covering them. As she reached her arms up to twine around his neck, he moved his hands up her taut belly to cup her breasts.

She tensed, and then as if willing herself to relax, slowly melted into his embrace. The night got more interesting all the time.

He bent his head, sliding his hands around to her back.

When his lips were close to her ear, he asked, "What's your name, sugar?"

She pulled away and stared into his eyes. "What do you want my name to be?"

"Mine," he replied. "Just say you're mine for the night."

"Still determined to fuck me."

"Not determined, sugar. Convinced."

He could swear fear flashed in her eyes for the briefest of seconds. But when he blinked it was gone, replaced by a sultry stare. Her lips twisted into a tempting pout. The kind that dared a man to taste them. He was never one to back down from a dare.

He hauled her against him, cupping her cheek in his palm. His lips found hers with a command to submit. She didn't surrender right away, but he deepened the kiss, demanding access. Finally, her lips parted and he slid his tongue inside. He'd been dying to taste her, wondered if she tasted as exotic as she looked.

He wasn't disappointed.

He scraped the tip of her tongue with his teeth, nibbling and sucking at her soft flesh. A groan worked from low in his throat. Forgotten for a moment was his curiosity over why she'd sought him out. He didn't care as long as she let him take her out of here.

Her chest rose and fell as she panted against his mouth. Her small hands gripped his shirt, but he could feel her touch all the way through the material. Damn, but he wanted her hands on his naked skin. Why the hell were they fucking around in this human wasteland when they could be miles away enjoying each other? And maybe he could find out who the hell she was and why she was looking for him.

"Let's get out of here, sugar."

A myriad of expressions flew across her face before she slowly nodded. He didn't waste any time waiting for her to change her mind. He took her hand and pulled her toward the exit.

A blast of hot, humid air hit him square in the face as he strode into the small alley that paralleled the club. By the time they made it to the sleek sports car parked a half block away, sweat dampened the T-shirt he wore.

He opened the passenger door for his lady then hurried around to slide behind the wheel. He keyed the ignition and revved the engine, the motor purring as he accelerated down the street.

She didn't say much, another point in her favor. He could think of a dozen better uses for her mouth than talking. They drove the rest of the way in silence. A few minutes later, he pulled into the parking garage of a downtown apartment complex.

"Home sweet home, sugar."

She turned her head, cocking an eyebrow. "Does that Southern boy charm work for you all the time?"

He flashed her a grin. "It worked on you."

She eyed him evenly. "Your charm had little to do with it."

She intrigued him. No two ways about it.

He got out of the car and started around to her door, but she slid out and met him halfway. As she moved closer to him, he started to curl his arm around her waist, but she shied away, keeping a foot of distance between them. He shrugged and walked into the building.

They took the elevator up, and a few seconds later, he unlocked the door to his apartment and ushered her inside where the welcoming blast of cooler air hit him in the face.

She walked into the small living room as he flipped on the lights. Her hands crept around her middle. As before in the bar, he sensed hesitancy on her part, but then she turned and let her arms fall to her sides. "Do you have something to drink?" she asked in a husky voice.

All he really wanted to do was get her into bed as fast as he could, but he supposed he could slow down and try to act a little civilized.

He walked over to the liquor cabinet and opened the beveled glass doors. "What would you like?"

She moved in beside him and laid her hand on his arm. "What would *you* like?"

Hell if that wasn't a loaded question.

"To drink," she said in an amused voice.

"Whatever you're having, sugar."

He stepped back and allowed her access to the cabinet. She pulled two glasses down then reached for the first bottle on the shelf. She didn't seem particularly discerning when it came to her liquor.

He almost missed what she did next. Almost.

It was done so quickly and efficiently, he almost thought he'd imagined her making the dump into his drink with an expert swipe of her hand. Conniving little wench had spiked it. The question was whether she was trying to kill him or incapacitate him. Neither option was particularly enticing. Not when the alternative was spending the evening between her legs.

She turned with a smile and handed the glass to him. He took it and raised it to his lips, watching her as he did. A subtle spark of satisfaction and triumph lit her eyes.

As she tilted her own glass back to take a swallow, he lowered his and set it on the sideboard. She frowned.

"Is something wrong?"

"Not at all, sugar. I'm just not very thirsty. I find I'm craving something else altogether."

To her credit, she didn't let her thwarted attempt bother her. She set her drink down then sauntered over to him and slid her fingers into the waistband of his jeans. He sucked in all available breath when the tips delved into his underwear and scraped over the ridge of his dick.

Slowly, he squeezed the air back out of his lungs and gripped her wrist in his hand, gently pulling her away.

She raised that eyebrow again, an action that was starting to get on his nerves.

"What's your hurry, sugar?" he asked.

She shrugged. "Well, if you don't want me..."

He yanked her against him in one swift motion. She let out a small gasp when he swung her up into his arms and headed for the bedroom.

When he shouldered past the door, he nudged the light switch with his elbow then moved toward the bed where he dumped her in the middle.

Her lips quirked into a smile as she rose up on her elbows. "You going to stand there all night, cowboy?"

When he didn't move, she edged off the bed and reached for him again. This time he didn't stop her. She obviously had a desire to dictate the action, and he could be a reasonable man. When a gorgeous woman wanted to call the shots, he didn't object. At least not until he could get her naked and underneath him.

He allowed her to start peeling his clothes away. She started with his jeans, hiking them down his legs. He kicked off his shoes and did a little dance step until he was free of the confining denim.

She moved forward again, sliding her hands underneath his shirt and pressing her palms against his abdomen. He flinched as a thousand teeny tiny needles assaulted his skin. The chemistry between them was off the hook. At this rate, he'd go off like the Fourth of July before he ever got between her legs.

With tantalizing slowness, she edged the shirt up and over his head. She rose up on tiptoe, straining to reach, but he wasn't about to help her. Not when she was at full stretch, her breasts plumped against his chest. Hell, he'd sit back and enjoy the view.

Finally, she wrestled the shirt from him and tossed it aside. Then she went for his underwear. He let out an agonized hiss when her fingers brushed across the sensitive skin of his groin. Her palms smoothed down his legs as the underwear inched lower.

His cock sprang free as if it had a life of its own, and half the time it did. It strained outward, begging for her touch. When he was free of his underwear, she ran her hand back up his leg and cupped his heavy sac in her hand.

God, he ached. Her fingers all wrapped around his balls was enough to make him explode. Then she let go, and he groaned.

She stepped back, her eyes running up and down the length of his body.

"You like what you see, sugar?"

"Very nice," she purred. "Nothing wrong with your

equipment."

He grinned and wrapped a hand around his straining cock. He pulled gently, working his hand up and down as he grew even harder.

"Lie down," she murmured, gesturing toward the bed. He wondered what her back-up plan was now that he wasn't passed out or dead from whatever drug she'd slipped him.

He wagged his ass over to the bed like an obedient stooge, but really, what red-blooded man wouldn't be jumping to do this woman's bidding? Hell, right now, he'd leap out the window naked and bark at the moon if that's what it took.

He flopped onto the bed, legs spread, hands behind his head. If she wanted to run the show, he'd let her. For the time being.

She reached into her back pocket and pulled out a foil-wrapped packet. Came prepared, did she? It was then it registered that she didn't carry a purse. Combat boots and no purse. He might have just lost his heart.

As she moved to the bed, she ripped at the edge of the condom pack with her teeth. She threw the foil away and slipped the tip of the condom between her lips. A red condom. What the hell?

Okay, he wasn't arguing. Really. She could put a pink rubber on him, and he wouldn't bitch, but the idea of a colored dick set his teeth on edge.

All complaints ceased when she crawled up between his legs and lowered her head to his thighs. Oh hell, she wasn't.

Fuck. She was.

She slipped the condom over the tip of his cock with her mouth. And she didn't stop there. Warm, moist lips surrounded him as she slowly eased her way down.

Fuck, she was well on her way to deep-throating him. He liked head as well as the next guy, but he'd never had a woman slide a condom all the way down his dick with her mouth.

The head of his cock bumped against the soft flesh of her throat, and her tongue unrolled the remainder of the condom. Unbelievable.

Slowly, she began inching her way back up, her mouth

working its magic over the thin latex. If ever there was a time he cursed condoms, that time was now. What he wouldn't give to feel that tongue and nothing else.

"Get your damn clothes off," he growled.

The corner of her mouth quirked in amusement as she stared up at him. "Now who's in a hurry?"

"You can take them off or I'll tear them off," he said calmly.

Annoyance flitted across her face, but she set to work untying the little string that held her shirt on. When the scrap of material fell away, his pulse sped up. God almighty, the woman had gorgeous breasts. And her nipples. Perfect.

He reached out to palm one, wanting to feel the slight weight in his hand, but she pulled away and climbed off the bed. She bent down to take off her boots, giving him a perfect shot of her breasts as they swayed with the motion. Then she stood and shimmied out of her tight jeans, no small feat, and hooked her thumbs in the waistband of her underwear. It was interesting to note that her panties were white and functional. Kind of like her combat boots.

She yanked her underwear down, and his eyes drifted to the curls that shielded her pussy. His cock tightened, became unbearably hard.

She noted his reaction and pinned him with her emerald stare. Her small, pink tongue darted out and ran across her upper lip as she moved back to the bed.

The mattress dipped as she climbed between his legs. Soft hands gripped his hips as she straddled him. In one quick motion, she arched over him then sheathed herself fully on him.

His body jerked in reaction, and he shut his eyes against the pleasure, sharp and exploding. God, she was tight. So tight and hot. Her pussy convulsed and quivered around his cock, sucking him deeper into her body.

He reached up to cup her breasts, rolling his thumbs over the pink nipples. They tightened under his touch, and when she would have pulled away, he slid one hand around her back, holding her in place.

She increased her pace, riding him as if she wanted to get him off quickly. And maybe that was her back-up plan. Too bad.

He trailed his fingers across her lean stomach and dipped lower to the curls of her pussy. She froze then pushed down against him. He wouldn't be deterred.

He eased one finger between them, seeking her hot, wet flesh. He circled her clit and stroked the taut bud. Her pussy spasmed around his cock, and despite her cool façade, he could see her start to falter.

Her entire body quivered against his, and she resumed her ride, rotating her hips as she bucked up and down on him. He'd had about enough of allowing her to call the shots.

He moved his hand from the small of her back to her hip, and before she could react, he rolled her underneath him. His cock slid out, but he reached between them and guided his dick back into her pussy.

She looked almost panicked as he thrust forward. And if she wasn't panicking before, she was when he yanked her arms above her head and held them there.

He grinned down at her, knowing he had her right where he wanted her.

"What are you doing?" she gasped.

"Not letting you call the shots."

She opened her mouth as if she'd retort, but he didn't give her the opportunity. He swooped down, capturing her lips with his.

She tasted sweet and spicy. He refused to hurry the kiss even as she squirmed beneath him. When he finally pulled away, she panted for breath.

The soft skin of her neck beckoned him, and he bent, nibbling a path down the curve of her shoulder. A soft moan filtered through his ears, and he smiled triumphantly. The little wench wasn't as unaffected as she'd like to be.

She stirred restlessly against him as he rolled his hips forward, diving deep into her warmth.

"Please," she whispered.

"Don't worry, sugar, I plan to," he murmured against her ear.

He licked the lobe then sucked it between his teeth. He nibbled his way around her ear before sinking his teeth into the soft skin of her neck.

She arched her back then wrapped her arms tight around him. Her nails scored his shoulders, and he moaned low in his throat. Little wildcat.

"That's it, sugar. Let it go."

He ran his hands underneath her back and held her close while his hips pumped against her. Damn, she felt incredible. If he didn't get a grip, he was going to shoot his wad before things got really good.

With reluctance, he withdrew. She whimpered in protest, but he moved his body down hers, kissing a path to her breasts.

He'd waited all night to sample her nipples, and he wasn't going to rush the experience. He flicked his tongue around the rigid peak, leaving a damp trail on her skin.

A soft sigh escaped her when he sucked the puckered tip into his mouth. He pulled at the nipple, suckling in a steady rhythm. With his free hand, he reached down to slide his fingers between her legs.

He eased inside her, stroking the inner walls of her pussy. Her breath hitched and escaped her throat in a ragged sound. He smiled.

"Like that, sugar?"

She moaned in response and spread her legs wider for him. Unable to resist the invitation, he let go of her nipple, licking it one last time before he moved his big body further down the bed.

His mouth hovered over the juncture of her thighs. He looked up to see her green eyes through the narrow slits of her eyelids. They glittered with need. Gone was the wall, the very visible barrier she'd worn the entire evening. In its place was a tangible yearning.

Gently, he parted the tender folds of her pussy. The pink skin glistened with the evidence of her need. He trailed a finger over the slick flesh, circling the soft bud of her clit.

Then he lowered his head and lapped his tongue over the quivering button. She jerked beneath him, arching her back in a spasmodic motion. He smiled but didn't move his head.

He loved her taste, sweet and silky in his mouth. With his fingers, he spread her wider, allowing his mouth easier access. He circled her tight entrance with his tongue, enjoying each and every time he made her twitch.

It'd been a while since he enjoyed going down on a woman this much. He could definitely stay between her legs for the better part of the night.

As he dipped his tongue inside her pussy, her thighs clamped around his head, and she trembled violently against him.

"You have to stop," she gasped.

Oh, hell no, he wasn't stopping. He wanted to make her come in his mouth. He couldn't wait.

He began to lick and suck in earnest. As his mouth moved back up to her clit, he slid two fingers into her pussy, stroking and gliding against the slick walls.

She let out an anguished wail, one that told him how hard she fought against the pleasure he was giving her. Her body convulsed and tightened around him. He pulled his fingers from her pussy and moved his mouth down, thrusting his tongue into the small opening.

She exploded into his mouth in a hot rush. He closed his eyes as she spasmed against his tongue. He licked and nuzzled until he felt her start to come down and relax. She finally went limp against the mattress, and only then did he raise his head to look at her.

She lay against the pillow, her long hair fanned out. Her eyes glittered, and her bottom lip was puffy, no doubt from being pinned between her teeth.

He ached to be back inside her, that velvet sheath of hers encasing his dick. Impatiently, he spread her thighs and moved up, shoving inside her with one hard lunge.

Her harsh exhalation shattered the quiet.

Unable to resist her swollen mouth, he swooped down, capturing her lips hotly. He forced his tongue deep, wanting her to taste herself, to know just how hard she'd come.

Her hands dove into his hair, wrapping tightly around the long strands as she held him against her. A sound of pure male satisfaction rumbled from his chest. She wasn't tender, and he loved that. She was about to pull him bald, but he didn't give a fuck.

He reached down, hooking his hands underneath her legs. Using his arms, he hoisted her legs higher, pushing her knees toward her chest.

The position sent him deeper into her, and he closed his eyes as he surged forward over and over. Her pussy still rippled with the aftershocks of her orgasm, clutching his cock in a staccato motion.

He moved his lips down to her neck again, sinking his teeth into the curve of her shoulder. He sucked in time with his thrusts, wanting to mark her.

She quivered underneath him, her body tightening with the promise of another orgasm. He smiled and kissed the spot he'd been sucking, feathering his lips over the area to soothe it.

Her nails raked his shoulders then dug into his back. He strained against her, trying to hold out, wanting her to come again before he gave in to the cascading force of pleasure rushing over him.

His eyes locked with hers. Then he bent to kiss her. Hot, open-mouthed, raging kiss. Their bodies arched and strained, and he captured her cry of release in his mouth.

He withdrew the tiniest bit then surrendered to the urge to bury himself in her again. He jerked his hips forward in a series of desperate plunges before exploding. He rocked against her over and over until finally he felt the firestorm begin to recede.

He carefully lowered himself until he was pressed close to her body. His chest heaved with exertion, and he gathered her tight in his arms. His lungs felt near to bursting as he dragged painful breaths into them.

After several long seconds, he reluctantly eased himself away from her and reached down for the condom. He tossed it into the garbage can by the bed then carefully pulled her back into his arms. He shifted so they lay side by side.

She breathed hard against him. Then she quieted. He could feel her heart beating wildly against his chest, but she didn't make any motion to remove herself from his embrace.

He reached up toward the headboard and slid his hand along the wall until he felt the light switch. He flipped it, bathing the room in darkness. Then he settled down to wait.

ꝏ

She was patient. Eli would grant her that. He'd lain next to her for three hours feigning sleep, just as she was. She'd even perfected all the sleepy snuggle moves, occasionally stirring and nuzzling closer to him.

But he wasn't fooled.

Obviously her back-up plan was to blind him with mind-numbing sex, although he could swear she never planned to take things as far as she did. It was too bad, really. It figured that the best sex he'd had in at least five years had to come with a woman who may well be trying to kill him.

Thirty minutes later, he fought the urge to succumb to a restful sleep. Then he felt her tense against him. Just the slightest bit, but he knew she was awake.

He willed himself to stay relaxed. He even managed a soft snore as she began to ease away from him. She took her time, moving in incremental spaces, pausing after each movement to evaluate his level of consciousness.

Finally, after an interminable period of time, he felt the bed dip as she got off. He listened as she gathered her clothes, and he assumed she got dressed. Then he heard her soft steps as she left the room.

He cracked one eye open to survey the room, but she wasn't there. He stared up at the ceiling then closed his eyes, summoning the mental energy to shift to mist.

His body floated free from the boundaries and parameters set by his mind. A brief shock rolled over his system before he came apart, quickly reassembling into tiny molecules of water.

It was an addictive surge, one he never tired of. Shedding the constraints of his human body and embracing the freedom of the elements. It was powerful. It was a rush only rivaled by sex.

He hovered over the bed for a split second before shimmering from the room in his search for his mystery woman. He found her in his office rummaging through his desk drawers.

He settled in a small cloud just over her shoulder, intent on seeing just what it was she thought she'd find. He wasn't stupid enough to keep important information just lying around, but she didn't know that, obviously.

She cracked open his laptop, and after a few minutes of trying to access his files without success, she closed it. She pocketed the CD from the drive and moved on to the assorted papers littering the desk.

Suddenly she froze. She whirled around as if expecting to see someone behind her. Her eyes darted warily around the room, and oddly, she focused right where he hovered.

Her instincts were obviously good.

She turned back around, but her demeanor was cautious. She cupped something in her hand then suddenly rocketed from the chair and sprayed a tiny aerosol container directly at him.

"Shift your sorry ass so I can see you."

The spray managed to blow him a couple of feet from where he'd hovered. How the fuck did she know he was there, and how did she know he was a shifter?

And what the hell did she hope to accomplish with her aerosol assault?

She eased sideways, her feet moving her closer to the door.

He streaked to the space between her and the door then materialized right in front of her, granting her wish. If she wanted him, then baby, she'd get him. She just might not like the results.

He reached for her arm, and to his surprise, she allowed him to take it. Then she exploded in a flurry of movement.

She rotated into his body. His head snapped back as she connected with her free hand. She went completely kung fu on his ass, and in the next second he landed on the floor with a thud, staring up at the ceiling in shock.

She gave him no time to shift back. She was out the door in a split second. Crazy bitch had given him the fuck of his life, then laid his ass out on the floor.

He gingerly picked himself up, irritated and impressed all

at the same time that she'd been able to get the drop on him. Okay, yeah, he'd been fooled by the package. Even as toned and fit as she looked and felt, he didn't expect her to take him down with such speed and skill.

The question was, who was she and what had she been looking for? And the million dollar question was how the fuck had she known he was a shifter? That wasn't exactly something he went around broadcasting. For that matter, how had she known where to find him?

He moved around a lot. Never stayed in the same place for longer than a couple of days, and yet she managed to show up in Singapore within a day of his arrival?

This didn't bode well at all.

If she knew about him, did she also know about Braden, Ian and Gabe?

He walked back into the bedroom, rubbing his aching jaw. He delved into his jeans pocket to retrieve his phone and punched in Gabe's number.

It was time to get the team together and figure out just what threat Psycho Woman posed. He wasn't chasing her ass around Singapore, that was for sure. He'd wait until she quit running like a scalded cat and then he'd lock on to her position using the tracking device he'd planted when he was planting other parts of his body in hers.

Chapter Two

Tyana Berezovsky cupped one hand over the end of her pool stick as she watched Damiano Ruiz lean over the table to take his shot. The members of Falcon Mercenary Group were gathered in the game room of their island estate, a common enough practice between missions, but tonight things were strangely silent and strained.

Tyana had arrived back on the island a few hours earlier, and Jonah was itching with impatience to get a report on her mission. And what could she tell him? *How* could she tell him what had transpired?

She grasped a small glass in her other hand, raising it to her lips to drain the expensive whiskey.

She should be toasted by now. She'd never had a huge tolerance for liquor, well, not when compared to her brothers, anyway. But adrenaline still hummed along her veins, even a full day after fleeing Singapore. No matter what she did, how she tried to drown her rioting emotions, she couldn't douse the wildfire.

Off to the side, Jonah Pearson and Maddox St. Pierre watched in silence as D lined up his shot. Jonah took a swig of his beer while Mad Dog carelessly rolled a joint before lighting it up.

They were all indulging more than usual. For D, it was an attempt to leash the beast within him that struggled for control. The injections Tyana gave him were helping less and less, a source of panic and frustration for her. There simply had to be a way to help him. Her encounter with Eli had proved that.

The crack of the balls connecting broke the silence, and D stood up, motioning to Jonah to take his turn.

It wasn't usually so quiet, but an uneasy silence had fallen between the members of Falcon, and no one seemed willing to go out of their way to correct the problem. Jonah and Mad Dog were watching her closely, but neither would bring up her trip to Singapore in front of D. It was a secret they'd all decided was best kept from him, and instead they'd simply told him she was on a mission for Falcon. Which was the truth.

Mad Dog handed D another drink, and Tyana's chest ached as she watched him swallow it down, his eyes flashing in pain. The muscles in D's lithe body strained and spasmed. How much more could he take before he lost all control?

Tyana's eyes stung with unshed tears, and she turned her attention to Jonah as he bent over, his dark eyes narrowing in concentration. He ran one hand through spiked black hair before returning it to the pool stick. With careful precision, he lined up his angle then banked his shot. He grimaced and turned to Mad Dog.

Mad Dog shrugged and ambled over. He started to set his joint down in a nearby ashtray, but Tyana held her fingers out for it.

He blinked in surprise, his blue eyes crinkling in confusion. But he relinquished it to her before turning away to the pool table.

Tyana refused to look at the others who'd stopped to stare. She raised the joint to her lips and inhaled deeply. She kept the smoke in her lungs for a long moment before exhaling. Then she took another long drag, willing the drug to numb her shattered senses.

Her hand shook as she pulled the joint away from her lips. What had happened to her in Singapore? Forty-eight hours after seeking Eli Chance out and seducing him, she still carried with her the burning images of their bodies writhing and undulating.

He was a job, nothing more. It was just sex. Nothing to lose control over. But she had. And how.

He scared the living hell out of her, and there weren't too many things she could say the same about. She'd long ago learned to deal with her monsters. They couldn't hurt her anymore. But this man...

And she had to confront him again.

"What the fuck are you doing?" D asked as he jerked the joint from her hand.

Her head came up, and she stared into D's angry brown eyes. She could see the strain etched into his face. His battle was strong tonight, and she felt guilty for adding to his struggle.

"You don't do this shit," he continued. "What's got into you?"

He turned around and stalked over to Mad Dog, shoving the joint toward him. "I've never had jack to say to you about the shit you do, but keep it away from Ty."

Mad Dog held his hands up in surrender, his beefy arms bulging with a multitude of muscles. "She's never wanted it before, man."

Only Jonah studied her in silence, as if he could see the inner war she waged. She stood there, afraid to meet his stare, afraid of what he'd see if she did.

But now all three turned their attention to her.

She fidgeted slightly and moved toward the table, ready to take her shot. She bit her lip and eyed her target. When she struck the cue ball, it went sailing. Right off the table and through the window on the other side.

The sound of breaking glass made her wince. Shit.

"Everyone out," Jonah barked.

From the corner of her eye, she saw Mad Dog hustle D from the room. A move D wasn't happy about. But he'd had too much to drink to put up much of a fight.

Tyana laid her pool stick down and eased toward the door.

"Not you," Jonah said. "*You*, I want to talk to."

She closed her eyes and slowly turned around to face her older "brother". No, he wasn't her blood, but he might as well be. He certainly cared more about her than any blood relation she'd ever had.

She chanced a look up at him and found him boring holes through her with his stare. He crossed his arms over his chest. They stood, facing each other for several long minutes. She hated when he got all silent. He was a brooding bastard on his best day, but get him riled and he could be positively menacing.

Finally Jonah spoke. Just about the time Tyana was about to tuck tail and run for the hills.

"What the fuck happened, Ty?"

"Nothing," she mumbled. "I'm fine." They didn't normally indulge in too much personal shit, and this was fast encroaching on her comfort zone.

"Bullshit."

They both turned when they heard the door to the game room click open. Mad Dog ambled back in, his gaze assessing the tension between Jonah and Tyana.

"Where's D?" Jonah demanded.

"I put him to bed. He's had enough to drink that he ought to sleep well," Mad Dog rumbled.

Tyana's chest squeezed uncomfortably. "Is he having problems again?"

Mad Dog shrugged, his long hair rippling with the movement. In some ways, he reminded her of Eli. They both had a wild, untamed look about them. But where Mad Dog sported a row of earrings, Eli only had one. A single diamond stud in his left ear. Eli also didn't have any tattoos, and she'd certainly seen enough of his body to know.

An uncomfortable heat centered in her abdomen.

The similarities ended there. Beneath Mad Dog's tough-as-nails exterior lay a big ole teddy bear. He'd never hurt her. Eli...well, he was dangerous.

"No more than usual," Mad Dog said. "I got him drunk enough that he wasn't doing any weird shifting. He didn't try to turn into a bird or anything."

His attempt at a joke fell flat.

"What are you doing back here?" Jonah asked, his question pointed.

Jonah was used to giving the orders, and *most* of the time the rest of them obeyed.

"I wanted to know what the hell was going on with Ty," Mad Dog said evenly.

"And I'm waiting for her to tell me," Jonah said, turning his attention once more to Tyana.

"You guys worry too much," she said crossly. If she injected the right amount of sour indignation they just might buy that nothing was wrong.

Or not.

"What's going on with you, baby?" Mad Dog asked softly. "You're not yourself."

"Don't call me baby."

He crossed the distance between them and cupped her cheek in his hand. "It's kind of hard not to call you baby when I remember the first time I ever saw you. All of twelve years old, all big eyes and more fear than I've seen since. Until now. Now suppose you tell me what the fuck has you so afraid again?"

"Mad Dog. Back off," Jonah said.

Mad Dog slowly dropped his hand and moved back. Jonah walked forward until he and Mad Dog stood shoulder to shoulder in front of her.

"What happened in Singapore, Ty?" Jonah asked.

She looked down and then away. She squeezed her eyes shut, but all she saw was the way Eli looked at her, the way he commanded her body, the way he made her *feel*. Something she hadn't done in more years than she could count.

"You've never come back from a mission like this," Mad Dog growled. "You've been jumpy as hell and distant. What the fuck happened?"

"Spill it, Ty. Every damn word," Jonah said through gritted teeth.

She turned her back, walking to the window that overlooked the ocean, the one she'd just shattered with the damn ball. She curled her arms protectively around herself in a mad effort to draw comfort. It was little wonder the guys were so freaked out by her. This cracked-shell person wasn't her.

A warm, salty breeze blew in from the broken window. In the distance, she could hear the crash of the ocean swells. Moonlight shone and bounced off the dark sheet of water, casting an iridescent glow over the beach.

"I had sex with him," she said in a low voice.

"You did *what*?"

She didn't even know who said it. Both? She could hear two angry men heaving behind her.

Firm hands gripped her shoulders as Jonah turned her around to face him. "Why? Sex was not the plan, Ty. You were supposed to drug him. You were never supposed to take things that far."

She looked away. "I slipped the drug into his drink, but he didn't take it. I didn't see another way, and I made provisions for that possibility."

Mad Dog swore behind Jonah, his blue eyes flashing. "Did he force you, Ty? Did he hurt you?"

"N-no," she stammered. "It wasn't like that."

Jonah directed her gaze back to him. "So what if he didn't take the drug. Damn it, you're a highly trained operative. Taking this guy out should have been a piece of cake. You should have never crawled into bed with him. Do you honestly think D would want you to prostitute yourself for him?"

She yanked away, tears gathering in her eyes. "It doesn't matter what D wants. He's done far worse for me. There is nothing I wouldn't do for him, to help him. Nothing."

Mad Dog ran a hand through his hair, pulling it behind his neck in a ponytail. Then he let it go. "And what did you find out, Ty?"

She closed her eyes. "Nothing."

She found herself being dragged to the couch.

"Sit," Jonah ordered. "Then you tell us everything that happened."

With a resigned sigh, she related the events of the night down to her escape from Eli's apartment.

Again, Jonah swore while Mad Dog muttered under his breath.

When she finished, she chanced a look up at Jonah who regarded her thoughtfully.

"You should have aborted the mission at the first sign that things weren't going as planned. And you damn sure shouldn't have been climbing into bed with him. If D knew, he'd shit a brick, and you know it," Jonah said.

"You handled the situation," Mad Dog said quietly. "So what's bothering you? What's scared you so bad?"

She looked back and forth between him and Jonah, wondering if she should admit what was really bothering her. Mad Dog's eyes narrowed, and he arched an eyebrow expectantly.

"I enjoyed it. The sex, I mean," she said uncomfortably.

Those words shouldn't hurt so much to say. They shouldn't have such power over her. Shouldn't bring back such painful memories or highlight in stark clarity that she'd never had sex for the sake of enjoyment. No, sex was painful, dirty and shameful.

Jonah heaved a deep breath and looked upward in resignation. His hand rose as he motioned to Mad Dog. "This is your department," he muttered as he backed away.

It might have been funny in another instance. Jonah always left the girly stuff to Mad Dog. Patience and understanding weren't Jonah's strong points. Tyana still remembered the birds and the bees talks that Jonah had pawned off on Mad Dog as she had gotten older. Mad Dog had dealt with Tyana's first period. She was a late bloomer in that regard, and Damiano had been as clueless as she was when it came to the *natural* nuances of growing up.

Mad Dog had handled it with an ease that to this day she was grateful for.

"I'll be outside," Jonah said as he headed toward the door.

Tyana sighed and glanced unhappily up at Mad Dog. She didn't want to have this conversation. She'd much prefer him to go away and leave her to brood alone.

Mad Dog knelt in front of the couch and gently cupped her chin in his hand. It was so easy to remember all the times before, when she and D were so young and Mad Dog had soothed their fears and nightmares.

"Did he hurt you?" he asked.

She slowly shook her head.

"Ty, it's okay to have enjoyed it. I'm guessing he had a pretty good time too."

Her cheeks tightened uncomfortably.

"Sex is supposed to be enjoyed. You're not a little girl anymore. Those bastards can't hurt you. No one will ever hurt you while me or the others are around. Do you understand that?"

"It scared me," she admitted. "I lost it. For a moment..." She gulped, not wanting to relate just what had happened in that moment.

"For a moment what?" he prompted.

She looked down, shame crawling up her spine. "For a moment I forgot all about D, about why I was there, what I was after."

He chuckled softly and nudged her chin upward. "That's what good sex does."

"I don't know what to do," she said miserably. "I acted like some green moron on her first mission. I can't afford it to happen again."

"It won't happen again, because you're not going anywhere near him," he said pointedly.

"I have to go, Mad Dog. D can't hold out much longer. I won't lose him," she said fiercely. "And Eli was stable. I saw him. He shifted right in front of me. He even had clothes. How could he have conjured clothes? He obviously has great control over his abilities which proves there has to be a way to help D."

Mad Dog gave her a look so full of love and sympathy she flinched. "Ty, when are you going to stop punishing yourself?" he asked softly. "What happened to you and D wasn't your fault. The things that happened to him weren't your fault. You can't spend your life trying to make up for things that were out of your control."

"I can't forget that he gave up so much to protect me," she whispered.

He stood and gently pulled Tyana up in front of him. Then he folded her into his arms and held her against his strong chest.

"You have to stop blaming yourself," he said quietly against her hair. "D doesn't blame you. Neither should you."

Before she could muster a response, he pulled away from her and brushed his thumb across her cheek.

"You should head on to bed and get some rest. You're running on empty."

She nodded and turned away. She could feel his gaze as she walked out of the game room, knew he would be watching her closely over the next few days, if not weeks.

As she stepped out the door, Jonah straightened from his position against the wall.

She tensed and waited.

"We need to get something straight, Ty," he said with no preamble. "I'm pulling rank. Not as FMG leader, but as your brother. You know and I know there isn't an assignment you can't handle. I trust you implicitly. But as your brother, I'm shutting you down. You aren't going anywhere near Eli Chance again. Are we clear? I'll tie you to your bed if I have to, and you know I'm not bullshitting you. We'll find another way to help D."

Tyana stiffened. She wanted to scream. She wanted to lash out at Jonah. She wanted to cry. But she did none of those things. She stood there rigidly, hands balled into fists at her sides.

They stared at each other for a long moment. Finally Jonah broke the awkward silence.

"Are you okay?" he asked, and she knew he was referring to her conversation with Mad Dog.

She nodded. "Yeah, I'm cool. Heading up to bed."

He looked as if he wanted to say something further, but he nodded and walked back into the game room where no doubt he and Mad Dog would have a long talk about her discussion with Mad Dog. She cringed.

She'd always been treated as one of the guys, but now they were going to see her as a vulnerable sister. Just another girl who needed their overbearing protection. She should have just kept her damn mouth shut and lied through her teeth.

Emitting a disgusted sigh, she trudged up the stairs toward her room. When she got to D's door, she paused before sliding her hand over the knob.

She quietly pushed it open and walked inside. D was on the bed, his big body curled into a defensive gesture. It was a position she was intimately familiar with.

Even in sleep, he fought for control. Sweat beaded his forehead, and his muscles contorted and spasmed in his chest and arms. He let out a low moan, and Tyana bent to soothe a hand over his face.

There was no question of her offering comfort. She eased into bed beside him and wrapped her arms around him, just as she'd done so many other nights.

His arm crept around her even as he slept, an automatic motion born of years of habit. They held on tight to each other as Tyana drifted into sleep. The two of them against the world.

ᘓ

Jonah strode into the game room to see Mad Dog lighting another joint. There was a weariness to Mad Dog's face that Jonah hadn't seen in a long time. Mad Dog looked up as Jonah drew closer.

"What the fuck are we going to do about Eli Chance?" he demanded.

Jonah crossed his arms over his chest then relaxed them again and put his hands on the back of the couch. "Short answer? I don't know."

"Ty said he was stable, that he shifted at will and had complete control over his abilities. I'd say that's a big point of interest for us. What if Ty is right and he could lead us to a cure for D?"

"Ty is going to keep her ass out of this," Jonah bit out. He'd seen the fear and uncertainty in her eyes, and it was something he swore he'd never have to look at again once he and Mad Dog took her and D in. It pissed him off that Eli Chance had rattled her so badly. It pissed him off even more that his confidence in Ty's ability to handle herself was shaken.

"We've been gathering intel on Eli and his team for weeks," Mad Dog said evenly. "Ty was supposed to be on a simple fact-finding mission. Well, she found out plenty. The bastard is stable which means his team probably is as well."

"We don't know that for a fact," Jonah said.

Mad Dog made a rude sound. "They all got gassed by the

same chemical. D is a shifter, and we now know for sure Eli is as well. It's not a stretch to say that his team also developed the ability. And if Eli is stable, what are the chances that his team isn't? They obviously got help from somewhere. We just need to figure out how and where. I'm not one for walking up and saying *hey, buddy, can you help my brother out* after he left D for dead and skedaddled with his teammates."

Jonah's jaw ticked in anger. The truth was, he wanted Eli Chance's blood. Now more than ever. If it hadn't been for Ty intervening, Jonah and Mad Dog would have gone after the asshole and taken him out. But she viewed Chance as a means to help D, and so Jonah had allowed her to approach him in Singapore. Big mistake. One he wouldn't make twice. He was done allowing Ty any leeway when it came to Eli Chance.

He looked back up at Mad Dog. "We let things calm down a bit. Allow Chance to relax his guard, and then you and I will take him out. I don't want him to see us coming until he's staring death in the face."

"And if he does have information that can help D?" Mad Dog asked.

"Then he'll tell us before he dies."

Mad Dog nodded. "Good enough." He exhaled a thin plume of smoke then stubbed the joint out in the ashtray.

Jonah turned and walked out of the game room. He trudged up the stairs feeling a hell of a lot older than he had just a few hours before. The burden of responsibility for his family, his teammates, weighed heavily. Things were fast going straight to hell, and he didn't like the feeling of helplessness that gripped him.

As he passed D's room, he stopped and frowned when he saw the door slightly ajar. They were careful to keep the door closed. Usually locked. A measure as much for D's protection as their own.

He nudged the door open and peered inside. He swore softly when he saw Ty in bed with D, the two wrapped protectively around each other. It wasn't a new sight, but in recent weeks, he'd cautioned Ty to be more careful. D was growing more unstable. He couldn't control when and how he shifted, and he retained none of his human characteristics or understanding. He could easily hurt Ty, never meaning to, never realizing it until it was too late.

Overwhelming guilt squeezed Jonah's chest. He hated that Ty blamed herself for D's pain. Jonah knew whose fault it was D was in this predicament. It was Jonah's.

D should have never gone on that mission to Ahdarji. It should have been Jonah who led the American team. He had more expertise, more experience with all things Ahdarjian. He should, it was the country of his birth. But his anger, his vow never to return, had placed D in a position he should have never been in.

It should have been Jonah. And he'd live with that for the rest of his life.

He moved quietly to the bed, and he gently disentangled D's arms from Ty. Then he picked her up, cradling her in his arms.

He walked out of the room and down the hall to Ty's bedroom. He laid her on the bed and pulled the covers down, lifting her again before settling her back down on the sheets. He pulled the comforter over her and tucked her in. He kissed the top of her head before leaving the room.

He backtracked to D's room, checking on his sleeping brother one last time before retreating, locking the door securely on his way out.

Chapter Three

Tyana jogged along the beach, occasionally skirting the incoming surf. Usually she jogged a few miles as part of her daily workout, but today she pushed herself beyond her usual endurance.

She darted closer to the water then away again when the waves chased her back. Her shoes left deep imprints in the wet sand, and her legs ached from the strain of the sand sucking her feet downward.

The morning sun beat on her bare shoulders. Sweat beaded and rolled down her back, making the thin material of the muscle shirt cling to her skin.

She scrubbed her arm over her forehead and pushed herself further along the beach. Her mind centered and focused on the issue plaguing her.

Despite Jonah's insistence that she not go after Eli, she knew she had no choice but to confront him again. Somehow she had to find out how he maintained such control over his shifting abilities. Maybe they'd gotten their hands on a cure.

D had led Eli's hostage recovery team into Ahdarji to extract two prisoners. She knew from the file they'd compiled on Eli's team that they were a highly specialized, highly trained former military combat unit. With their contacts, it wasn't unreasonable that they'd been able to seek help when they all turned into unmanageable shapeshifters.

If they possessed the know-how to help D, then by God, she'd track them down. She'd sleep with the devil himself if it meant her brother would find peace.

The formula a trusted doctor friend had come up with had at first been successful in controlling D's shifts. But as more time elapsed, D had grown resistant to the injections. The aerosol that had prevented shifting for several hours at a time had long since failed to be effective.

It hadn't worked on Eli either, but then Eli had shifted with ease, his mastery of his body and abilities apparent in the way he'd taunted her.

The sun lifted higher in the sky as she continued to push her aching body. She rounded the eastern corner of the tiny island and headed down the southern strip of the beach.

When she raised her head to look down the sandy stretch, she saw Mad Dog step onto the beach from the rocky path leading up to the main house. He motioned her over then stood watching her, arms crossed over his chest.

She sighed and jogged toward him, irritated at the disruption to her solitude.

"Jonah's called a meeting," Mad Dog called out as soon as she drew within hearing distance. "We've got company coming."

On cue she heard the *whop whop* of an approaching helicopter. Mad Dog reached out to pull her close to him, and he urged her under the cover of the trees lining the rocky path to the house.

"What's the meeting for and who's coming?" she asked as they started the climb to the house.

It wasn't like Jonah to allow a meeting on their island. When they met a client, they always did so in a large international city.

"I don't know," he muttered. "It came through Burkett."

Tyana raised an eyebrow in surprise. Burkett rarely got involved in their jobs. Though if he'd recommended a client, she could understand why Jonah was at least entertaining the offer.

"Be on guard," he said as they neared the house. "I don't like that Jonah let them come here. Our location has always been a secret." He turned to look at her. "Are you packing?"

She shook her head. She'd left her gun in her room while she'd gone jogging.

He reached into his jacket and pulled out a Glock. She

nearly chuckled. He likely had two more guns and at least three knives stashed on his big body. Knives were his specialty. There didn't exist a way he couldn't defend himself with a blade.

He pressed the cool metal into her hand. Then he shrugged out of his jacket and draped it over her shoulders. "Come on. Jonah's waiting."

"And D?" she asked.

Mad Dog shook his head. "He's still sleeping. I gave him another injection early this morning. He's fighting..." He let his voice trail off as they entered the house.

"His body is fighting the injections," she said softly.

"Yeah, something like that. I've called Marcus to come out and take another look at him."

"He can't last much longer like this and you know it," Tyana said fiercely. "You know Eli Chance is our best hope right now. We need to go after him."

"If you hope to sway me against Jonah, it isn't going to happen. In this we're united. Call us overprotective older brothers, but we're not going to sacrifice our baby sister for our baby brother. It don't work like that. We'll find a way to help D. One that doesn't involve you getting yourself killed."

Tyana ground her teeth but didn't argue. When Jonah and Mad Dog made up their minds about something, there wasn't anything she could do to sway them.

She pushed her arms into the sleeves of Mad Dog's jacket and shoved the gun into the inside pocket as they headed down the hall to the meeting room. They stepped in to see Jonah standing behind his desk, arms crossed, a serious expression creasing his face.

"What's going on?" Tyana asked as she dropped into a chair in front of the desk.

"We've got company," Jonah said grimly.

She lifted one brow. "You let them come here?"

He returned her gaze. "I had our pilot pick them up. He flew a flight pattern that would have *you* confused about where you were going. And I made damn sure members of our security team frisked them for any GPS equipment. I think we're just fine."

She winced at his rebuke. He didn't like that she'd questioned his judgment, and in his defense, it certainly wasn't something she normally did.

"I'm sorry," she began. She was interrupted when the intercom beeped. Jonah leaned forward, pressing the button on his desk.

"Yeah."

"They're here. We're coming up."

Tyana recognized the voice as their head of security. Jonah employed a dozen men to maintain the tight security net around their island. In short, no one got on or off the island without Jonah's permission.

"*Who's* here, Jonah?" she asked.

"Someone about a job," he said shortly. "Burkett called and asked as a special favor for us to entertain what the man has to say."

She frowned. Burkett never asked for favors.

A few moments later, a knock sounded at the door.

"Come," Jonah called.

The door opened and Henderson, their chief of security, entered. Behind him walked a man in an expensive business suit. Smarmy was the first word that came to Tyana's mind. But then a lot of their clients weren't exactly the upper crust of humanity.

He was flanked by what looked to be two personal bodyguards who were in turn surrounded by members of FMG's security detail.

"Burkett said you were interested in hiring our services," Jonah said abruptly. But then he'd never been one for formalities or beating around the bush. He seemed on edge, and Tyana knew he wasn't keen on having clients on their home turf. Must be one hell of a favor he owed Burkett to allow people on their island.

The man pulled his sunglasses off, a flashy move that didn't impress Tyana. His gaze flickered around the room until it settled on Tyana, making her shift uncomfortably beneath his scrutiny.

Mad Dog moved closer to her and slid his hand over her

shoulder.

"I was under the impression there were four of you," the man said mildly.

Jonah scowled. "You're wasting my time. Either outline the job you want to hire us for, or leave."

The man raised an eyebrow but smiled, flashing straight white teeth. "Very well."

He reached inside his suit jacket and withdrew a folder. He flipped it onto Jonah's desk. "We'd like you to deliver these three men. One of them we want alive. It's imperative that he isn't harmed, merely immobilized. If you deliver, we'll be content to let you name your price."

Tyana raised her eyebrow in surprise. Money clearly wasn't an object, but she sensed desperation in the man's tone. Whoever the men were he wanted them to find, they must be bad news.

Jonah opened the folder, glancing over the contents before passing it over to Mad Dog. Tyana leaned forward to peer over Mad Dog's shoulder, her curiosity piqued. She sucked in her breath when she saw the photos. She recognized two of the men immediately as part of the team that had hired D, and the third... She was on intimate terms with the third, also a member of that same team. Eli Chance.

"Why do you want them?" she spoke up.

The man turned glittering eyes on her. The corners of his mouth quirked upward in a fake smile. "You needn't concern yourself with my use for them. All I need from you is their delivery. Eli Chance alive. The other two..." He shrugged. "Dead or alive. Doesn't really matter."

"No," Jonah broke in.

The man turned in surprise back to Jonah. "No?"

"That's what I said," Jonah said evenly. He snapped his fingers at Mad Dog and held out his hand for the folder. When Mad Dog handed it over, Jonah shoved it toward the man. "We have no interest in taking the job."

Tyana leaned forward. "Jonah—"

He held out a hand to silence her, his expression black. He turned back to the man. "I'm sorry you've wasted your time, but we don't have any interest in this assignment."

The man studied Jonah for a long moment before turning his gaze to Tyana. Then he shrugged and turned away. "Let's go," he said.

Tyana watched him leave, a sense of frustration beating against her temple. As soon as the man had disappeared from view, she rounded on Jonah.

Before she could spit out a single word, he held up his hand. "There won't be any arguments, Ty. Not over this. At the moment I don't even want to ponder the coincidence of this man appearing from nowhere asking us to deliver Eli Chance on a silver platter."

"But—"

"But nothing," he said firmly. "The subject is closed."

She sighed, shutting her eyes against the overwhelming urge to throttle him. He was like a freaking steel beam when he made up his mind about something.

She got up and stalked over to the window, watching as the helicopter lifted into the air. She'd never felt so damn helpless in her life. Not even during the days in the orphanage when she and D had lived every moment in fear.

Warm hands gripped her shoulders, kneading and soothing.

"We'll find a way to help D, baby," Mad Dog murmured. "You've got to relax. You can't take on the world by yourself."

Her shoulders slumped underneath his hands, and her head bowed.

"What do you say you and I head to Paris for a little R and R? It's been a while since we cut loose and had a little fun together."

"I can't leave D. He might need me."

Mad Dog turned her around to face him. "Jonah will be here with him, and Marcus is coming out tomorrow to check D over. He'll be fine."

Tyana reached out to twirl a strand of Mad Dog's hair around her finger, indecision wracking her brain. "You know Paris is my weakness."

He grinned charmingly. "I'll even take you to Aviation Club

de France and let you lose some of my hard-earned cash."

She looked beyond his shoulder to Jonah. She raised a brow in question.

"I've never tried to keep you on a leash, Ty," Jonah said dryly. "You don't need to ask my permission. You and Mad Dog go and have fun. D will be fine here with me."

Impulsively, she threw her arms around Mad Dog's neck and hugged him tight. He wrapped his beefy arms around her waist and squeezed her just as hard. Then he smacked her on the ass.

"Go get packed. I'll get the chopper ready, and Jonah will call and make sure the jet is fueled and ready when we hit the mainland."

ꙮ

Eli watched her across the intimate club setting as she collected chips from another pot she'd won. Her eyes glowed with excitement as she stacked her winnings. The man at her side grinned and nudged her on the shoulder. She laughed and turned her wide smile on him. The two were obviously close, and Eli wasn't fooled by the man's easygoing demeanor. He hovered protectively over her.

Which begged the question. If she was intimately involved with the rather large guy glued to her side, what the fuck had she been doing in Eli's bed just days ago?

He felt a surge of irritation.

He knew exactly why she'd been in his bed. She was using him. For what he didn't know, but he was going to find out what the hell she wanted. And if she was a threat to his team.

His team. His lips drew into a thin line. He didn't have a team. A team implied an organized unit. Something with a network. Back-up. What he had were three men he felt a deep responsibility for. Members of his former *team*. A team that used to be recognized by his government.

Now they were a group of men without a country. Cut loose and ignored as long as they played by the unspoken rules. Play dead. Disappear.

Only now, his mystery woman threatened their obscurity.

When he was sure he was unobserved, he recorded a few shots of the couple with the mini camera chip concealed in his palm. He'd upload them and zap them over to Gabe at the first opportunity.

He picked up a glossy magazine and held it up as he saw her rise from the table and head presumably to the ladies' room. With a quick glance to make sure her bodyguard hadn't spotted him, Eli moved in the woman's direction.

He followed her discreetly until she ducked into the bathroom. He stood, waiting at a distance, and wondered for the hundredth time who she was and what her story was.

The Aviation Club de Paris catered to a rather exclusive crowd. Mostly bigger names in poker. The wealthy and the famous. Judging by the amount of chips he'd seen in front of the woman and her escort, she wasn't short on cash.

When she reappeared from the bathroom, he watched as she returned to her table. A few minutes later, she and her escort collected her chips and left the table. They cashed out then exited the club. The man hailed a taxi, and they clambered in.

Eli stepped outside as the taxi sped away. He hurried down the street until he could step into an alley and shift.

The rush burned over his skin. He didn't stop to savor the sensation as he usually did. There wasn't time. Even before he was fully transformed, he streaked toward the distant cab. He rode the wind, coalescing into tiny particles of gasses.

Ten minutes later, the taxi pulled to a stop in front of the Royal Hotel on Avenue de Friedland. The couple stepped out and walked laughing into the hotel.

Eli wrapped around the strands of her hair, absorbing her fragrance until his every molecule smelled of her. He rode the elevator up with the couple. Stayed glued to his mystery woman until she stopped in front of her room.

To his surprise, her escort ruffled her hair, forcing Eli from his perch. Then he gave her a quick kiss on the cheek before walking a few feet down to the next room.

So they weren't sharing a room. Interesting, indeed. And very convenient as far as Eli was concerned. Certainly made things easier for him.

When she entered her room, Eli swirled to a corner, shimmering there as mist as he watched her prepare for bed. She stripped from the silk sheath, and as much as he liked the view of her in just lingerie, he was damned sorry to see the dress go. It fit her like a dream, adhering to her every curve.

The room pulsed and vibrated around him as she pulled her bra and panties off and slipped a satin camisole over her head. For the first time he could remember, he had difficulty maintaining his form.

His human form called to him, begging him to shift so he could touch her, caress her skin. Who was he fooling? Yeah, he wanted, needed, to know who she was and what she was up to, but he was interested in her in a far more personal way.

She'd gotten under his skin as few women in his lifetime had. He should be pissed that she'd laid him out at their last meeting, but instead he was more amused by the little spitfire. He wouldn't underestimate her again, and that would even the playing field.

As she settled among the covers, her soft, even breathing filled the room. Still, he waited patiently, wanting to make sure she had drifted off to sleep. Why, he wasn't sure, since he intended to wake her, but he wanted the element of surprise.

When he was sure she was sleeping, he floated over to the bed, becoming a wisp of smoke, so thin he would barely be visible.

He feathered across the hollow of her throat, circling her neck and back around before sliding lightly over her full lips. He stroked her cheek, imagining it was his lips following the curve of her jaw.

He chuckled to himself when she brushed her hand across her face and turned her head to the side.

You won't escape me so easily this time, little firebrand.

He continued his smoky seduction, sliding underneath the neckline of her satin nightie. The material lifted the slightest bit and rippled as he swirled around her nipple.

She sighed and twisted restlessly against the sheets. He licked at the turgid point, leaving a damp trail as he shifted between smoke and mist.

Soon, he floated lazily up her body again and danced across her lips. They parted and a gasp escaped her mouth. He allowed himself to tighten, straining between his human and elemental form. He hovered above her, flashing eerily transparent. If she opened her eyes now, she'd see a faded image of his human form.

Unable to resist, he lowered his lips to hers. His touch was light. He wasn't fully shifted so his body conformed to hers, a ghostly apparition flush against her.

He kissed her again, licking over her lips, inhaling her sweet moans. When she stirred again, he gave over to his elemental form, coalescing as a plume of smoke once more.

Suddenly her eyes flew open and she rolled off the bed in a heap of legs and covers. Eli shot upward, hovering over the bed as he looked down at her.

She scrambled up, looking warily around her, her pupils dilated. She fumbled with the lamp on the nightstand and soon the room was bathed in soft light.

Her chest rose and fell with exertion.

"You're going nuts," she muttered. "Have great sex one time and your brain becomes mush."

Eli chuckled to himself. So she was thinking about him, or maybe, like before, she sensed his presence. He certainly couldn't fault her instincts. And he damn sure didn't fault her performance in bed.

She slowly rose from the floor, hauling the covers back onto the bed. She stared around the room, taking her time assessing every nook and cranny. Then she looked up. Right at him.

How on earth did she manage to pinpoint his location every single time?

Her eyes narrowed as she cocked her head to one side.

"Fucking pervert," she growled. "Get your ass down here so I can kick it again."

Chapter Four

Tyana balled her fingers into tight fists at her sides and readied herself for the coming confrontation. The hairs at the nape of her neck prickled and stood on end, just as they had that night in Singapore, and there was a chill in the air. She knew he was here. She *felt* him.

A slight shift in the air alerted her to Eli's movement just seconds before he materialized at the end of the bed.

He stood in a relaxed pose, studying her indolently. She glared and sized him up.

"How did you know I would be here?" she demanded.

He cocked one eyebrow at her. "How did you know I'd be in Singapore?"

She shrugged. "Lucky guess?"

"What do you want?"

Her eyes narrowed. She eased sideways, putting more distance between her and the bed. Eli backed a step away, his stance growing more wary. Maybe he remembered the last time she put him on his ass.

She smirked. "Afraid of a girl?"

His eyes glittered with amusement. "Afraid I'll make you want me again?"

She didn't dignify the remark with a response.

She closed in and the two circled each other, hands up, feet barely making a sound across the floor.

"You know, I'd much rather fuck you than fight with you."

She lashed out with a fist only to have her punch blocked by his forearm.

"Well, if you insist," he murmured.

Annoyance bubbled just under the surface, not that she'd give him the satisfaction of reacting. He irritated the piss out of her, and nothing would give her greater pleasure than taking him down again.

She feinted right with her fist then kicked low with her foot, catching him just below the knee. She grinned when he stumbled back and caught himself on the desk.

"Feisty little wench."

She glared him down and closed in again. He was toying with her, and that pissed her off. Hell, everything about the man made her want to grind her teeth.

When he made a move toward her, she danced back, then kicked again, this time connecting with his thigh. Inches from his groin. She grinned when he covered his privates and backed off.

"Now, sugar, we can't have any fun tonight if you damage the goods."

She rolled her eyes. "If I had meant to kick you in the balls I would have, cowboy. Now shut the hell up and fight. Or are you too much of a pussy to fight with a girl?"

Before she could blink, he rotated and executed a sweeping kick. She landed on her ass and quickly scrambled up before he could take advantage.

She rubbed her butt as she cautiously circled him once more. He gave her a lazy smile and winked.

"My mama always taught me it wasn't respectful to hit a girl."

"What about a bitch?" she challenged.

"Are you just wanting me to hit you?" he asked.

"Who says you'll get the chance?"

She purposely let him get close and then she punched him right in the chin. His head snapped back, and he wiped his face with his hand. He lost some of the teasing look, and she smirked again.

And then he disappeared.

She whirled around, trying to get a bead on his location. Damn shifter.

A prickle of awareness skated down her spine, but before she could react, two very human arms snaked around her from behind and trapped her arms to her sides.

"Now, sugar, why do you want to be all violent?" he purred in her ear.

She reared her head back, satisfied when she made contact, and he grunted in pain. She twisted and kicked, but he held on to her.

He picked up her struggling body and tossed her onto the bed. She landed with a thump and rolled over just as he came down on top of her.

An electric shock scorched up her body as his heat bled into her skin. He yanked both her arms high over her head and held them as he stared down at her.

"I believe this round goes to me."

It shouldn't be legal for a man to be this sexy, and worse, to know it. Perfectly straight, white teeth flashed as he grinned. Bastard had probably read her thoughts.

"Yeah, so what are you going to do about it?" she demanded.

He transferred her wrists to one hand and propped himself up off her body with the other. It wouldn't be too hard to escape since he was only holding her with one hand, but damn it, she had no desire to go anywhere at the moment. Not until he did something about the unspoken promise in his eyes.

Without speaking, he lowered his head and closed his mouth around her nipple, through the satin material of her camisole. She flinched when his teeth grazed over the point. To her dismay, a small moan escaped her lips.

His head came up, and he grinned again. Cocky bastard. It was time to change the dynamics of this little rendezvous. She wanted him. No sense denying it. But she was going to have him on her terms. He'd dictated the action the first time, but screw that.

She slid her knee between his legs, wrenched her arms free and rolled hard, landing on top of him with her knee jammed against his balls.

He didn't fight, much to her disappointment. He just lay there staring at her with those sexy dark eyes. The earring glinted in the lamplight, and his black hair lay strewn on the pillow.

"This begs the question, now that you've got the man at your mercy, what *are* you going to do with him?" he drawled.

"Oh, shut up," she muttered. She lowered her lips to his and took him. Hard.

Their tongues tangled, wet, hot. His hands yanked at her camisole as her fingers tugged at his shirt. She fumbled with the fly of his jeans, becoming impatient when she couldn't get it unbuttoned.

He tossed her camisole across the room, and then he pushed her aside. "Give me just a second, sugar, and I'm all yours." He rolled over and shimmied out of his jeans. His shirt, shoes and underwear went sailing through the air and hit the wall.

He flopped back onto the bed. "Now, where were we?"

She straddled his body just below his groin and stared down at his turgid erection. Unable to resist, she reached out and touched it. It bobbed and jerked in reaction.

She closed her hand around the base, warm, soft, yet so hard. "I hope you brought your own condoms this time, cowboy. I wasn't exactly planning to run into you again."

"If you'll let go of that, sugar, I'll run into the bathroom and get one. In case you didn't notice, these highfalutin hotels come stocked with all the necessities."

She eased off of him and sat on the edge of the bed as he got up. He strode naked to the bathroom, giving her a prime view of his ass. His very nice ass.

Tyana groaned and closed her eyes. Since when did she go around eyeballing a man's ass? And why this man? Why was there such a powerful attraction? He irritated her, even as she wanted to bite him, lick him and explore all those nice sexual feelings he inspired.

She was determined not to analyze this. Just go with it. Enjoy it. The closer she got to him, the more she could learn about his stability and if there was a way to help D.

Satisfied with her reasoning, she reclined on the bed to

await Eli's return. Not that she needed a reason to have sex. She could enjoy it just like the other billion people on the planet.

"Shut up," she muttered.

She looked up when she heard Eli. For a moment, she second-guessed her decision to indulge in sex with this man. Was it the end of the world? No. But she'd feel better if she just beat him to a pulp and pried what information she needed from him.

"Now where were we?" Eli said as he lowered his body onto the bed next to her.

She shoved him onto his back and resumed her position astride his hips. "I believe we were here."

He held his hand out, the condom package between his fingers. "By all means."

She tossed the condom onto the bed beside them, in no hurry this time. If she was going to indulge, then she was going to opt for more than a quick tumble. She wanted to touch, explore, experience what she'd been missing out on.

She scooted down his legs but kept her knees on either side. She placed her palms on his thighs and slowly moved them up his body, enjoying the roughness of his skin and the slight scratch of hair.

When her hands reached his firm stomach, she leaned down and gently blew over the head of his cock. He sucked in his breath—in anticipation? Her tongue darted out, and she tasted him. No condom interfered this time.

She ran her tongue around the blunt head and then down the length of his shaft. His hands balled into fists at his sides as he moaned.

Addicted to the feel of him against her lips and loving the sounds of appreciation he made, she became bolder and took him into her mouth.

She sucked deep and smiled as he arched into her. He filled her, and she wanted more. Her tongue stroked up and down as she continued to tease and taunt him.

His hands, no longer content at his sides, tangled in her hair, pulling her down to meet his impatient thrusts. She gripped his hip with one hand and curled her other hand around his cock. She squeezed and worked her fingers up and down, following the motion of her mouth.

"Jesus Christ, you have to stop."

The statement sounded ragged. Like it had been ripped from him under duress. She stopped her upward motion and held the tip in her mouth as she looked at him. He stared down at her, his fingers gripping her hair. His eyes glittered with need and had an almost pained quality to them.

"Am I doing it wrong?" she asked huskily as she let him fall from her lips.

"God no. If you do it any better, I won't be able to stay conscious."

She smiled. "Well then, why did you want me to stop?"

He rose up and grabbed her by the shoulders, rolling until she fell under him. "Because, you little wench, it was about to be all over before it began."

She hooked her leg over his and shoved, rotating them back over until she was on top. "That would be a great shame, since I plan to enjoy you for quite a while."

He arched a brow and reached out to her breast. "I do believe I like the sound of that," he murmured as he rolled a thumb over her nipple.

She shuddered and arched into his caress.

"Like that?"

"Mmm hmm."

"Come here," he said. He reached behind her and cupped her ass then pulled her closer to him. His hands smoothed up her back until they touched her shoulder blades, and he pressed her down so that his mouth captured her breast.

She closed her eyes as he licked and nibbled at one nipple and then turned his attention to the other. His erection was sandwiched between his stomach and her pussy, and each movement, no matter how slight, sent spasms through her groin. Her clit buzzed and tingled, and she shifted, trying to bring him into closer contact.

"You want top or bottom?" he asked.

"I'm surprised you're giving me a choice," she murmured.

He rolled them again, until he was positioned over her. "I

can go that route. I just figured you'd kick my ass if I got too pushy."

She shoved and rotated until she was back on top. "Who says I won't? I merely said I was surprised you offered."

"You still haven't answered the question."

"Hmmm, why don't I get the condom out and then we see where things lead?"

"Good idea."

She reached for the wrapper and tore it open. Moving her body back until she straddled his knees, she reached down to roll the condom over his straining cock.

"At least it's not red this time," he muttered.

She laughed. "Did I scar you for life with the colored cock?"

"You have a sick sense of humor," he said darkly.

She scooted back up his body and placed her hands on his taut belly. "You have such a great body," she murmured.

He ran his hands over her shoulders and down until he cupped both breasts. "The feeling is entirely mutual."

He moved lower until his fingers dug into her hips. He lifted her as though she weighed nothing and settled her over his cock. For a moment he held her there, prolonging the sensation. Then he lowered her until she sheathed him completely.

They both sighed with satisfaction.

"I could die happy," he said.

"Be careful what you wish for," she warned. He moved so quick she barely had time to blink before she was underneath him, pinned to the bed. He was so deep inside her that she could barely breathe. Both her hands were above her head, held tight with one of his. And now she knew he'd merely been playing with her before.

She narrowed her eyes. "I was only joking."

He rolled his hips against hers, driving deeper. "Funny, but I don't believe you."

Dizzying heat bloomed in her abdomen, raced through her pelvis. Each time he withdrew and rocketed forward again, her body tensed a bit more. Pressure built and squeezed until she writhed helplessly beneath him.

"If I wanted you dead, you would be," she gritted out.

He slid out of her until the head of his dick barely rimmed her entrance. He palmed her breast with his free hand and tweaked her nipple until it stood stiff and erect. Then he bent down and nipped sharply just as he slammed back into her.

"Am I supposed to be grateful?" he murmured around a mouthful of her breast.

"I'm going to change my mind about killing you if you don't start moving."

He chuckled softly against her nipple then lapped it with his tongue.

"Fuck me, damn it."

He reached down, grabbed her right leg and hooked his arm underneath. He pulled upward, spreading her wider. It made her feel vulnerable. Way more exposed.

"Oh, I'll fuck you, sugar. Buckle down for a long, hard ride."

Finally.

She whimpered when he slammed into her, her elevated leg giving him deeper access into her pussy. God, it hurt, but the pain was delicious.

He showed absolutely no mercy, and she loved every minute as he pounded into her over and over.

Suddenly her hands were free as he let go and grabbed her other leg. He shoved both legs up, over his arms, higher as he thrust.

She gripped his shoulders and dug her nails into his skin. He moaned and tensed between her legs as he surged deeper. She licked over the column of his neck, and when she reached his ear, she sank her teeth into the cord below his lobe.

He shuddered and bit out a curse. "Are you close?"

She closed her eyes and gripped him tighter. Sucked his skin into her mouth. Marked him. Her body tightened. "Yes. God, yes."

"Thank, God," he muttered. "I'm not going to last. Come with me, sugar."

He rode her, hard and unrelenting. The slap of flesh on flesh filled the room. She bit him again and felt him stab deeper into her. The pressure mounted unbearably. The pleasure was too much. She arched into him, every muscle in her body seizing. And then she burst, and a thousand little spasms erupted in her groin. Wave after excruciating wave blew over her.

Eli strained against her, his body quivering as he pushed himself further into her, like he wanted to invade every inch. He fell forward, covering her. They both lay shuddering in the aftermath, his body a blanket over hers.

She should push him away, avoid such intimacy. Sex was sex. But it felt good. *He* felt good. And she didn't want the moment to end just yet.

"Holy Mother of God. I think you might have killed me after all."

She smiled against his shoulder.

He shifted his weight and rolled to the side, and she had to bite her tongue to still the protest that sprang to her lips. His arm snaked over her side and pulled her close to his chest.

"If I go to sleep, you're not going to off me are you?"

Did she want him to stay? Sleep implied he'd stay over. She bit her lip. The truth was, she didn't want him to leave. She needed information. Needed some way closer to him. But she knew those weren't the reasons she didn't want him to go.

"I'm too tired to murder you," she mumbled as she snuggled deeper into his arms.

He stroked her hair then let his hand glide over her back and to her bare bottom. "Let me get rid of the condom."

She relaxed as he rolled away, and a moment later, she was back in his embrace. They both wanted information. She knew it and he knew it. But for the time being, they were content with mind-blowing sex. They'd deal with the rest tomorrow.

Chapter Five

Tyana awoke to Eli's hand stroking up and down her spine. He was flat on his back, and she was curled into the crook of his arm, her head pillowed on his chest. It was nauseatingly cozy.

"We've fucked twice, and I still don't know your name," Eli said.

She stiffened, but his hand continued its caress.

"Or why you came after me in Singapore."

She clenched her jaw.

He reached down, cupped her chin in his hand and tilted her face up so that their eyes met. "Care to enlighten me?"

A loud knock on the door interrupted her response, not that she'd planned to give one.

Mad Dog's voice followed the bang. "Tyana, come on. It's late. Get your ass up."

She scrambled up and searched frantically for her clothing. Eli also slid out of bed, but he calmly collected his clothes and then stood watching her as she hopped around on one foot. She finally got her other leg into her pants and yanked her shirt over her head.

When she glanced over at Eli again, he started to fade.

"Damn it, don't go yet," she protested.

His smile quivered and stretched as he became a transparent apparition and then disappeared altogether. A fine sheen of mist streaked for the air vent above the bed, and he was gone.

She swore and balled her fingers into a fist. She wanted to hit something. Hard.

Mad Dog knocked again, and she hurried for the door. She opened it a crack to see him standing impatiently in the hallway.

"Hey, give me a few minutes, okay? I slept in and I need a shower."

He grinned. "Meet me down in the lobby café. We'll have brunch then head over for some more action."

She smiled back and nodded.

Closing the door, she leaned against it for a moment before trudging into the bathroom. She took a quick shower and lamented for a moment rinsing Eli's touch and smell from her body.

Idiot.

Angrily, she dried off and wrapped a towel around her head and then walked out of the bathroom to get clean clothes from her suitcase. As she was dressing, the room phone rang.

She yanked her head up in surprise. No one would be calling on her hotel phone. Jonah would have used her cell phone or just not called at all. They didn't share chatty phone conversations.

Unless there was something wrong with D and Jonah couldn't reach her on the cell?

Even as she frantically looked around the room for her cell phone, she rushed to pick up the still ringing phone on the nightstand.

"*Allo*?"

"Miss Berezovsky, so glad I caught you."

The accented English grated on her nerves. It was a voice she recognized and one that sent warning bells clanging.

"What do you want?" The more obvious question would be how he knew she was here, but fuck, Eli Chance hadn't had a problem tracking her down. There was some serious cause for concern when FMG was so predictable.

"Meet me at Chez Didier's. There are things we should talk about."

She made a rude noise. "Jonah already told you we weren't

interested in the job."

"I'm not asking Jonah," he said. "I want to talk to you. Before you refuse, let me say this. I know how to help Damiano Ruiz."

She was stunned into silence.

"I'm offering a trade. You meet me. I tell you how to help Ruiz."

"I'll be there," she said shortly. "What time?"

"Just ditch your companion and come. I'll be there."

The phone went dead in her ear, and she dropped the receiver. Shit, shit, shit. She ran a trembling hand over the towel on her head and jerked it away. Mad Dog would shit a brick over what she'd just agreed to.

"He can't know," she muttered. He'd drag her kicking and screaming back to the island and never let her off again. Hell, he'd do that anyway if he knew that Eli had found her.

She hurried for the bathroom to dry her hair. A few minutes later, she slid the room key into her pocket, retrieved her cell phone and stuffed it into the small backpack with her passport, money and the knife Mad Dog had given her.

With a sigh, she went down to meet him.

He was sitting at one of the small tables drumming his fingers impatiently on his leg. When he looked up and saw her, he flashed her a grin.

"You're buying breakfast, by the way. You won the most last night."

She laughed and allowed some of the tension to escape her shoulders. "I always win the most."

He shrugged. "I ordered you an omelet the way you like it."

She took the seat across from him and shoved her bag underneath the table. "Thanks."

"You feeling any better yet?"

If she hadn't got the phone call a few minutes ago, she could honestly say yes. Apparently a night of great sex was a great way to unwind. But now her nerves were fried.

So she lied and nodded.

"I need to call D," she murmured as she pulled out her cell

phone.

Mad Dog reached across the table and put his hand on her arm. "Ty, he's okay. I talked to Jonah a few minutes ago. D's resting so you'll just disturb him."

Reluctantly she put the phone down. "Sorry. But I worry about him."

"We all do, baby."

"Yeah, I know, it's just that..."

Mad Dog nodded. "I do know, Ty. I do. But chasing Eli Chance all over Asia isn't going to help D, not to mention he'd be pissed as hell if he knew what you'd done. Best just to leave it alone."

Her cheeks grew warm, and she struggled to keep the guilt from her expression. Yeah, Mad Dog would go ballistic if he knew who had been in her hotel room.

They ate and talked about last night's poker game. Tyana could tell he was eager to get back over and play some more. She fiddled with her food then realized her sleeping in and reluctance to eat could be in her favor.

She pushed the plate aside and slouched in her chair.

Mad Dog's fork paused midway to his mouth. "Everything okay?"

She sighed. "I'm just tired. I don't feel very well. Would you mind going over to the club by yourself and letting me catch some sleep?"

His gaze narrowed as he contemplated. "You sure? I can hang out here if you prefer."

She smiled. "You know you're dying to go play. I just want a nap. I didn't sleep too well last night. Too hyped up from playing. I'll catch up to you later."

"Okay, if you're sure."

She reached down to gather her bag in her hand. "Yeah, I'm sure. I'll feel better after some sleep."

She ignored Mad Dog's questioning stare and walked away from the table.

ꙮ

Tyana. The name hovered in Eli's mind as he settled into his own hotel room just a block from the Royal. Her companion had called her Tyana. Unusual name and he'd only heard it once before. His team's guide into Adharji, Damiano Ruiz, had mentioned a sister named Tyana.

A weary sigh escaped him as he flopped onto the bed. He needed a shower and a shave. And about twenty-four hours of sleep. Not necessarily in that order.

If the woman who'd sought him out in Singapore was Damiano's sister, he could only come to the conclusion that she blamed Eli for his death and had revenge on her mind.

He shook his head. No, that didn't make sense. She would have gone for his throat, not fucked him senseless then snuck through his belongings.

He dug into his pocket for his cell phone, flipped it open and punched a button. He'd fucked around long enough. It was time to figure out what the hell Tyana wanted. And how Falcon Mercenary Group played into the picture. The last thing he wanted was a damn merc group on his ass.

"Ian," he said when the other man answered the phone. "I need some fast intel."

"Do you have any idea what time it is?" Ian growled.

Eli checked his watch and did a swift calculation. "You lazy shit, it's only six a.m. in Argentina."

Ian grunted. "Only? What the fuck do you want so goddamn early?"

Eli grinned. "I need whatever info you can dig up on Falcon Mercenary. And I need it fast."

Ian was quiet for a moment. "Isn't that who we got to…"

"Yeah, it is."

"What's up, Eli?"

"Don't know yet, but I'll let you know when I do. Give me a buzz when you have details on the group." He paused for a moment. "How are you and Braden doing?"

Eli heard a sigh.

"We're making it," Ian finally said.

Eli gripped the phone tighter. "I'll find help for you, Ian. I swear it."

"I'm not sure you can. Let me go. I'll get back with you as soon as I have what you need."

Eli let the change in topic slide and quietly closed the phone. There wasn't much he could say. There wasn't a way for him to ever make up for what happened to Ian, Braden or Gabe.

Before, he'd lamented being the only freak of nature. An elemental shifter. An accident of birth. Something born of science fiction movies and bad action adventure flicks. But now he realized having others like him didn't make him feel any less isolated.

While Gabe didn't seem to have the instability issues that Ian and Braden did, he knew Gabe wasn't any happier with his newfound abilities.

Eli was fortunate. He nearly laughed at the irony of that statement. But it was the truth. He had complete mastery of his shifts. He'd been born with the ability. His team wasn't so lucky.

Set up on a false mission, they'd been ambushed and an unknown chemical had been unleashed on them. They'd managed to escape, but within months, Ian and Braden began to randomly shift into animals. Cats. A jaguar and a panther, while Gabe could make himself invisible.

Bizarre didn't even begin to cover it.

In light of those developments, Eli no longer felt compelled to hide his own abilities from his teammates. With Gabe's stability, Eli's could be explained as well. And the truth of his past remained hidden.

Eli reached over to the nightstand and turned on the small GPS unit. In a moment, a small blip lit up the screen.

So, she was still in Paris. A smile crossed his face. Maybe he could arrange to run into her again. After he got more information from Ian.

ꙮ

Damiano stood on the deck, hands braced against the wood

railing as he stared over the ocean. A cool evening breeze blowing off the water washed over his face, filled his nostrils with a salty tang.

"You okay, man?"

Damiano turned his head to see Jonah watching him from the open doorway. He eased around and leaned his butt against the wood. "Yeah, I'm fine."

Jonah ambled out holding two beers. He tossed one of the cans into the air, and Damiano caught it in one hand. Jonah popped the tab on his and came to a stop a few feet away.

Damiano studied him for a moment and opened his own beer. For once he didn't feel edgy and out of control. For a few blissful hours he'd enjoyed a normal existence. He almost felt like his old self. He wanted to be in Paris with Ty and Mad Dog, playing poker and drinking like a fish.

His hand trembled as he held the beer to his lips.

"Today was a good day," Jonah said.

"Yeah."

Damiano turned back to the view of the ocean. He set the beer down on the railing. He glanced over at Jonah and voiced what was uppermost on his mind. "She went after him, didn't she?"

Jonah's breath came out in a hiss, but he didn't look at Damiano. "You know me better than that, D. I'm not going to discuss what Ty may or may not have done."

Damiano ground his teeth together in anger. "Damn it, Jonah. Don't fuck with me. Not over this. She has no business risking herself like that. If you can't control her then by God, I will."

Jonah turned, his eyes glittering dangerously. "Stand down, D. Last time I checked, I was still responsible for Falcon...for this family."

"I was responsible for Ty—and myself—way before you were. I won't let her go down for me."

Jonah's anger eased, and he laid a hand on Damiano's shoulder. "Ty cares about you, D. She'd do anything for you. Put yourself in her shoes. If she needed it, you know you'd put yourself out there, no hesitation."

Damiano turned with a growl and grabbed Jonah's shirt in his fist. "Tell me you haven't gone along with some crazy scheme of hers. Damn it, Jonah, I'll kill you for this."

Jonah grasped Damiano's wrist and pulled his hand away from his chest. "You go too far, brother," he said quietly. "Do not think to question my authority. As long as I'm the head of this family, you won't challenge me."

Damiano stumbled back and felt the uneasy crawl of change creep over his skin. He closed his eyes and sucked in air as he tried to control the urge to change to something wild and feral. Frightening images flashed in his mind. Wild beasts. Predatory creatures. A low snarl escaped him.

Strong arms surrounded him, hauled him toward the door. "Focus, D. Don't leave me. Hang on. Don't give in."

A few minutes later, he felt the prick of a needle and warm oblivion seeped into his veins. The fiery itch eased, and the urge to claw at his skin in an effort to free the predator inside abated.

"Listen to me," Jonah said close to his ear. "You insult me by suggesting I'd ever let Ty place herself in harm's way. She won't be going after Eli Chance. If I have to tie her down and drug her ass, I'll do it. Your only concentration needs to be on defeating this thing that has you in its grip. Do it for yourself and for those of us who love you."

"I won't...let her sacrifice...herself...for me."

"Neither will I. Now sleep, D. You need your strength."

Chapter Six

Tyana scanned the occupants of the outdoor café until her gaze alighted on her target. Her eyes narrowed, and her lips formed a tight line as she strode toward the table on the far end of the patio.

Two bodyguards stood on either side of the man, and Tyana sneered as she approached.

"Not exactly subtle, are you?" she said as she slid into the chair opposite the man who had phoned her.

He flashed her a sleazy grin and raised his hand to snap his fingers. Pete and Repeat slunk away and stood at a distance.

"Take off the sunglasses," she directed. "I like to see who I'm speaking to."

He paused for a moment before he slowly raised his hand to remove the expensive shades. Dark, soulless eyes stared back at her, and she resisted the urge to shiver.

"So glad you could make it, Miss Berezovsky."

"You have me at a disadvantage," she said sweetly. "We were never introduced."

"Esteban Morales. You may call me Esteban."

"I may call you asshole," she muttered.

He laughed and sat back in his chair. "You're fortunate I have a sense of humor, my dear. Another man might not be so tolerant of your snideness."

She made a show of checking her watch. "Look, can we get on with this?"

"By all means," he said smoothly.

She leaned forward. "How the hell do you know anything about Damiano Ruiz?"

His eyes glittered with amusement. "Ah, your shifter friend. Not doing well, is he?"

"How do you know anything about him or how he's doing?"

His teeth flashed again in a smirk. "Because my company engineered the chemical that made him into what he is."

Tyana exploded across the table, her hands wrapping in the collar of his shirt as she yanked him toward her. "You son of a bitch!"

"Get your hands off me at once," he said calmly. "Or I'll have my friends give you a few lessons in manners."

"Fuck you and your friends," she snarled.

"Remove yourself or I don't give you the information you need."

She slowly uncurled her fingers from his shirt. Then she shoved him back in his seat before retaking her own.

"Talk and make it fast."

He chuckled. "Quite demanding aren't you? You see, Miss Berezovsky, I hold all the cards. If I were you, I'd be very nice. And exercise some restraint."

She sucked in a breath through her nose and blew it out around tightly clenched teeth.

"There, much better. Now, I have something you want, and you have skills that I want to utilize. I see no reason we can't come to an agreement."

"What do you want?"

"Ian and Braden Thomas. Dead or alive. Preferably dead. They're a liability. Eli Chance, on the other hand, I'd like alive. If he dies, the deal is off."

She studied the worm closely. He was adamant about Eli Chance. As adamant as she was about Eli. Which left the question why? What did Esteban want with them?

"In return," he continued, "I'll give you what you want most."

"And what is that?" she drawled.

"A cure for your brother."

She sucked in her breath. Was the bastard telling the truth?

"I own the largest pharmaceutical corporation in Europe. In the last few years, I've branched into other interests. I find human experimentation rather fascinating. I wanted strong men. Warriors. The Covert Hostage Recovery team fit the bill. Your brother was just an unfortunate victim. Wrong place, wrong time. I'm willing to rectify that mistake if you give me what I want in return."

"Why do you want Ian and Braden Thomas dead and Eli Chance alive?" she asked bluntly.

His eyes flickered. "I don't have to explain myself to you, Miss Berezovsky. Either you take the job and help your brother, or he'll be added to my termination list of failed experiments. He'll be hunted down like the others."

She surged to her feet, fists clenched at her sides. "Fuck you. You'll have to come through me, and I swear to God, you come after Damiano and I'll hunt you down, cut off your balls and shove them down your throat. You'll choke to death on your own dick."

His laughter carried, causing people to stop and turn their way. "Do sit down, Miss Berezovsky. You're causing a scene."

"I've had enough of this." She turned to leave, but he stood and reached across the table to snag her wrist. His fingers bit painfully into her skin. She moved to strike, but he thrust a business card at her with his other hand.

"In case you change your mind."

She snatched the card from him and stalked away, fury igniting her steps. Rage billowed and rolled through her body. Angry tears burned her eyelids as she strode back to her hotel.

She wanted to hit something. Make something bleed. What she really wanted to do was go back and pound fucking Esteban into the pavement. Arrogant, slimy asshole. Who the fuck gave him the right to play God? Because of him, D was fighting a losing battle. How much longer could he possibly hold out until he lost all vestige of humanity?

A woman leaving the hotel bumped into Tyana and proceeded to dress her down in French.

"*Va te faire foutre*," Tyana muttered. The woman's eyes grew round, and she walked away, grumbling about arrogant Americans.

"*Va t'empaler encule*," Tyana called after her. "And I'm not American!" She turned and shoved her way by more people exiting the hotel.

She jammed her thumb over the elevator button and twitched with impatience as she waited for it to arrive. Her head pounded like someone had taken a jackhammer to it, and damn she needed a drink.

Bastard. *Fils de pute. Fickakopf.*

As she entered the elevator and the doors closed behind her, she rammed her fist into the back wall, shaking the car as it rose.

She muttered expletives in six other languages before the doors opened on her floor. Upon arriving at her door, she dug into her pocket for her room key and jammed it into the slot. In her agitation it took three attempts before she could get it open.

Finally the light turned green, and she yanked at the handle. She shouldered her way in and slid her bag from her shoulder, ready to toss it across the room. She came up short when she saw Mad Dog slouched in the chair by the window, his eyes stormy.

"*Fick mich*," she whispered.

"Yeah, I'd say so," Mad Dog said in a near growl as he stood. "Where the fuck have you been, Ty? And who the hell was here with you last night?" He waved a hand at the bed that still looked like it had hosted a wrestling match, and in fact, it had. With his other hand, he held up the torn condom wrapper. Oh hell.

Freaking maids would have to pick today to be lax on the job. Any other time, they would have been knocking on her door at an obscenely early hour in their haste to clean the damn room.

She closed her eyes and flopped on the bed, letting her bag fall to the floor. Of the two things she could tell Mad Dog, her meeting with Esteban was not one of them. Which only left telling him about Eli. Not much of an improvement, but he wasn't going to buy that no one had been in her bed and that she'd just happened off on a stroll through the streets of Paris on some sightseeing tour.

"I'm waiting," he bit out.

"Eli Chance was here," she said dully.

Mad Dog swore then swore again. Anger vibrated from him, and Tyana glanced worriedly up at him. He gathered his hair into a ponytail in one hand and stood there, gripping the mane at his neck. His features were a study in trying to maintain control. He wanted to rage at her, and what prevented him, she wasn't sure.

Guilt pricked her conscience. She'd never kept things from her team. Until now. They were her family. Her only family.

"How did he find you, Ty?"

His nostrils flared with each breath, and his jaw was set in stone.

Uncertainty gripped her. She wasn't sure how he'd found her. But then how had Esteban?

"Son of a bitch," Mad Dog muttered. "You're going to get us all killed."

She stared down at her hands.

"Get into the bathroom and strip," he ordered. "Go over every inch of your body. He must have planted a tracking device in Singapore. Do it, or I'll do it for you."

She stumbled to her feet and hurried into the bathroom. Dread pumped through her veins. Her stomach swelled and rocked with nausea. Jonah would kill her. And she'd deserve it. She'd put them all at risk.

She shed her clothes and began at her feet, feeling every inch of her skin. As she moved up her body, she tried to remember the night she'd spent with Eli in Singapore. Heat raced up her spine. He'd not left a single inch of her skin untouched. The damn thing could be anywhere. But where wouldn't she easily find it? Accidentally knock it off?

Standing to her full height, she stared back at herself in the mirror. The most logical place would be on her back or another such place she couldn't easily reach and wouldn't pay much attention to. She sighed. She'd have to get Mad Dog to help.

She grabbed a towel to cover her front then went to the

bathroom door and called softly for him. He was there in a second.

"Did you find it?" he demanded.

"Not yet. I need your help. It has to be somewhere on my back. Someplace I wouldn't easily find it or accidentally knock it off."

"Turn around."

She complied, holding the towel tightly to her. His hands skimmed over her skin, and then he pushed her further into the bathroom where the light was better.

"Lean against the counter," he said as he felt along her spine.

She glanced into the mirror and saw him frown.

"Hold your hair up."

She reached back with one hand and gathered the strands. Mad Dog's fingers slid up her neck into her hairline and felt around. He paused in the slight hollow at the base of her neck. His lips came together, and she felt a slight twinge.

She whirled around to see him holding a tiny needle-like device, much thinner than a toothpick and only about a quarter inch long.

Mad Dog stared grimly back at her as he held the tracking device between his thumb and forefinger. "He must have planted it when you were otherwise occupied."

Tyana closed her eyes and leaned against the counter. "I'm so stupid," she whispered. "I can't believe..." She didn't even finish the thought, because she knew full well how she'd allowed it to happen.

"I'm sorry, Mad Dog."

He sighed and cupped her chin in his hand. "Let me go take care of this little piece of technology, and then I'm taking you back to the island. Jonah's going to have to know, you realize that, don't you?"

She nodded miserably. Jonah would flip out, and he'd lock their island down tighter than Fort Knox.

"Is there anything else you want to tell me, Ty?" He stared at her with piercing blue eyes, his expression thoughtful. "Like about what happened last night?"

"You can imagine what happened," she muttered.

Mad Dog raised one brow. "That was all? He followed you all the way to Paris for a quick fuck?"

Her cheeks tightened, and she glared at him. "He wanted to know why I went after him in Singapore. We didn't get into details. We might have if you hadn't interrupted us this morning."

His eyes narrowed and his lips pursed. "I'm only going to say this once, baby girl, so you listen, and you listen good. Stay away from Eli Chance. *Comprende*? If you see him, if he comes near you, if he so much as breathes in your direction, you get your ass to me or Jonah and let us handle it."

Her teeth dug into her top lip as anger lit fire to her cheeks. "I can take care of myself. I don't need you or Jonah acting like goddamn babysitters."

"Normally I'd agree with you, Ty. But this time you're in way over your head. You've lost perspective. You lost it a long time ago when it comes to D. Now get dressed and get your stuff packed. We're out of here just as soon as I get rid of this." He held up the device.

Tyana watched him go, helpless fury swarming her. The last thing she wanted to do was go home and face Jonah. But she wasn't a coward, and she deserved what was coming to her. She'd stand up and take it like a big girl and hope Jonah didn't hold a grudge forever.

ꟙ

Eli wasn't fooled by the GPS coordinates. He knew Tyana wasn't heading into Germany. She'd obviously found the tracking device, and he'd lay odds that her big friend had snatched her back to whatever island they hung out on.

Tyana Berezovsky. "Sister" to Damiano Ruiz, or so Damiano had claimed. Only female member of Falcon Mercenary Group. Specialties were hand-to-hand combat and languages. She was proficient with knives and knew her way around explosives. She could also pick off a fly with a rifle at four hundred yards.

Eli leaned back into the soft leather seat of his private jet as the pilot began taxiing down the runway. Next stop: Argentina. Despite Gabe's assurances that Ian and Braden were okay, Eli wanted to see them for himself. He owed them that much. He owed them more than he could ever repay. And so far he'd come up with nothing in the search for a possible cure.

Everywhere he turned, he encountered a door shut in his face. In a way it was his own damn fault. He'd put too much trust in the U.S. government and their extensive web. All of his contacts were in some way connected to the military. When he was part of the fold, things had run smoothly. If things went to shit, he could pick up the phone and call in back-up. Now that he was no longer a recognized entity by Uncle Sam, it was as if Covert Hostage Recovery had never existed. It was damn eerie.

Now he faced rebuilding his network from the ground up, but his first priority had to be finding a way to help Ian and Braden.

He closed his eyes and allowed sleep to come. He hadn't rested in more nights than he could count. Even as he floated away, the tantalizing image of Tyana Berezovsky whispered at the edges of his mind.

What did she want? What game was she playing?

He could have followed her back to the island, but no doubt it would be an impenetrable fortress now that she'd found his tracking device. And besides, it was her move. She'd come to him. He was as sure of that as he was anything.

He didn't yet know what she wanted with him, but she'd find him again. And when she did, he'd be ready.

Chapter Seven

Jonah was pissed. Oh yeah, he was hanging on to his temper by a thread. He hadn't even said anything to her. He just stared at her with that tick in his jaw, his dark eyes furious.

And as predicted, he picked up the radio. "I want the entire island in lockdown," he ground out to his security team. "No one gets on or off unless it comes directly, and I do mean directly, from me."

He dropped the radio and folded his arms across his chest. He continued to stare her down, but she didn't flinch. She stared back at him as Mad Dog stood to the side, no doubt trying to figure out if he'd have to jump in and separate them.

"You've compromised every single one of us with your actions."

Still, she didn't say anything. An apology wouldn't cut it at this point, and he wasn't done with his lecture.

"You can't keep this up, Ty. Your attempts to help D are only going to bring trouble to our front door."

She looked down, no longer able to meet his gaze.

"You're out of commission until I can figure out what the hell to do about Eli Chance."

She yanked her head back up. "You can't do that."

Fire blazed in his eyes. "I just did. You aren't leaving this island. You'll stay where I can see you at all times. Are we clear?"

She glared at him, her teeth and lips so tight together her jaw ached.

"I said, are we clear?"

She nodded.

"I want to hear it, Ty."

"We're clear."

"I suggest you go find D. He's not that happy with you either at the moment. If I can't talk some sense into you, maybe he can."

She turned away, guilt and worry nagging at her. Why had he told D?

"He's not stupid, Ty," Mad Dog said in a low voice. "You tend to think if you don't talk about it, it doesn't exist. Jonah didn't have to tell D anything. He knew."

She walked out of the room, avoiding Jonah's gaze. She went to find D. She'd missed him. Lately they hadn't spent much time together. Between her search for Eli, and more recently her jaunt to Paris, she hadn't had time to do much else.

She found him on the deck, staring out over the ocean. She walked past the open sliding glass doors. He looked up when he heard her approach.

"Hi," she said in a soft voice.

He opened his arms, and she walked into his embrace. She wrapped her arms around him and held on tight. Just like so many times before.

His lips brushed across the top of her head. She turned her face up so she could see him. "How are you?"

"I don't want to talk about me."

She closed her eyes and buried her face in his chest. Strong fingers slid under her chin and forced her gaze back up to meet his.

"I want to talk about you, Ty."

She closed her eyes and shook her head. "Don't spoil things, D. Let it go."

He tapped her cheek with his finger, causing her to open her eyes again. "I'm not letting it go."

"There's nothing you can say that will change anything. I don't want to fight with you."

He sighed and gripped her a little tighter. "I won't let you do this. Stay away from him, Ty. I won't let you kill yourself for me."

She pulled away and gripped his shoulders in her hands. "I'm not going to get myself killed. You know I'm better than that. But if you think I'm going to sit back and watch you suffer, then you know nothing about me."

Damiano turned his back to her to stare over the ocean again. "What you don't understand, Ty, is that I'd suffer more if something happened to you. Maybe you should think about that instead of trying to fix things you can't change."

She curled her arms around his middle and laid her cheek to his back. She could feel the tremors rippling through his muscles. The resignation in his voice made her want to scream. Never had she felt so helpless in her life. Not in the orphanage, not when they came for her and Damiano, not when Damiano stood in front of her, determined to take whatever he could for her.

"He's stable, D. He has absolute control over his shifts. He has connections we don't. Someone or something helped him. If it can help him, it can help you. I won't accept that I can't make this right for you. I won't."

His hands closed over hers and pulled them up over his heart. "I'm asking you to stand down, Ty. Don't do this."

She closed her eyes and kept her face buried in his back. He never asked her for anything. But this was one promise she couldn't make him. So she said nothing, because she wouldn't lie.

☙

Jonah stared down at Damiano and Tyana lying on the couch in the game room. Ty was on the inside of the couch, curled into D's body. D had a protective arm around her midsection and both were asleep.

Even in sleep, D was tightly wound, his body tense. His breaths came erratically, seemingly torn from him under duress. Nerves twitched and muscles jumped.

The two looked vulnerable. Despite their toughness. Despite the fact that Jonah knew they could take on just about any challenge. They wouldn't be on his team if he had any doubts about their capabilities.

But right now they reminded him of the two scared, starving kids he and Mad Dog had found on the streets of Prague so many years ago. They were running on empty.

Jonah turned to look at Mad Dog who stood a few feet away. Helplessness he wasn't accustomed to flickered uncomfortably in his mind. He was used to being able to meet any challenge no matter how great. But Tyana and Damiano mattered to him. They were his family. For the first time, he was faced with a situation where he wasn't sure he could provide a solution.

"How much of a threat is Eli Chance?"

Mad Dog scowled. "To us? Not great, even if he did manage to locate the island. He's nothing we can't handle. To Ty, however..." He shook his head. "I'm afraid this has become more than a simple matter of her searching for answers. He's gotten to her twice."

"Fuck waiting for him to relax his guard," Jonah said coldly. "I want to know when he eats, sleeps, takes a piss and where he does it. When you have everything compiled, bring it to me. We're going after him. I won't take chances with Ty's safety."

Mad Dog nodded. "I'll get on it." He paused for a moment then looked over at Jonah. "What are we going to do about Ty when we go after Chance?"

Jonah fixed Mad Dog with a stony stare. "If I have to tie her up and have the Falcon secondary sit on her, I will. She's not to leave this island again."

ꙮ

Damiano's guttural cry woke Tyana from a deep sleep. He rolled from the couch and hit the floor. She was beside him in an instant, her arms curling around his spasming body.

"D, stay with me," she pleaded.

"Get away from him, Ty," Mad Dog ordered as he strode into the room.

"No. I won't leave him."

Damiano arched and jerked. His hand caught her in the face. Pain exploded through her head as she sailed backward several feet. She lay there, stunned at his strength.

"Jonah! Get the hell in here," Mad Dog yelled.

She stared at Damiano in mute horror as his body contorted. When his eyes opened, he stared at her without recognition. The pupils constricted and changed shape. They were no longer human.

"No," she whispered.

Jonah and Mad Dog fell on him in an attempt to subdue the raging beast. Two more of their security personnel ran through the door. One carried a syringe.

"Stun him," Jonah barked.

"No!" Tyana scrambled over to Damiano as he struggled beneath the men. "Don't hurt him."

Mad Dog plucked her from the floor and held her kicking, writhing body away from the others. "Ty, stop. It's the only way."

She twisted and fought, but Mad Dog held her fast. Finally, he pushed her to the floor and put one knee in the middle of her back and held her arms behind her with his hand.

"Goddamn you, Mad Dog."

With his other hand, he stroked her hair, the action at complete opposition to the force he was using.

Damiano let out a cry of pain, and Tyana jerked beneath Mad Dog's body. Then all went quiet.

"D!" Tyana's cry split the room.

"He's all right, Ty," Jonah said as he got up from the floor. He looked over at Mad Dog. "Let her go."

Mad Dog eased off her body, and she crawled over to where Damiano lay, his breaths coming in quiet spurts. Tears filled her eyes as she gathered him in her arms.

"I want him confined to quarters," Jonah said to the security men.

She shot to her feet. "Why are you doing this? I won't let you treat him like an animal."

"Am I supposed to stand by and let him kill you, Ty?"

"He won't hurt me."

Jonah reached out and cupped her bruised cheek. "He already has."

"It wasn't his fault," she said desperately. "It wasn't him. You know he wouldn't hurt me."

"That's just it. He's not himself. I won't allow him to endanger you just because you've lost all objectivity."

"We can't all be the cold-hearted bastard you are," she spat. She whirled around to see Damiano being carried out of the room. Jonah followed close behind. She started to go after him, but Mad Dog caught her wrist and held tight.

She stared at him with accusing eyes. "You too?"

"You're not being fair to Jonah and you know it," Mad Dog said quietly.

Rage simmered underneath her skin, begged to be let loose.

"Will it make you feel better to hit me?" he asked.

Her chin sagged, and she looked away. "No, goddamn it, it won't."

"Jonah is doing his best, Ty. Cut him some slack. He wants to help D just as much as you do."

She sank onto the couch and held her hands over her face. "I know. Damn it, I know."

Mad Dog sat down beside her and for a long moment neither of them spoke. She turned to him, finally breaking the silence.

"I don't know what to do, Mad Dog," she whispered. "I don't know how to help him, and it's killing me."

Mad Dog touched her face. "You need some ice on that or it's going to swell."

She sighed as he got up and walked over to the minibar to get some ice. Her head ached like a son of a bitch.

"Get me a drink too. Hell, and fire up one of your joints."

Chapter Eight

"You're getting sloppy, Eli."

Eli raised one eyebrow as he stared at Ian Thomas over his beer. "Sloppy? I think I might be insulted."

Braden strolled in, a baseball cap shoved over his eyes, and sat down next to Ian. Concern flickered in Ian's eyes before he shifted his attention back to Eli.

"You didn't exactly cover your tracks very well. Registering your flight plan from Paris? Flying into frickin' Buenos Aires? Making enough noise to wake the dead? Shit, we'll have the damn U.S. government back on our asses. We're supposed to lay low, pretend to be dead or something, according to Uncle Sam."

A smile curved Eli's lips. "My actions were purely intentional, I assure you."

"That's what bugs me," Braden muttered, speaking for the first time.

Eli stared at the two brothers and sighed. And then another thought occurred to him. "Where the fuck is Gabe? He was supposed to be keeping an eye on you two."

"We don't need a goddamn babysitter," Ian growled.

"Who needs Gabe when Ian fulfills those requirements perfectly?" Braden muttered.

Ian glanced sideways at Braden. "You're more unstable than I am, little brother. Someone has to look after your ass."

Braden snorted. "I haven't shifted in three days. But gee, I happened to see a fucking jaguar skulking around the grounds yesterday. I wonder who that could be."

"Shut the fuck up," Ian said.

"Both of you shut the fuck up and listen," Eli interjected. "Not that I don't love listening to you two argue, but we have things to do."

"Such as?" Ian asked.

"Preparing for a visitor." Eli couldn't keep the grin from his face.

He had their full attention now.

Braden stared at him for a moment. "So the sloppiness was to lure someone here, I take it?"

Eli nodded.

"Who?" Ian demanded.

"Tyana Berezovsky."

Braden frowned. "The name is familiar. Am I supposed to know who she is?"

Ian drummed his fingers on his knees then gave Eli a sharp look. "Damiano Ruiz's sister? Doesn't she belong to Falcon?"

Eli nodded. "Yep. And she's after me. She looked me up in Singapore. I returned the favor in Paris. She'll come after me next."

"You seem so sure of that," Braden said.

"Oh, she'll come," Eli said softly. "And I plan to be ready for her."

"What does she want?" Ian asked.

"That I don't know. But I intend to find out."

ꟾ

Tyana settled into a cross-legged position and rubbed her eyes in an attempt to ease the wooziness brought on by too much to drink and a few too many joints.

The salty ocean breeze helped clear her head some as she focused her stare at a distant point on the horizon. She'd crawled down to her favorite getaway spot to do some hard thinking and plotting.

From the deck, she'd had to climb over the railing, drop

down to the rock outcropping and shimmy around the face of the cliff. Several feet below, a boulder jutted out from the rock face. The flat surface offered an area large enough to sit on and enjoy the view of the ocean crashing below her.

It was her one seclusion away from everyone else. No one ever bothered her here, though she had no doubt Jonah knew of its location. He made it his business to know everything.

A deflated sigh escaped her. True, Jonah made her angry, but she couldn't bring herself to stay that way. He'd saved her and D, taken them from scraggly street kids to honed fighters. She'd always owe him for that, and for that reason, he had her loyalty. Loyalty that would be sorely tested by what she had to do.

After seeing what had happened to D earlier, she knew she couldn't wait to act. If there was any chance, no matter how slight, she had to seize it. He wouldn't last much longer.

Grief knotted her throat and pressed painfully against her chest. She couldn't lose D. She wouldn't. He'd been hers since she was a child. Her earliest memories were of the orphanage and of Damiano, an older boy, skinny, with big brown eyes and enough courage to sustain them both during their rough years at the institution.

He'd fought for her more times than she could count, and now, when he couldn't fight for himself, she would. Or die trying.

She stayed out long after the sun had slipped over the horizon. She watched as, one by one, the stars popped into the night sky. Instead of being soothed by the sounds of the waves below her, she grew tenser the longer she sat.

Plans rolled and formulated in her mind. Jonah presented a huge obstacle, but not an insurmountable one. Seeing Damiano in pain, writhing on the floor, had provided her all the motivation she needed. He was running out of time.

Finally content with the plan of action she'd formed, she uncurled her stiff limbs and stood. She dug her hands into the side of the cliff and prepared to climb back up to the deck.

A few minutes later, she hauled herself over the railing and fell with a thump.

"Climbing up and down a cliff is never a good idea after

drinks and marijuana," Jonah said dryly.

She stood, brushing herself off as she looked over to see Jonah sitting in the dark. When he continued to stare at her, she let her shoulders sag and braced herself for a lecture.

When he didn't say anything further, she leaned against the railing and propped her weight on her hands.

"What are you doing out here?" she asked.

"Waiting for you."

She stiffened again.

"I know you're angry with me, Ty. In your shoes, I would be too."

She stared uneasily at him. The only thing worse than a brooding, pissed-off Jonah, was dealing with a Jonah she wasn't used to. An understanding, *nice* Jonah.

"I would have done the same thing you did," he said quietly.

She went completely still.

"I'm not condoning what you did, but I understand why. Even though I can't allow you to continue this crusade to help D."

A frustrated sigh spilled from her lips.

"If this was a mission, if it was anything else, I'd place my confidence and my trust in you. You've never let me down. You're damn good. Our team relies on you."

Even as her cheeks tightened with pleasure from his rare praise, disappointment settled heavy in her stomach. "Why don't you trust me now?"

He sighed. "It's not a matter of trust, Ty." He stood and covered the short distance between them. He stood just inches from her and looked down. In the pale moonlight, she could see tension and fatigue etched into his hard features. "You, Mad Dog and D are the only family I have. The only people I care about. I'll do whatever it takes to keep you safe."

Her fingers curled into tight balls against the coarse wood railing. "But D needs help. By not allowing me off the island, you're hurting him."

Jonah shook his head. "I won't trade you for D." His words echoed Mad Dog's statement of a few days ago. "We'll find a way to help him that doesn't involve you chasing after Eli Chance or his team of shifters."

He reached out and gripped her shoulders. "Do you understand that, Ty? Do you honestly think any of us could be happy that Damiano was saved at your expense? It doesn't work like that, and if you think it does, then you don't know us very well."

Shame crept up her spine. Tentatively she circled Jonah's waist with her arms and pressed her cheek to his chest. He hesitated for a moment then slid his hands from her shoulders and hugged her tightly against him.

After a few seconds, she shifted uncomfortably and pulled away. He stepped back and shoved a hand to the back of his neck. It was more up close and personal than either of them felt comfortable with. She chuckled softly. Boneheads, the both of them.

"Thanks, Jonah," she said.

He reached out and ruffled her hair. "Get some rest, okay? You look like hell."

"Gee thanks."

She watched him walk back inside and expelled a pent-up breath when he closed the sliding doors behind him. It was as if he'd read her goddamn mind and knew exactly what to say to make her feel about six inches high.

For a brief moment, she contemplated chucking her carefully thought-out plan, but the image of Damiano writhing on the floor, in so much pain, shut the door on any guilt she felt.

Jonah's anger, his disapproval, she could face. She couldn't face herself if she let Damiano down. Jonah might well toss her out on her ass once this was all over with, and she wouldn't blame him. No one in FMG crossed him. What he said went. But as long as Damiano got what he needed to survive, she was okay with the fallout over her actions.

Chapter Nine

It wasn't easy to pick a time when either Mad Dog or Jonah wasn't skulking about. Tyana sometimes wondered if they slept at all.

She picked an hour before dawn, typically when Mad Dog had just gone to sleep and Jonah was holed up in his office doing what he did best. Brood.

She put on a muscle shirt, a pair of shorts and her running shoes then walked out of her room, prepared with a story that she couldn't sleep and was going on a run. Something that, as it happened, occurred frequently.

First she'd swing by and check on D.

When she found two guards posted outside his door, she frowned. When she tried to move past them and open the door, they moved to block her.

"Sorry, Jonah's orders. No one goes in without his say so."

Anger exploded within her. She wanted to kick their asses and then go tear a strip off Jonah's hide, but she had to remember her objective.

She glared at them both before she stalked down the hall to the stairs. When she was stopped by another of Jonah's security team, she let out a hiss of impatience.

"I'm going running. Or is that allowed?"

"Let her go," Jonah called from his office door where he stood watching Tyana.

She turned her resentful stare at him and had to make herself forget about the fact he'd barred her from Damiano's room. Otherwise they'd be in each other's faces again, and she wouldn't get anything accomplished.

Squaring her shoulders, she walked calmly down the stairs and headed for the French doors leading to the back patio. She stepped outside into the cool morning air and jogged down the path that led to the beach.

She knew despite Jonah's acquiescence that she was being closely watched. She'd have to be fast.

As she rounded the northwest corner of the island, she slipped between two large rock outcroppings, inaccessible when the tide rolled in. She dropped to one knee to fiddle with her shoelace and carefully looked around to see how visible she'd be from the house or other lookout points.

Feeling that she was as obscure as she was going to get while on the island, she reached into her shorts, slid the earpiece into her ear and palmed the tiny receiver, bringing it to her mouth in a casual gesture.

"Tits, you there?"

There was a long moment as she waited for a response.

"Tyana, my girl. What brings you knocking?"

She breathed a sigh of relief. "How much would it be worth to you to annoy the piss out of Jonah?"

Tits chuckled. "For that pleasure? Consider whatever it is you need on the house."

"I need a boat on the east side of the lesser island. Tonight. Oh two hundred. Arrange for a helicopter exchange five miles out. I need cash, a fake passport and the first flight you can get me on to Paris."

"You got it." There was a slight pause. "You can catch me up on the whys and wherefores later."

"Will do," she said before removing the earpiece and tucking it back into her shorts.

She set back out on her run, and just to make it look good, she circled the island twice before she headed back up to the house.

When she walked in, she saw Mad Dog standing at the breakfast bar, rummaging through the M&M bowl.

"You better not be eating my orange ones," she grumbled as

she walked over. “I saved the green ones for you.”

“And I appreciate it,” he said around a mouthful of chocolate as he turned in her direction. “All oranges are accounted for, see?” He pointed at the bowl that now only housed the brown and orange M&Ms.

She reached for a handful and plopped on a barstool to stare at him. “Don’t you ever sleep? I could swear you just went to bed.”

He grunted in response and dug back in the bowl, looking for another green one. He gave a disgruntled sigh and snagged a brown one instead. “I got an hour. That’ll do for now. What about you? What’s got your panties in a knot this morning?”

She lifted an eyebrow. “Can’t I go for a run without you and Jonah on my ass?”

His eyes widened and then narrowed as he looked her over suspiciously. “Get up on the wrong side of the bed this morning?”

“I’m pissed because I tried to go see D and got blocked by two of Jonah’s henchmen.”

“Ahh.” Mad Dog turned back to the M&M bowl and fingered one of the orange ones.

She shot him a quelling glare, and he picked a brown one instead. “Ahh? Is that all you can say? This sucks, Mad Dog, and you damn well know it. Locking him up like a fucking animal? Forbidding me to see D like I’m some kind of goddamn child he has to babysit?”

Mad Dog stared pointedly at her.

She blew out her breath in frustration. “Okay, forget the babysitting part. I know I fucked up, but the keeping D locked up and me away from him bites, and you know it.”

He reached out and chucked her lightly on the chin. “I know it sucks, baby. But in this...this time I support Jonah’s decision.”

Tyana looked away, trying hard not to be angry with him. It wouldn’t change anything, and she really didn’t want there to be bad feelings between them. Or with Jonah for that matter, though after tonight, she knew there wasn’t a lot she could do about that.

"I want to see him today, Mad Dog," she said softly. "I need to see him and make sure he's okay. If I have to fight my way through that goddamn door, I will."

He sighed. "I'll make sure you see him after Marcus has been through to check things out, okay?"

She nodded.

"Did you and Jonah make up last night?" he asked in an abrupt change of subject.

She made a face and hoped to hell Mad Dog hadn't seen her and Jonah get all mushy. "Yeah, we're cool. That is until he pissed me off again this morning."

He laughed. "Yeah, well him pissing you off is nothing new and vice versa. When you two start being nice to each other is when I'm gonna start looking for a new job."

She grinned. Their relationship...well, it just worked. It always had. She had a deep and abiding respect for Jonah that had started as hero worship and evolved as she'd grown older. Which made it so difficult for her to disregard his orders for the first time.

Mad Dog cocked his head to the side. "I think I hear the chopper now. That must be Marcus."

She stood eagerly, but Mad Dog pushed her back down. "Let Jonah handle it. You'll only get in the way, start butting heads, and D doesn't need that right now. Be patient. I promise you'll get to see him afterward."

With a resigned sigh, she settled back on her seat and stuffed more orange M&Ms in her mouth. When Jonah rounded the corner, their gazes connected for a moment before he walked out to the helipad to greet Marcus.

"Down, girl," Mad Dog murmured.

She threw an M&M at him which he caught and promptly popped into his mouth.

A few moments later, Jonah returned with Marcus, along with two men carrying a whole host of medical bags and equipment.

Her panicked gaze found Mad Dog's, and he reached out and covered her hand with his.

"He'll be all right, baby. Trust in that."

She closed her eyes against the pain and fear that threatened to slice her in two. Damiano had to be all right. She simply wouldn't accept anything less.

"Come on, let's go shoot some pool. It'll get your mind off D for a while."

She reluctantly followed Mad Dog into the game room, but her attention was focused on what was happening upstairs.

ꙮ

After three frustrating rounds in which Mad Dog kicked her ass, Tyana was ready to concede defeat. She was solidly on edge, and with every minute that passed, she was more tempted to charge upstairs.

Then Jonah appeared, standing in the doorway, his expression giving nothing away.

"You can go up and see him, Ty."

She tossed aside the pool cue and shouldered by Jonah without a word. When she reached the stairs, she vaulted up two at a time. Marcus was just walking out of Damiano's room with his assistants in tow.

Though she wanted nothing more than to see D for herself, she stopped and grabbed Marcus's arm.

"How is he?" she demanded.

Marcus regarded her steadily. "I've upped his dosage of the serum, though I'm not sure how much good it will do. I've taken more blood samples to bring back to the lab for further testing. His instability doesn't seem to be physiological. I have a suspicion that it's psychological and that his triggers stem from his brain activity."

She frowned. "What does all of that mean? Is there a way to help him?"

"I'm working on it, Ty. I'm adding a regimen of mild sedatives. If he remains calm, I think there's a better chance he can control the random shifting." He paused for a moment then stared intently at her. "I think more and more that this is something he's going to have to beat on his own. From the beginning, I've approached this as a medical condition and treated it as such, but despite the manner in which he contracted his abilities, they fall in the realm of the supernatural, and as such, the key to conquering or controlling them is going to manifest itself within him. Basically he's been given powers that he's going to have to learn to use."

She shook her head. "That's not logical, Marcus. There has to be a scientific cure, some explanation, some way to fix what happened. It was a chemical agent, not some act of a supernatural being. God didn't come down and gift him with superpowers. Science did this to him, so science has to be able to fix him."

Marcus's expression grew grim. "This wasn't science, Tyana. It was men playing at being God, and maybe they succeeded to a degree. Whatever was in that chemical agent altered his DNA. I can't fix that. I can only bandage it."

She fell back against the wall, tears stinging her eyes. She scrubbed angrily at her face with her sleeve. "I won't accept that. I won't accept that there isn't something we can do."

Marcus reached out and lightly touched her arm. "I'm sorry, Ty. I know this isn't what you want to hear, but I won't lie to you. You have to accept that Damiano may always be this way, and if he can't learn to harness his powers, they might destroy him."

She pushed past Marcus and into D's room. He was sitting on the edge of his bed, his gaze directed out the window. He looked up when he heard her enter, and she could see the haunted shadows in his eyes.

She fell to her knees in front of him and gathered him tightly in her arms. His arms came around her and held on just as tightly.

"We'll beat this," she said fiercely. "Goddamn it, D, we'll beat this. Do you hear me?"

He slowly pulled away, and his gaze flickered over her face. His expression tightened in pain when his hand brushed over the bruise on her cheek. "I hurt you," he said hoarsely.

She kissed his hand and shook her head adamantly. "You didn't hurt me, D. You would never hurt me. It wasn't you."

"You should probably stay away from me," he said in a low voice. "It's for the best."

She framed his face in both her hands and forced him to look at her. "I'm never leaving you, D. Never. You don't have to do this alone. I'm going to find a way to help you. I swear it. We'll do this together, just like we've done everything else. You and me against the world."

He smiled then, his brown eyes warming with love and affection. "How is it you turned into my fiercest protector when I spent so many years looking out for you?"

"Because now it's you who needs protecting. It's time I took care of you."

He yawned and frowned. "Marcus gave me a sedative. It's making me a little woozy."

"Then rest," she said softly. "And know that you'll always have me with you. No matter what."

"I know, little sister, I know."

She hugged him once more then heard Jonah at the door.

"He needs to rest, Ty."

She rounded furiously. "Back off, Jonah."

He stared hard at her but didn't leave. She slowly turned back to Damiano and hugged him tightly. "I love you," she said fiercely.

"Love you more," he said with a soft laugh. "Now go before Jonah has a coronary."

She touched his cheek one last time, knowing this would be the last time she'd see him for a while, longer if Jonah tossed her out of FMG after she pulled off her latest plan.

Then she turned, her eyes burning, and walked past Jonah and down the stairs. She needed air. She needed to be alone to grieve.

Chapter Ten

This was the part of her plan that sucked. Not the sneaking out of the house with a wetsuit, radio and GPS or the quick change she'd done crouched among the rocks dodging the incoming surf. It was the swimming.

Tyana swam through the dark waters toward the adjacent island with precise strokes. Her radio and GPS were stuffed into a waterproof bag and secured to her waist. The knife Mad Dog had given her was strapped to her leg. Everything else had been left behind.

Midway, she paused and flipped onto her back to rest, thankful that her rigorous training kept her in shape. The water wasn't rough, but she knew it would get hairy when she neared the rocky island. She'd need all her wits and strength to make sure she didn't end up a rock ornament.

After a few moments, she flipped back over and struck out again. She was on a tight schedule and needed to be on that boat before Jonah or Mad Dog discovered she was gone.

She'd left a note for D, not that Jonah wouldn't know exactly why she was gone, but she wasn't so callous as to simply disappear without explanation.

Jonah would know, and he'd come after her. She'd just have to make sure she stayed one step ahead of him and accomplished her goal as quickly as possible.

The current began to drag more forcefully at her, and she didn't try to fight it. She swam hard as it pushed her to shore and rested when it began to suck her back.

Three steps forward, two steps back.

She chose the angle of entry and put all her concentration into making sure she wasn't yanked off course. The waves pounded at her as she swept between jagged rock outcroppings. Pain shot through her leg when her knee cracked into a rock just below the surface, but she gathered her wits and used it to push off and propel her closer to shore.

Her feet glanced off the bottom, and she reached down, digging for a foothold, only to be dragged back and slapped again against the rough surface of the rock.

With the next wave, she plunged beneath the surface and grabbed at handholds to pull herself forward. She was almost there, damn it.

She broke the surface, gasping for air, and planted her feet on the bottom as she fought the current. Then, with the next oncoming wave, she lunged for the shore, finally crawling and collapsing onto the sand.

Her leg ached like a mother, but she didn't have time to evaluate her injuries.

She hauled herself up and limped up the incline and into the dense foliage and rock that sheltered the tiny island. She hit the button on her watch, and the green neon glow illuminated the time. She had twenty minutes to make the rendezvous point.

She made it to the opposing beach with five minutes to spare, bursting out of the thick, vine-ridden underbrush. She breathed a sigh of relief when she heard the boat in the distance.

Right on time.

The boat stopped a quarter mile from shore and flashed a single beacon toward the beach. Ignoring her pain and exhaustion, she plunged into the surf and waded out to do battle again with the rocks and current. At least this side wasn't as bad as the western front.

Several long minutes later, she reached the boat and threw her hand up to grasp the side. A strong, male arm hoisted her up and over, and she collapsed on the bottom, sucking air like a fish out of water.

The boat sped off as she caught her breath and mentally took stock of her condition. Aside from a few bumps and bruises and the pounding her knee had taken, she'd escaped relatively unscathed.

She pulled herself up, clutching the side as they rolled over a swell, and took position beside the guy manning the boat.

"How far until we rendezvous with the chopper?" she shouted.

He pointed to the onboard navigational system that charted their course, and she could see their ETA was fifteen minutes. Enough time for her to collect herself and prepare for the next leg of this insane venture.

She examined the tear in her wetsuit and wiped at the blood seeping from the cut. It stung like hell, but it didn't appear too serious. She slouched in her seat and tried to relax as much as possible as the minutes ticked by. Finally the boat slowed, and the guy cut the engine. They came to a stop, rocking and dipping with the waves.

A few seconds later, the sound of a chopper heading in their direction echoed through the night. When it hovered overhead, Tyana heard a thump as the rope ladder hit the deck of the boat. Her driver grabbed the lower rung and motioned her to hurry.

He held it in place while she gripped the rungs and hauled herself up. Another pair of hands gripped her wrists when she neared the top, and she found herself lying facedown on the floor of the helicopter as it soared away.

Damn, what a night. In other circumstances, she would have enjoyed the rush. Right now she was just trying to get her bearings.

Really big hands wrapped around her arms and jerked her upright. She found herself looking into the dark brown eyes of Tits, a bald-headed, bad-assed, mean-tempered son of a bitch. He liked to call himself a cross between an African American and a European mutt, whatever the hell that was.

He gave her an earpiece with a mic extending around to her mouth, and she grinned tiredly up at him as she put it in place. "Tits, love the earring, dude. When did you get it?"

He fingered the gold hoop dangling from his fleshy earlobe. "You like it? Did it myself."

She tried not to shudder. "It's you. Definitely you. Now

what's up with the meet and greet? Had no idea I rated such special treatment."

He flashed his perfectly straight, disgustingly perfect white teeth at her in what looked more like a snarl than a smile. "And miss out on this story? Hell, girl, this will only get better when I get the call from Jonah asking me where the hell you are. That's when the fun begins."

She gave him a sour look. "Don't egg him on. It'll only make things worse for me."

He patted a thick envelope on the seat beside him. "I got your stuff here, but you don't get it until you spill."

"Blackmailing bastard," she muttered. With a resigned sigh, she gave him the much abbreviated version of the story behind her run-in with Eli Chance and her subsequent meeting with Esteban in Paris.

"And you trust this dude?" Tits asked incredulously. "I seriously gave you more credit for smarts, Ty. I might need to knock some sense into that pretty head of yours."

She bared her teeth and snarled. "Don't get condescending on me, asshole. I don't trust the dickhead further than I can throw him. He has his purpose, though. He can tell me where Eli Chance is."

"You could find that out on your own," Tits said calmly.

She nodded. "I could, but I'm on a tight timeline here. If I don't already have Jonah hot on my ass, he'll be there shortly. The less time I spend fucking around trying to find Eli, the better off I'll be. I don't believe for a minute that Esteban has shit that can help Damiano, but I do believe Eli does. He's who I want, and if I have to go through Esteban to get to him then I will. I need him to think I'm working for him, though, because he's made threats against Damiano I can't ignore. When I'm done with Eli, I'll take Esteban's sorry ass out."

Tits whistled. "That's quite an agenda you got there, girl."

She shrugged. "It's nothing I haven't done before."

"You'll be glad I brought this along, then," he said as he stuck his hand under the seat and pulled out a bag.

She reached for it, the weight of it forcing her to rest it on her lap. When she looked in, she found a variety of weapons. All her favorites. She looked up at Tits and gave him a wicked grin.

"You're the shit, you know that?"

Tits laughed. "I really need to teach you better American slang. You sound ridiculous. Now do I get a kiss?"

She rolled her eyes, leaned forward and planted her lips against his. She tried to pull away just as fast, but he held her firm, deepening the kiss into a hot, lusty mix of lips and tongues.

She balled her fist and punched him in the gut. He broke away, laughing his fool ass off.

"*Ein geiler Wicht*," she muttered.

"I love it when you curse at me in foreign languages. Gets me all hot and bothered."

"Asshole."

He grinned again. "Consider that payment for services rendered."

She shot him a dark look and was tempted to punch him again, but damn, the man was built like a brick house and her hand hurt like hell from her last hit.

"When's my flight to Paris?" she muttered. "And how the hell am I going to get all this shit on my flight?"

"I'm the shit, remember?" he said with a cocky grin. "Private jet. Only the best for you, Ty baby."

She briefly considered giving him another kiss, but he looked too damn hopeful.

"I don't suppose you thought to bring me any clothes, did you?" she asked, pissed that she hadn't put it on her list of required items.

He grinned again and shoved a pair of jeans and a T-shirt at her. "As long as I get to watch you peel out of that wetsuit, I'll even throw in a pair of boots."

"*Casse-toi.*"

"Oooh, French now. My life's ambition is to get you to curse at me in Russian while we make love."

She laughed. Honest to God, how could you do anything else around this irreverent bastard.

"My Russian is rusty. I'd probably just end up telling you what a small dick you have."

He looked affronted. "Hey now, no need to get all personal on me."

"Besides, my tits aren't big enough for you, tit-man." Tits had gotten his nickname way back when for his affinity for big-busted women. His type had little in the brains department. Tyana was convinced that smart women scared him. It made no sense to her that a guy as intelligent as Tits would be so terrified of a woman with a brain, but then men were a mystery to her. One she didn't have any real interest in solving.

"For you, I'd make a sacrifice."

"I'd have to dumb down too much for you," she said sweetly. "Now turn your head while I turn my back so I can get out of this damn wetsuit."

She swiveled around, knowing full well he wouldn't do the same, but the most he'd see was her ass, and it wasn't as if he hadn't saved it enough. She figured he deserved a glimpse.

He proved her right by whistling when she wiggled out of the wetsuit. She shook her head and thrust her legs into the pants and then pulled the T-shirt over her head. When she turned around, she threw the wetsuit at him, smacking him on the chest.

He grinned, tossed it aside then shoved a pair of boots toward her, complete with a pair of socks. There was a reason he did so much work for Falcon. He never missed the details.

"You realize this is going to put you into hot water with Jonah," she said as she pulled on the socks and proceeded to lace up her boots.

He leaned back, adopting a casual slouch look that fit him perfectly. "Nah. He'll be pissed. Ain't no doubt about that. He'll threaten to kick my ass. I'll threaten to kick his. We'll scratch our balls, but at the end of the day he knows he needs me."

Her shoulders shook with silent laughter. For all the hilarity, it was a pretty accurate description of what would happen. Jonah would be furious, and he'd threaten all sorts of things, and with anyone else, he'd totally carry them out. But Tits? No way Jonah was going to bite the hand that had fed them on too many occasions.

"Well, thanks. I would have had a hell of a time getting off the island without your help."

His expression darkened, and the light teasing was gone in a second. "I'm only doing this because I want to help D. If you think I'd let you put that pretty ass of yours in this kind of danger for any other reason, you're short a few brain cells that I've always attributed to you. You're a big girl. You can take care of business, ain't no doubt, but I don't like it. I don't blame Jonah a bit for shutting your ass down. But D and I are tight, and I'll do anything to help my brother out."

"You and me both," Tyana whispered.

He held out a beefy fist, and she balled her own fingers into a fist and bumped it against his.

"You holler if you get into any trouble, you hear?"

"Yeah, I hear. Don't worry. I'm hoping this doesn't take more than a few days at most. Then I can go back so Jonah can toss me out of FMG, and I can come to work for you."

"You'd have to have bigger tits," he said with a slow perusal of her chest.

"You are such an asshole," she muttered.

Chapter Eleven

When Tyana touched down in Paris, she immediately called Esteban to set up a meeting. He didn't sound surprised to hear from her, but then he thought he held all the cards.

She checked into a hostel with the fake passport Tits had arranged and took a hasty shower to wash the sea grime from her body. She was starving, but she'd take care of that problem after she met with Esteban.

She shoved her stash of weapons under the bed but armed herself with the knife Mad Dog had given her, something she never went anywhere without. Deciding a couple more wouldn't hurt, she slipped two into the sleeves of her boots.

Hastily pulling her hair into a ponytail, she then donned a light jacket over her muscle shirt and headed out to her meeting with Esteban. Dusk wasn't too far off, though there was still plenty of light for her to stay aware of her surroundings.

She hated hotel meetings. Too closed in. Not open or public enough for her tastes. But Esteban had given her instructions to meet him in his suite at a swank hotel near Avenue des Champs-Élysées. Pretentious bastard.

She made a careful sweep of the area as she left the hostel and began walking casually down the street. She pulled a backpack over one arm, giving the appearance of just another college kid hiking across Europe.

After three blocks her neck prickled, and she fought the urge to do the clichéd stop and check. She didn't want to give away her suspicions, but she was certain she'd picked up a tail.

When she crossed the street at the next intersection, she glanced right to observe the sidewalk she'd just come from. Nothing immediately jumped out at her, but then a man wearing a leather coat, expensive Italian loafers and what looked to be tailor-made slacks made eye contact with her.

She grinned flirtatiously and gave him an appreciative look, but he didn't respond. No acknowledgement. Just a cold stare, straight through her.

The question was, who did he work for? Esteban? Eli Chance? Someone else entirely? It so wasn't Jonah's style to hire a henchman. No, he'd come after her himself and haul her ass back to the island.

For that matter Eli didn't strike her as the type to hire others to do his dirty work, either. He'd looked her up personally after the deal in Singapore.

That only left Esteban, and maybe he was making sure she hadn't set him up. She'd find out soon enough.

She didn't want to take the impending confrontation too public, so she veered off the main stretch and ducked into the narrow alleyways lining the back streets. It was quieter back here, though certainly not noiseless.

She kept her stance casual as she rounded the next corner, but as soon as she was out of sight, she flattened herself against the building and waited.

Suave Guy turned the corner a few seconds later, and she lashed out with a kick to his midsection. He doubled over and stumbled back. She launched herself at him, but he recovered quickly, landing a fist to her mouth.

Her head flew back in pain as her lip split. The metallic taste of blood filled her mouth. She spit, and it spattered on the street.

"At least you don't hit like a pussy, despite appearances to the contrary," she taunted.

His eyes flashed at the insult, and he swung again, but this time she was prepared. She blocked his fist, planted her boot in his balls, and when he folded over with a bellow of pain, she slugged him and sent him sprawling to the pavement.

She wrenched her knife from the inside of her jacket and followed him down, pressing the blade against the crotch of those nice, expensive slacks. She rotated her wrist in one of those flashy moves Mad Dog had taught her that was more for intimidation than anything else.

"Unless you want to lose the jewels, you tell me who the fuck you are and what you want."

His eyes betrayed him. His gaze skittered beyond her face, and she saw a glint of satisfaction.

She reacted solely on instinct, whirling and thrusting with her knife. It collided with a muscular arm, and she lost her grip on the handle as the blade slipped deep.

A hand snaked around her ankle and yanked. She fell forward, scraping her palms on the jagged cobblestones. She rolled and arched upward, snapping back to her feet.

She faced not one, but two pissed-off men, desire for her blood burning bright in their eyes.

She backed cautiously away. "Not that the knife doesn't look good on you, but I'm rather attached to it. It was a gift. So I'd like it back if you don't mind."

The second attacker calmly reached up and gripped the handle and yanked the knife out of his arm in one clean motion. She winced. That had to hurt.

She reached down to slide the two knives from her boots. She rose gracefully, twirling the handles expertly in her palms, letting the smooth leather dance between her fingers.

They circled each other, the unarmed man taking refuge behind the man with the knife.

He swiped first, testing her. She easily leaped away. He pressed in closer, trying to box her in. She kept a wary eye on Mr. GQ as he sidled over to the left.

When he reached down for a piece of metal pipe lying in the alley, she threw one of the knives. It landed with deadly precision right in the side of his neck.

He went down like a rock, blood spewing like a geyser from his carotid.

"That leaves just you and me," she said calmly as she sidestepped to keep a safe distance between her and the remaining man.

He grunted in response and whipped the knife in an

intricate pattern in the air.

"Is that supposed to scare me?" she asked. "Come on, slick. You'll have to do better than that."

To his credit, he refused to let her bait him. He continued to stalk her, and Tyana knew she needed to end things quickly before they were discovered.

The man rushed her. She felt the slick steel cut through her skin as his knife slashed through her upper arm. Refusing to allow the pain or surprise to make her falter, she dropped to one knee and rammed her fist into his balls at the same time she slashed at the hand that held the knife.

Her blade met bone, and she heard the clatter as the knife fell from his hand. She dropped and rolled, reaching for the other knife. She lunged to her feet a few yards away, ignoring the pain in her shoulder and the overwhelming odor of blood.

She tensed, prepared for another attack, but the man merely glared at her then turned and sprinted down the alleyway, blood dripping from his arm.

She didn't waste any time herself. She yanked the knife from the neck of the dead man and wiped it clean on his pants. She looked down at herself, and apart from the blood smeared on her jacket, she wasn't too much of a mess.

She slipped the jacket off, put her knives back in her boots and covered the remaining knife with her jacket. At the end of the alleyway, she found a bucket of dirty water and rinsed the blood off her boots so she wouldn't track it out of the alleyway.

Her arm hurt like hell, but a quick glance told her it wasn't too bad. The blade had just glanced off her skin, cutting a shallow gash about two inches long. It could have been a hell of a lot worse.

She hurried on to the hotel and snarled at the doorman when he took one look at her, turned his nose up and wouldn't admit her. She gave him Esteban's name and waited with ill-disguised impatience as he called up to verify her identity.

A few moments later, he uneasily escorted her to the elevator and ushered her in. The lift opened into a penthouse where she was met by two men who looked like poster children for steroid use.

When they tried to pat her down, she yanked the blade out

from under the jacket and pointed it under the chin of the one with his hand on her shoulder.

"I suggest you back the fuck off," she hissed. "I've had about all I can take this afternoon. You touch me one more goddamn time, and you'll lose that hand."

"Jorge, let her go."

Tyana looked up to see Esteban standing across the room, an amused smirk on his face. Then she saw the man who'd cut her in the alley standing just beyond Esteban.

She stalked over to Esteban.

"You sleazy motherfucker. What's your game? You want to hire me, I say yes, and then you try to kill me?"

She pulled back to punch him but a hand gripped her wrist and squeezed painfully. She turned to gut the son of a bitch when again Esteban barked a command for his man to back off.

"Leave us," Esteban ordered.

The three men complied, and she was left alone with Esteban.

"Come, sit down," he said as he walked into the lavish sitting room.

She followed but opted to remain standing so she could see every entrance to the room.

"Why'd you try to kill me?"

"I wasn't very successful," he said pointedly.

"Your men are inept and fight like damn pussies," she sneered.

Esteban chuckled. "Which is why I hired you to go after Eli Chance instead of sending them. You impress me. Maybe I just wanted to see what kind of muscle I was hiring. I'd say you passed with flying colors."

"You gave up one of your men for a test?"

He shrugged. "He was expendable."

"Nice," she drawled.

"Enough about him," Esteban said with a wave of his hand. He sat and crossed one leg over the other as he extended his arm along the back of the couch. "We have other matters to discuss. Like Eli Chance."

She nodded. “Eli Chance in exchange for the antidote or cure or whatever you want to call it for my brother.”

“Alive,” Esteban said. “He must be alive or the deal is off.”

“I think you made yourself perfectly clear when we spoke before. Now tell me where to find him.”

Chapter Twelve

Jonah surveyed Tyana's empty room and barked a directive into his radio. One by one his security team checked in. No one had seen Tyana or knew her current location.

He let out a vicious curse and turned and stalked down the hallway toward Mad Dog's room. He flung open the door, and Mad Dog, never one to sleep much or very deeply, rolled out of bed, silver glinting in his hand.

"What the fuck?"

"Tyana's gone. Any idea where she is?"

A flash of fear speared Mad Dog's blue eyes. "She's not on the island?"

Jonah shook his head. "Last time she was seen was last night around ten when she went up to see D before heading to bed."

Mad Dog got up from the floor and tossed his knife back onto the pillow. Then he reached for his pants and yanked them on. He turned back to Jonah. "Let's go see if D knows anything."

Jonah hesitated. "It might not be a good idea to upset him."

Mad Dog swore. "If she's gone, he's going to know it soon enough. Those two are attached at the hip. You can't protect them from everything, Jonah."

Jonah nodded curtly and walked into the hall. Mad Dog was right, and he wished he could stop the knot that was growing in his stomach. Ever since Damiano had taken the Americans into Adharji, things had slowly spiraled out of control. And now Jonah feared he was no longer able to protect his team. His family. Just as he hadn't been able to protect so many others from his father all those years ago.

He and Mad Dog walked past the guards at Damiano's door and entered quietly. D was awake, standing at the window, staring unseeingly over the water. His hand dangled at his side, a piece of paper held between his fingers.

He turned slowly to look at Jonah and Mad Dog, dullness edging his dark brown eyes.

"She's gone," he said simply and held the paper up.

Jonah yanked it away and read the short note written in Tyana's neat scrawl.

We're going to beat this, D. Believe that. Don't worry about me. I can take care of myself, and this time I'm going to take care of you. Be back soon. Ty.

Jonah balled the paper in his fist and sent it flying across the room. Mad Dog, who'd been reading over his shoulder, cursed and ran a hand through his shaggy hair.

"How can she be so stupid?" Jonah gritted out. "She's going to get herself killed. How does that help any of us?"

Raw helplessness seeped into his chest and paralyzed him.

"You don't understand," Damiano said, and he sounded as helpless as Jonah felt. "Ty feels like she owes me. She's always felt like she's owed me. No matter what I say or what I do to try and make her understand, she looks at where we were and everything I did to protect her, and she feels guilty. But God, how could I not? She was a child. A tiny little thing too young and innocent for the hell we lived in. I was all she had, but she was all I had until you and Mad Dog.

"As crazy as it makes me for her to feel the way she does, I understand it, because if the positions were reversed, I'd do whatever I could to help her, fuck you and anyone else in my way."

Jonah saw the pain, the uncertainty in Damiano's eyes. He knew that he and Tyana had been through hell before they'd struck out on their own. After two scraggly kids attempted to pick his and Mad Dog's pockets on the streets of Prague, Jonah hadn't ever stopped to examine the reasons why he took them in.

Running from his own past and mistakes, Jonah had

teamed with Mad Dog under the patronage of Burkett, a wealthy businessman with more shadows than dusk. With Burkett's money and Jonah's determination, he'd turned two misfits into honed fighters. Later they formed Falcon Mercenary Group, first only doing work for Burkett, but as their reputation grew, they expanded beyond Burkett's umbrella and became independent.

Still, they owed him a lot, which was the only damn reason Jonah allowed Esteban on his island. He needed to glean what information he could from Burkett about Esteban and his connection to Eli Chance, but first he was going to give Tits a call.

"We'll find her, D," Jonah said quietly. "And I'm going to haul her ass back here where it belongs. After I'm done with her, she won't have much of an ass left, but at least it'll be here where she's safe."

"I want in," Damiano said in a determined voice.

Mad Dog muttered a no even as Jonah was shaking his head.

"I know how important Ty is to you," Jonah said. "But we can't afford any distractions. The best thing you can do for her and us is to stay here and concentrate on beating this thing."

Damiano's face twisted in a sneer. "Don't fucking patronize me, Jonah. I know what I'm dealing with here. There isn't a cure, no matter what Tyana wants to believe. No serum, no antidote. I'm stuck like this. I have to learn to deal with it. That's on me. No one can do it for me. For Ty I can do whatever it takes. You're not leaving me in the dark. Not when it comes to her."

Jonah and Mad Dog exchanged frustrated glances. It was obvious that if they left him, he'd pull a Tyana and go off on his own. And that wasn't an option. The last thing they needed was an unstable wild shifter on the loose. He'd get his ass killed.

Goddamn, but there were times when Jonah wished to hell he'd never laid eyes on those two gangly kids.

Mad Dog shrugged. "He's a big boy, Jonah. Time to cut the apron strings."

"Hey, fuck you," Damiano growled. But a glint of humor lit his eyes, the first sign of the old Damiano Jonah had seen in a long time.

In that moment, he realized that maybe this was what D needed. Not to be treated like a freak. To give him back his position on the team and ride his ass just like Jonah had always done.

They'd all been so wrapped up in their worry that they'd started treating him like he was damaged. Less than human. An animal.

Tyana's accusing eyes and her furious words flashed back to Jonah. She was right. He'd treated D like an animal.

He glanced sharply up at Damiano. "You've got a half hour to get your act together and meet us downstairs. I'm going to be on the horn with Tits because I know that bastard was the one who helped Tyana off the island."

He turned to Mad Dog. "I want all the intel you've collected on Eli Chance, and get the chopper out here pronto. If we can get to Chance before Tyana then we can eliminate the threat and be there when she shows up."

"And if we don't beat her to him?" Mad Dog asked.

"He dies," Jonah said simply. "He's already signed his death warrant. You and I have been over this already. Tyana's leaving had nothing to do with it. He was going down regardless. As long as he exists, Tyana's never going to stand down."

Mad Dog nodded then clasped Damiano's shoulder. "Glad to have you back, brother. Now get your ass in gear. We've got some ass to go kick."

Jonah turned and walked out, and Mad Dog followed closely behind. As they hit the stairs, Mad Dog bumped Jonah on the arm.

"Now you mind telling me what the hell we're going to do if he spazzes out on us?"

Jonah sucked in a deep breath. "Call Marcus. Ask him what we need to bring, whether it's drugs, tranquilizers, sedatives, and ask his advice on how much stress he thinks D can take. We'll just have to keep a close eye on him."

Mad Dog nodded and trotted down the remaining steps, disappearing around the corner. Jonah stalked into his office and picked up the phone.

A few moments later, Tits' distinctive drawl bled over the line.

"Jonah, my man, what can I do you for?"

"Cut the bullshit. Where is she?"

"Where is who? You lose your girlfriend?"

Jonah clenched his jaw. "You know damn well who I'm talking about. What the fuck were you thinking, Tits? She's going to get her ass killed. And I swear to God, if that happens, I'll fucking gut you and feed you to the sharks."

"Ty's a big girl, dude. Chill the fuck out."

"You don't seem to get it," Jonah snarled. "She's in way over her head. The guy she's after has already gotten to her twice. She's lost all perspective. She's gone off half-cocked riding high on emotion. You tell me, Tits. Would you want someone like that working under you?"

There was a long pause. Then Jonah heard several indecipherable swear words.

"She's not going to forgive me for this one, man."

"I don't give a shit. All I care about is making sure she stays alive."

Tits sighed. "I put her on a private jet to Paris. Gave her money, weapons and a fake passport. That's all I can tell you. She wouldn't say much more."

"Much, you said much," Jonah said, latching onto that little tidbit like a pit bull. "Which means she did say more. You tell me every goddamn word."

"She was hooking up with Esteban, the guy who wanted to hire you guys to take out Eli Chance and his team."

Jonah swore. "If you hear from her, if she asks you for anything else, you fucking sit on her until I get there, you read me?"

"I don't take orders from you," Tits growled.

Jonah hung up before he hurled any more curse words into the phone. Next on his list was a call to Burkett to find out his connection to Esteban and why Burkett had arranged the meeting between Esteban and Falcon.

He sat down and stared at the phone for a long moment before picking it back up. He punched in Burkett's private number and waited.

"Jonah, what can I do for you?" Burkett's gravelly voice bled over the line, harsh, like rocks.

"You're so sure it's me," Jonah said dryly.

"No one else has this number."

Jonah leaned back in his chair. "I need information, Paul."

There was a surprised silence.

"What kind of information?"

"Esteban Morales. What is your connection to him, and why did you turn him on to us?"

There was another long pause.

"Is Esteban a cause for concern?" Burkett asked.

Jonah simmered impatiently. "That's what I'm trying to determine. I need to know whatever you can tell me about him."

Burkett sighed. "He's an old friend. Well, not a friend exactly, but I owed him a favor. He came to me and asked if I'd put in a word for him with you. He wanted a job done, and I knew you were the best at handling discreet matters."

"How the hell would he know you were in any way connected to Falcon?" Jonah bit out.

"That's a very good question," Burkett said softly. "One I don't have an answer to. I take it from your tone that you didn't accept the job?"

"No."

"Then why do you want information on him? Is there a problem? I have a few favors I can call in if Esteban has become a nuisance."

There was too much eagerness in Burkett's voice, as though he'd like nothing better than to do away with Esteban.

"Thanks, Paul, but this is one we'll be handling ourselves."

"Just be careful, Jonah. Esteban's influence is far reaching. He won't be easy to take down." There was another hesitation. "If you need anything—"

"I won't," Jonah said shortly. "But thank you."

He hung up in frustration. He didn't know anything more now than he had before calling Burkett. If anything the waters had just gotten muddier. No matter how Burkett played it out, there was obviously some connection between him and Esteban. Why else would he have been so accommodating when Esteban came calling? Burkett was a cagey bastard who didn't pay much attention to staying inside the lines. It wouldn't surprise Jonah to discover that Burkett and Esteban had a much more detailed history than Burkett let on.

At any rate, he couldn't afford to expend the mental energy on trying to figure Burkett out. He, Mad Dog and Damiano were going to haul ass to Paris and hopefully shut Ty down before she ever got off the ground.

Chapter Thirteen

Tyana wasn't stupid enough to think Eli Chance wouldn't be expecting her. She didn't trust Esteban and his motives, and Eli had proved adept at tracking her location. In the end, it wasn't about the element of surprise. It was about beating him anyway.

She tugged her backpack into place against her chest and cinched the straps tight. She did a final pat down of her parachute and made sure her GPS was strapped to her wrist.

Two minutes to drop.

The pilot radioed for her to get into position, and she moved to the open exit, steadying herself with one hand.

Eli probably had his entire compound booby-trapped in a mile radius around the remote station in the Patagonian Mountains. Which was why she was going to drop right into its heart.

The pilot announced all go, and without hesitation, she jumped. For a moment, panic gripped her as it always did when she first hurtled out of a plane. But then she collected herself and folded gracefully into a freefall.

She dove downward, gaining speed as she kept a close eye on her altimeter. Her timing had to be just right if she didn't want to open the chute too soon and risk being spotted as she floated to the ground. Wait too long and she'd become a permanent fixture of the landscape.

The wind blew against her face, her hair streaming upward as she gave herself momentarily to the exhilaration of her freefall.

Three seconds. Two seconds. One.

She pulled the rip cord and waited that infinitesimal second before she was jerked upward and her progress halted. The chute billowed and slowed her as the ground came hard and fast.

She curled her knees, bracing for impact, and rolled as soon as she touched down. Still, the sudden landing knocked the breath from her even as she scrambled upward and immediately began disentangling herself from the cords.

In the darkness, she bundled the parachute, wrapping it as tightly as she could. When it lay on the ground at her feet in a wad, she unlatched her pack and pulled out her night vision goggles.

She took stock of her weapons, touching the places she'd secured her knives and the pistol in her shoulder harness. Then she picked up the assault rifle and slung the strap over her shoulder.

She shoved as much of the parachute into her pack as she could and began looking for a place she could hide it from view. After several minutes searching among the rocky nooks and crannies of the valley she'd landed in, she found a suitable place and piled rocks over the bag.

Her GPS lit up and calculated her position as she thumbed it on. Bingo. Right on target.

A quick smile quirked her lips upward before she squared her shoulders and surveyed the terrain surrounding her. The compound was over the next rise, and she'd successfully breached the outer perimeter.

Still, she was careful, keeping low, moving on silent feet as she crept through the trees. Her meeting with Eli might be on his own turf, but it would be on her terms.

ꟸ

And so it began.

Eli bit out a curse as one of the silent alarms was triggered. Though he'd been expecting company, he hadn't expected it so soon.

She certainly could have picked a better time. One when

both Ian and Braden weren't off prowling the grounds looking for kitty food.

Then again, he might do well to be more worried about them than Tyana Berezovsky. She might shoot first and ask questions later.

Gabe was God knows where, having decided yesterday to disappear into the village down the mountain, probably in search of pussy. His parting words had been something to the effect that since Eli was so keen for Tyana to find his ass then he could deal with her when she got here.

Good help was hard to find and harder to keep.

None of the others seem to think Tyana posed any sort of threat. Eli knew better. To them she was just a woman. Easily handled, easily subdued.

He smiled. He was looking forward to the challenge.

Pulling his hair behind his neck, he secured it with a leather tie then reached for his shoes and tugged them on. He might as well either go save her from the cats or save the cats from her. One way or another, someone better damn well be grateful.

A quick glance of the infrared monitor told him she was slowly making her way toward the south entrance. The most obvious course would just be to meet her, but where would the fun be in that?

No, he was going to enjoy this. Savor it. He smiled again. And maybe before the night was over, he'd take the impending confrontation to the bedroom.

He stepped into the night and breathed deep of the chilly air. Quietly he slipped beyond the shadows cast by the glow of the interior lights. He went east, cutting a direct path to intercept her...from behind.

He closed his eyes and let go, embraced the faint mist, let it curl around him, and then he became the very air he breathed.

A faint breeze carried him through the trees. Ahead, he saw movement. He looked down as he floated above the figure clad in black.

She moved with grace and stealth, her movements slow and calculated. She made no noise, left no disturbance in her wake.

He contented himself with watching her, gauging her patterns as she stopped and patiently observed the area around her. He saw her shiver then look quickly back, and he wondered if she'd sensed him again.

He ventured closer, wrapping around her hair and whispering softly against the nape of her neck. A slight shift in the air alerted him to her movement. Silver glinted in moonlight as a knife appeared in her hand. With the other, she grasped the barrel of her rifle and hauled it over her shoulder to cradle in front of her.

A faint apparition, he wrapped himself around her in a veil of mist, faint trails of smoke curling around her wrists. Then he jolted back to his human form, his fingers like bands around her small bones.

She exploded in a flurry of motion. He went sailing over her shoulder and wondered again how the fuck she always managed to get the drop on him no matter how prepared he was. He was starting to take it personally.

There was the wee little matter that he honestly wasn't trying to hurt her, but still. He could have simply slit her throat, and he consoled himself with the fact that if he was a real bastard, he could have broken her neck.

But no, instead he was lying on the ground feeling like a goddamn sissy for being beaten up by a girl.

He started to pick himself up and found a boot pressed against his neck. He grabbed her ankle, yanked the knife out of the side sleeve then wrenched her back, making her fall.

They both bolted to their feet, knives in hand, and began circling.

"You're late," he said, though he wasn't about to admit he hadn't really expected her for a few more days.

"I had a few technical difficulties," she said, and it was then, when she turned her head and a sliver of moonlight hit her face that he could see her split lip.

"Piss off one too many people, my love?"

She bared her teeth. "The last man to piss me off died in a Paris alley. I wouldn't push my luck if I were you."

"Isn't that what you're here to do, though? Kill me?"

He watched intently for any change, any flicker, some sign of what was going round that pretty head of hers. That incredibly stubborn, obnoxious, gorgeous head of hers.

"I'm pretty sure we've had this conversation before," she said in a bored voice.

"Then what are you here for?"

He blinked, and she was in his face, her knee planted in his stomach and one fist buried in his ribs. He let out a growl of pain but didn't budge. Instead he yanked her against him. She gasped in surprise and the knife fell from her hand.

When she brought her other knee up, he blocked it with his.

"You're getting too predictable, love," he murmured. "You have a morbid fascination with a man's balls. Is that any way to treat such delicate equipment?"

She cursed in what sounded like four different languages. He recognized at least two and raised his eyebrows.

"And to think I've kissed that mouth."

Her eyes glittered in the moonlight. Just before she reared back and head butted him.

Pain exploded over him. He let go and stumbled back, holding his nose as blood gushed. Jesus H. Christ. Bitch was vicious!

She took off in a dead run. He watched her leap like a damn gazelle over rocks and roots and disappear into the night.

He vaporized into smoke and streamed after her.

He materialized in front of her this time, stopping her in her tracks. She let out a disgusted grunt.

"Can't beat the weak woman without resorting to your little smoke tricks?" she taunted.

He grinned and wiped more blood from his nose. "If you want me to apologize for pressing my advantage, you'll be waiting a long time. If you'd just play nice, I'd invite you in for a drink..." he made a slow up and down sweep of her body with his gaze, "...and maybe show you just how hospitable I can be."

"And you say *I* have an obsession with that part of the male anatomy."

"I'm a man. We think with our dicks, remember?"

She responded with a quick jab. He dodged and punched back, connecting with her shoulder. It wasn't enough to even knock her back, but he heard her quick intake of breath, and he frowned.

Then once again, he found himself staring up at the stars when she executed a lightning roundhouse kick to his jaw. And she was off again.

Damn but he must have it awfully bad for this chick to put this much effort into getting into her pants.

He got up, rubbing his jaw, and set off. She was making steady progress toward the house. What did she want? She wasn't trying to kill him. Hurt him? Taunt him? Yes. But she was pulling her punches every bit as much as he was, and she hadn't tried to filet him with the damn machete she called a knife.

Chasing after women wasn't his style, but damn if he wasn't wagging his ass after her like a fucking lap dog. He had a sneaking suspicion the feisty little wench just might be his dream woman.

The constantly trying to do him bodily harm could put a serious kink in their relationship, though.

He shifted again and streaked after her, suddenly weary of the chase. It was time to end it. He wanted her. Wanted to taste her again. To get so deep inside her that he lost all sense of himself.

A low growl echoed across the night.

As he rounded the corner of the west wing of the house, he saw Tyana frozen, staring at two pacing cats.

Chapter Fourteen

Tyana didn't even bother with her knife. She gripped the rifle with both hands and quietly brought the muzzle up. A big-ass jaguar and only a slightly smaller black panther, so black that all she could really make out was the iridescent glow of his eyes, paced a few feet away, their eyes never leaving her as they moved back and forth in obvious agitation.

"It would seem you have two choices," Eli said mildly from behind her. "You can give up like a good girl and come inside with me. Or you can be kitty food."

Her fingers tightened around her rifle, and before she could breathe, Eli was in front of her, his hand gripping her wrist so tightly she was forced to loosen her hold on the stock.

"I won't let you hurt them." His voice was deadly, laced with no bravado whatsoever. "Not that I think you'd have a chance with them anyway. You might get a shot off, but you'd be hamburger in a nanosecond."

Her hand was growing numb. She knew better than to make any sudden moves. She didn't want any teeth or claws in her ass if she put Eli on his butt. Was she looking at Ian and Braden Thomas? The two men Esteban wanted dead?

"What's it going to be, sugar?" Eli asked in a quiet voice. "You going with me or do I leave you out here for them? I don't usually like to share my treats with the house pets, but I might make an exception this time."

"I'm not your fucking treat," she snarled.

White teeth flashed in the moonlight. "Oh yes, sugar, you're my treat, all right. I just have to dig for the sweet."

The jaguar hissed and stalked closer. Eli pushed into her body, moving her back several steps. His body surrounded hers. *Protecting* her, for God's sake.

She shoved angrily at him and yanked her wrist from his grasp. "All right, let's go."

"Give me your weapons," he said calmly.

"Fuck you."

He stood, arms crossed then looked back over his shoulders. "They look hungry to me."

She slammed the rifle against his chest, backing him up one step. She yanked a pistol from her shoulder harness and offered it to him. Then she took the two remaining knives she had and dropped them on the ground.

"Damn, girl. Have I ever told you how sexy you look in commando mode?"

She glared at him. "Let's go, pretty boy. You and I have things to discuss."

He took her arm and herded her toward the house. She almost laughed. How ridiculous was this, anyway? Pride wouldn't allow her to just show up and ask for his help. Instead she had to posture, show how tough she was and that while she might suggest a partnership, she didn't *need* his damn help.

That whole pride goeth before a fall thing came readily to mind. She could swallow it for D, she reminded herself.

They entered through two gates that Eli had to punch security codes in for. He led her through a small courtyard then punched yet another keypad before they entered the house.

"Got something against visitors?" she asked as he continued to push her further into the house.

"Depends on who's visiting. You have an open invitation, sugar. But next time, just call. It'll save a lot of pain in my ass."

They stopped in what looked suspiciously like Eli's private little domain. All it lacked was a bed, though she wouldn't be surprised if one didn't fold out of the wall somewhere.

There were two leather couches, dark brown with an invitingly comfortable look. She was dead tired and the idea of melting all over one of them was making her work up a drool.

To the back, there was a desk littered with papers, a

laptop, a desktop, two phones and a shitload of electronics. Organization was obviously not his friend.

She didn't wait for an invitation. She wrenched her arm free of his grasp and trudged over to the couch, turned around and flopped onto it, closing her eyes as her head hit the back.

Eli gazed intently at her. There was trust in that action, though he doubted she intended for it to be perceived as such. Now in the light, he could see the shadow of a bruise around her jaw and the dark red cut on her lip, just at the corner.

Her face was pale with a hint of vulnerability in her obvious exhaustion. The leather jacket she wore was torn in at least two places, and there was old blood smeared on the sleeve. He frowned as he remembered hitting her there.

He crossed the distance between them and knelt in front of the couch. Her eyes flew open as he tugged at her jacket.

"Relax," he murmured. "Just getting your jacket off."

She watched warily as he maneuvered the coat off and tossed it aside. There was more blood on the black muscle shirt, how much was hard to tell as it faded into the dark material. Then his gaze lit on the gash on her arm.

He leaned forward and pressed his lips lightly to the wound.

She yanked away, her brow furrowed, a dark frown on her face. "What the hell did you do that for?"

"Didn't your mama ever kiss your booboos to make them all better?"

Her eyes became emerald ice. "I don't have a mother."

He withdrew slowly, watching as an impenetrable shield surrounded those beautiful eyes. He rocked back on his heels then finally stood, purposely using his position over her to indicate subtle power.

"So, you're here. Care to tell me why?"

Something flickered in her eyes. Brief uncertainty. And then the cool, unflappable look was back. She turned her chin up and stared unflinchingly at him.

He wanted to smooth his hands over the bruises on her face, but more than that, he wanted to track down the motherfucker who'd put them there and beat his ass.

"Esteban Morales wants you. Alive. Your friends? Not so much. He hired me to take them out and bring you in."

It was hard not to react to a statement like that, but he kept his gaze steady and stared back at her. "And here you are. I can't wait to hear how you're going to pull off killing my team and hauling me in alive."

Her gaze skittered sideways. "Where are they?"

"Who, Ian and Braden? I imagine they're still outside pissed because I took their kitty treat from them. They'll be even more pissed when they hear you want to kill them."

"I never said I wanted to kill them," she said calmly. "I said Esteban hired me to kill them."

"So you're here out of the goodness of your heart? Forgive me if I don't quite buy that."

She got to her feet, her hands fisted at her sides. "I'm here to save Damiano. I don't give a damn about you or your cat friends."

Eli cocked his head in surprise. "Damiano Ruiz?"

Her lip curled. "Yeah, you know, the guy who led your team into Adharji and took a shot of the same chemical agent you did."

"I thought he died," Eli said quietly. "When we got out..." He dragged a hand to the back of his neck and down his ponytail. "We wouldn't have left him. We considered him one of ours."

"He didn't die," she said icily. "We got him out. And now he's got the same problem the rest of you do."

"And that is?"

"Don't play stupid mind games with me. He's a shifter. Only he can't control his abilities like you. He's..." Her voice broke off, and her shoulders shook as she fought to compose herself. Then she looked back up at him, resolve burning brightly in her eyes. "I have to save him, and you're going to help me."

Fuck. What a goddamn mess.

He checked his watch as he realized that Ian and Braden should have been in by now. Not that they were predictable by a long shot, but he could usually time the duration of their shifts, just not when they'd happen.

"Stay here," he said. "I need to go see about Ian and Braden."

She frowned. "I'll go."

"Fine." He wasn't going to argue with her.

He turned and hurried toward the back again, hoping they hadn't gotten behind the high security fence he'd had installed. It should do the job of keeping them contained, but then a wild cat didn't always play by the rules.

"Why are you checking on them?" she asked as she hurried to catch up. "What's wrong with them?"

"They've been out too long."

She caught up to him again as he opened the last security gate and stepped onto the grounds. He listened intently for any sounds, any indication they were near. When she started to speak again, he silenced her with an upraised hand. Surprisingly she complied and kept to his side, as quiet as he was.

He hurried to the last place he'd seen them, where Tyana had come across them. When he got close, his pulse ratcheted up as fear gripped him.

Braden was lying on the ground while the jaguar prowled close by. When the jaguar scented them, he turned his head and hissed, his teeth flashing and his ears flattening.

"Oh shit," Eli murmured.

"What's wrong with him?" Tyana whispered. "Why doesn't he just shift back?"

He didn't answer. His attention was fixed on Braden, trying to see if he was moving. He prayed to God Ian hadn't attacked him in jaguar form.

"Ian," Eli called. "Ian, goddamn it, you have to let me go to him." He felt stupid for talking to the damn cat. There was nothing of Ian inside, not when he was in shifted form. But he was starting to feel desperate. How could he sacrifice one brother for the other? He couldn't hurt the jaguar. Ian had no control over his actions. He became the predator.

The jaguar snarled again and stalked slowly toward Eli and Tyana. Eli shoved Tyana behind him and held her there with one arm. He could shift and easily evade the cat, but it would leave Tyana unprotected.

Braden stirred and Eli heaved a sigh of relief. At least until the jaguar turned when it sensed Braden's movement. The cat padded back to Braden, and Eli knew he was going to have to intervene. He wouldn't stand back while Braden was mauled.

"If this goes bad, you get your ass back to the house," he hissed in Tyana's direction.

Then he let go, let the air swallow him whole. He streaked toward the jaguar as he bent his head to sniff at Braden's chest.

Eli curled around the muscular neck of the jaguar, but to his surprise, the cat nuzzled against Braden, licked his cheek and backed off.

And then he began the shift.

Eli retreated, materializing a few feet away as Ian fell to the ground, his muscles contorting. The cat hissed in pain as his limbs elongated. His body rippled as fur and skin stretched and faded. Eli winced as the human face stretched in agony as Ian finally came back to himself.

Ian panted and a groan worked itself from the depths of his chest. He opened his eyes and looked first at Braden lying beside him and then turned his tortured gaze to Eli.

"What have I done?" he whispered.

He struggled to get up and collapsed to the ground again. Eli rushed forward to help him, but Ian shrugged him off as he fought desperately to get to his brother.

"Ian, he's alive. I'm not even sure he's hurt."

Still, Ian pulled himself to his brother, and Eli knelt beside them both.

Braden blinked with glazed eyes. His muscles twitched and spasmed, and a heavy sweat bathed his entire body.

"Braden," Ian croaked. "Are you okay? Talk to me, man."

"I'm good. I think," Braden whispered, his voice hoarse and laced with pain.

Eli felt Tyana walk up behind him. "Back off," he growled.

The two brothers looked up at Tyana in confusion.

Eli stood and whirled around, anger and his need to protect his men uppermost in his mind. "I said, back away."

She stared past him, not even absorbing his demand. Confusion simmered in her eyes as she stared at the brothers in a mixture of sympathy and horror.

"What's wrong with them?" she asked. "Why didn't they just shift back?"

"Because they can't. You should know this, Tyana. You said Damiano was the same. They're as unstable as he is."

She shook her head, tears swimming in her eyes. "But you're stable. You can control it. I thought...I thought they would be able to as well."

And then Eli knew. That was what she wanted. It was why she'd risked her ass to chase him across the globe. She thought he had answers that would help her brother. How could he tell her that there was no answer? That *he* was the freak, not Damiano. Not Ian and Braden.

Ian rose unsteadily to his feet, pulling Braden up with him. Eli gave them his attention then shot Tyana a sharp glance. "Help me get them back to the house."

She didn't hesitate to wrap an arm around a naked Braden as he leaned heavily on her. He didn't seem to care that a complete stranger was hauling him toward the house. He looked too washed out and exhausted to process much of anything.

Eli grabbed on to Ian and slung Ian's arm across his shoulders. Then he started forward, dragging Ian's weight with him.

As he watched Tyana struggle with Braden's much larger form, he wondered if she'd make it back, but she didn't complain, nor did she let go of Braden.

Eli cursed when he realized she was taking the brunt of Braden's weight on her wounded shoulder.

Several long minutes later, Tyana and Eli hauled the brothers into the house and toward their bedrooms.

"Hold up right here," Eli instructed Tyana as he reached over and leaned Braden away from Tyana and against the wall. "Sit tight a second and I'll come back to help you get him into his room."

Tyana nodded wearily.

Eli grunted as he heaved and tugged at Ian. He finally got him muscled over to the bed and leaned him down. Ian sagged against the pillow and his eyes opened, dull and shadowed.

"Did I hurt Braden, Eli? Tell me the truth. Did I attack my own brother?"

"No, man. I wouldn't lie to you. You know that. You were protecting him. From us. He was out of it from the shift. You watched over him."

Ian closed his eyes in relief. "Tired," he murmured.

"Rest, dude. You'll be hungry as hell when you get up. I'll try to make sure there's something to eat."

Ian cracked a half smile. "Won't you be too busy with your lady friend?"

Eli rolled his eyes. "Noticed her did you."

"I'm not dead," Ian said dryly. "Nice ass. I got a good view on the way back. Think she'd hold the fact that Braden and I are cats against us?"

Eli gave a disgusted snort. "She's not here to be your kinky plaything. You two get your own damn woman to sandwich."

Ian smiled faintly. "Yeah, I know. You don't share."

"And don't you forget it," Eli warned.

Ian struggled to keep his eyes open, and Eli put his hand on his shoulder. "Get some rest, bro. This was a bad one."

Ian nodded and closed his eyes.

Eli hurried back out to the hallway where Braden was still propped against the doorframe to his bedroom. Naked as a damn jaybird. He glanced over at Tyana but she seemed oblivious to Braden's nudity.

"I'll take it from here," he told her. "Go wait for me in my office. You remember the way?"

She nodded, her eyes subdued. To his surprise, she didn't give him any lip. No defiance. She just turned around and walked back down the hallway, a defeated slump to her shoulders.

Chapter Fifteen

When Eli walked into his office, he found Tyana gathering the weapons he'd tossed onto one of the couches. Her torn jacket was back on, and she was shoving her knives into place.

Her back was rigid, her movements mechanical, as though she were hanging on to control by a thread.

"What are you doing?" he asked softly.

She turned, casting her gaze briefly over him before returning to what she was doing.

"Leaving," she said shortly.

He moved closer to her but was careful to keep some distance between them.

"You just got here."

She slung the rifle over her shoulder and turned around again, her stance defensive and impenetrable as hell.

"I found out what I needed to know. You can't help me." She paused for a long second then stared hard at him. "Why you?"

He lifted his brow in confusion. "Why me what?"

She sighed with impatience. "Why are you stable? How is it you can control your shifts, even conjure clothing when you shift back? You're in complete control of your abilities. The inhibitor I used on you was ineffective."

"Dumb luck?"

"Until now, I assumed you'd found a cure, that you and your team had found a way to fight what happened. I wanted that for Damiano. I've killed for it. I would kill again. I'd do anything to save him from what I fear will happen if he doesn't get help soon."

"Join the club," Eli murmured.

"I was hired by Esteban to kill Ian and Braden and to bring you in alive. Any idea why he'd want you alive?"

"Sweetheart, I don't even know who the fuck Esteban Morales is, so how the hell would I know why he wants my team dead and me alive?"

Realization lit fire in her eyes. "Because he's the bastard who unleashed the chemical agent on you. You're stable. The others aren't. He wants to know why. You're the one thing in his experiment that didn't go wrong."

Eli held his hands up. "Whoa. Slow down. Back up and tell me what the fuck you mean by he's the one who unleashed the chemical on us."

Her shoulders sagged and fatigue blew over her. She looked like a sapling swaying in the wind. He moved into her space, took her by the arm and pulled her toward the door.

"What are you doing?" she asked.

"Fixing you something to eat. You'll eat. Then we'll talk. You're no good to me unconscious. You look like you're about to fall over."

Her quiet acquiescence was starting to bug the shit out of him. He was much more comfortable when she was threatening to kick his ass, kicking his ass or pulling a weapon on him.

He shoved her toward the kitchen, parked her butt in a chair by the table and went to rummage in the fridge for leftovers he could warm up.

Through it all she never said a word. Her gaze was focused across the room, unseeing, like she was a million miles away. Plotting her next move? Who knew with this woman.

He was beginning to understand her motivation a lot more now. Her loyalty to her brother mirrored his own toward his team. If he thought Falcon Mercenary Group held the answers to helping Ian and Braden, he would have been after their asses just like she'd latched onto his.

He warmed some soup on the stove, poured it into a bowl and plunked it down in front of her. Then he sat down across the table from her and told her to eat.

She fiddled with the spoon for a minute before she dipped in and started to eat. The silence grew between them as did Eli's impatience. He wanted answers.

Not that someone, some group being after him was anything new, not since the shit that had gone down in Adharji, but Esteban was a newcomer to the mix. And if Tyana was right, and he was behind the chemical attack, the shit was going to hit the fan and quick.

When he heard the clink of the spoon against the bottom of the bowl, he looked up and saw her push the bowl away. She looked like she was about to say something, so he kept silent, waiting on her.

"This sounds so stupid," she mumbled.

"Just say it, Tyana."

Her eyes met his again. "For some inexplicable reason I feel like I can trust you." She held up her hand. "That came out wrong. I don't trust you. I don't trust anyone outside Falcon. But I don't see you as the enemy.

"And there's this attraction thing..."

He raised his eyebrows. Somehow he didn't see her as having the balls to own up to the tension between them.

"I'm attracted to you in a way that leaves me baffled."

"The feeling is entirely mutual, sugar."

She glared until he fell silent.

"I looked you up in Singapore for information. I wanted a way to help D. I didn't intend for things to go as far as they did."

"I'm certainly not complaining," he offered.

Again she silenced him with a fierce scowl.

"Then you caught up to me in Paris and again, I lost sight of what mattered, what was important." A faint light of shame passed over her eyes. "I compromised Falcon because I couldn't keep my hormones in check. But when I'm around you..."

She put a hand to her forehead, a delicate gesture that contradicted her outer steel. "I get crazy. I feel stupid. I do stupid things. And quite frankly, it pisses me off."

"I'm assuming there's a point to this sharing of deep

thoughts," he said dryly. He wasn't about to admit that he was doing a mental double fist pump and already plotting how to get her get all stupid with him again.

"Yeah, there is," she bit out. "Esteban offered me a cure for D in exchange for killing Ian and Braden and bringing you in."

He was beginning to understand. "But instead you came here, knowing full well you had a snowball's chance in hell of pulling off the job."

She cut him off with a derisive snort, and he rolled his eyes. "Let's not go over the whole if I wanted you dead you'd be dead thing, okay? We've both had ample opportunity to kill each other. We haven't. Obviously you have no more desire to see me or my team dead than I do to see you die."

She nodded grudgingly.

"And you feel like you're betraying Damiano because you aren't willing to give Esteban what he wants?"

Her eyes flashed coldly, and he saw raw resolve there, simmering, angry.

"If I believed for a minute the bastard was telling me the truth I'd kill your men and package you and deliver you to him in a heartbeat."

"So you think he was lying."

"I think he knew exactly what buttons to push in order to get me to do his dirty work for him. Now what I want to know is why he's so fixated on getting rid of Ian and Braden and why he wants you alive."

Eli sat back in his chair. "My guess? If what you said is true, and we were all part of his little experiment then he wants me because I'm what *worked*. Just like you said." He frowned and leaned forward again. "What it doesn't explain is why he doesn't want Gabe."

Tyana gave him a perplexed look. "Isn't he the fourth member of your team? Why would Esteban want him?"

"Because he's stable," Eli said calmly.

Gabe was the sole reason Eli's secret hadn't been exposed. It also meant that Gabe was *really* the only experiment that worked. Had Esteban just overlooked him on his radar?

Tyana's eyes rounded with shock. "So you aren't the only

one after all?"

Eli shook his head.

"Maybe Esteban wasn't lying, then," she murmured. "Maybe there *is* a cure." Her chin came up and she looked at him, her eyes just a little bit lighter. "What went on during your captivity, Eli? Were you and Gabe given injections? Did they give you any serum? Tests?"

Eli's jaw tightened. "They didn't have time. We got out." He couldn't tell her that his natural shifting ability was what got their asses out of a sling in the prison camp. Not when the others didn't start exhibiting symptoms until much later.

"We didn't get in to rescue Damiano until three days after you guys split. He doesn't remember what happened." Her hands shook slightly on the table as she balled her fingers into fists. "He was in bad shape when we found him."

The area right behind Eli's eye began to pound. It felt like someone was shoving an ice pick right through his eyeball. He didn't leave men behind. He'd watched Damiano go down. Seen his lifeless body dragged out of the cell.

"That bothers you."

He looked up at her. She hadn't posed it as a question. "Hell yeah, it bothers me. I don't leave a man behind. I saw him die. I watched them take him away."

"He was more dead than alive when we found him," she said softly. "I won't lose him to this. Not after saving him once."

A silvery apparition shimmered and coalesced beside Tyana. Before he could utter a warning, not to Tyana, mind you, but to Gabe's stupid ass, Tyana bolted from her chair and grabbed Gabe's now solid form.

They fell to the floor, Tyana on top, knee dug deep into Gabe's crotch and her knife across his throat.

Eli stood and leaned over the table. "Dumbass. It would serve you right if I let her carve you up like a turkey. Tyana, back off. The moron you're about to kill is Gabe. I figure you at least want to stop and ask questions first."

Tyana pressed her knife just a little harder until a fine stream of blood slithered down Gabe's neck. "Don't you ever try and sneak up on me again like that, fucker."

Gabe held up his hands. "Yeah, yeah, I get the message. Get off, for God's sake. I have a policy about hitting girls."

Tyana kneed him in the groin even as she stood to her full height. Gabe rolled up in a ball, grunting in pain.

Eli chuckled and Gabe glared up at him. Then Eli grew more serious and fixed Gabe with a scowl. "How long have you been here?"

"Long enough."

Tyana speared them both with furious eyes. "So what's his gift?"

"Invisibility," Gabe said as he finally got himself to an upright position. "Damn convenient, wouldn't you say?"

"Or damn inconvenient if it gets you killed," she said sharply.

Gabe folded his arms over his chest. "Damiano. You said he was alive."

She nodded. "No thanks to you and your team."

"That's low and you know it," Eli said.

She lifted a brow. "Do I? It seems to me that you and Gabe here have a good deal. Maybe Ian and Braden were just collateral damage along with Damiano."

Eli bolted around the table and got up into her face quick. He wrapped his hand around the back of her neck and yanked her up close. "If you're insinuating that we somehow signed on for this gig, you better think again. We took a job to recover hostages. We hired Falcon to get us there. There were no hostages. It was set up from the start. How the fuck do we know that Falcon didn't lead us right into Esteban's hands?"

She gazed unflinchingly at him. "I guess neither of us has reason to trust the other."

"And yet here you are with the proverbial olive branch," he murmured.

"Maybe I just think our energies are better spent as a team rather than at odds."

"And I couldn't agree more." He bent and licked gently at the cut at the corner of her lip.

She jerked away, her eyes blazing with fury. She cast a sidelong glance at Gabe and frowned even harder. Eli laughed.

"He heard our entire conversation, sugar. Don't go getting all shy on me now."

It was probably the wrong thing to do, remind her that Gabe had been privy to her bloodletting. And he had a feeling that any time Tyana got in touch with her innermost thoughts it *was* the equivalent of shedding blood.

She turned and stalked out of the kitchen, and Eli turned on Gabe. "Stay the fuck away from her."

Gabe gave him a bored look. "You seem to forget she was sent here to kill at least some of us. Quit thinking with your dick, Eli. Get rid of her and fast."

Eli sighed. "To quote a saying that has become increasingly more common around here lately, if she had wanted to kill you, you'd be dead."

"That's it?"

"What do you want, Gabe? Want me to go slit her throat? How does that help us? She has information we need. We now have the name of the jerk-off who gassed us to begin with. He wants us out of the picture. I think we ought to be a little more concerned with taking this asshole out than pissing off the entire Falcon Mercenary Group by killing their little sister."

Gabe shrugged. "I'm with you, man. You know that. I just don't agree with her being here. And I'd hate to think your judgment was clouded because of your desire to get into her pants."

"I believe you've made yourself abundantly clear."

Gabe turned and went the opposite direction toward the stairs, and Eli went in search of Tyana.

He found her in his study, pacing.

It was interesting, the myriad of reactions she elicited in him. Yeah, he wanted to fuck her. But when he looked at her, all hard edges with just a hint of vulnerability that he got the barest glimpses of, he had the strange desire to shelter her. To protect her, though God knew she could take care of herself.

And it was that urge that had him crossing the room.

He slid his hand over her shoulder, cautiously, not wanting to spook her. When she didn't react, he added his other hand, cupping her arms and pulling her back against his chest.

She trembled in his arms, and he slowly turned her around.

"So what do we do with this thing between us, Tyana? Do we ignore it? Make it all business, keep trying to kick each other's asses and forge an uneasy alliance? Or do we stop fighting the inevitable, give in, spend the night in each other's arms and figure out what the fuck we're going to do tomorrow?"

Chapter Sixteen

Tyana didn't try to pull out of Eli's arms, though the feeling of being this close to someone was alien. It felt...right, and that should scare her to death.

She crooked her mouth up into a half-hearted attempt at a smile. "I'm too tired to fuck."

He leaned in close, his mouth hovering precariously close to hers. Their noses did a subtle dance as they moved to allow their mouths access.

"I'm more than willing to do all the work," he murmured. "All you have to do is lie back and enjoy the ride, sugar. Let me love you, touch you, kiss you, stroke that beautiful body of yours."

She shivered uncontrollably. A low throb, warm and steady, settled into her stomach and spread through her groin until her pussy strained and ached. How could such simple words do such a number on her?

He touched his lips to hers. Soft. It was an offering, not a taking. There was a gentleness to his movements she wasn't used to. Fear fluttered, distant, in her chest, but she pushed it aside. She wanted this. She wanted him.

"Take me to bed," she whispered.

She heard his sudden intake of breath as his hands came up to frame her face. His thumbs brushed across her cheekbones, like a feather, light, sensual.

He kissed her. Harder this time. Their mouths melded together, melting like ice on fire.

His teeth caught at her bottom lip and pulled outward until he sucked it into his mouth. His tongue licked over the full flesh, tasting before he released it again.

Then he reached down and took her hand, twining their fingers together. He took a step back, still holding her hand. Like a lover. Like someone who cared about her.

Her confidence fled.

Fucking she could handle, but she felt in her bones that this was not the sort of sex she was accustomed to. When she indulged—bad choice of words. When she had sex, it was out of necessity, done mechanically like a job, a necessary task. This...this was different, and she wondered if this was what it was like to be made love to. To be cherished by a man whose interest went beyond a quick lay and an orgasm.

He pulled her toward him as he simply turned and walked toward a doorway at the back of his study. When they entered, she realized this was his bedroom. It was dark and masculine, like him. A bit of wild and exotic mixed in.

He stopped a few feet away from the bed and fingered the strap of her rifle.

“Undressing you should be fun. Brings me back to my boyhood days of playing with GI Joe action figures,” he quipped.

She smiled and allowed him to divest her of her weapons one by one. They landed with a clatter, one after another on the floor, and finally he reached for her jacket, slipping it over her shoulders and letting it also fall to the floor.

“I thought we’d start with a hot shower,” he said. “I kinda like you all dirty and bloody. It’s a serious turn on. But there’s my sheets to consider.”

A low chuckle escaped from her throat. It felt good to laugh, to escape for a moment into lightness.

She trembled as he undid her pants. Instead of pulling them off, he guided her back until the backs of her knees met the bed. He gently pushed her down, and when she was sitting, he knelt and began unlacing her boots.

“You know when I knew I was a goner?” he asked.

She cocked her head in question.

“When you walked into that Singapore nightclub like you

fucking owned it, and I looked down and saw those combat boots."

"You're a sick puppy," she muttered.

He took the boots off and let them fall with a clunk. Then he stood and pulled her up again. His hands circled her waist, and his fingers dug into the waistband of her pants, skirting down into her panties.

He tugged downward, letting his hands glide across her bare ass as her clothing worked lower. When the material pooled at her ankles, she stepped out, disentangling herself from the pant legs.

His hands skimmed back up her legs, over her hips and then tunneled under her shirt, pushing upward.

"Raise your arms, sugar," he whispered, a sexy, husky catch to his voice.

Slowly, she moved her arms up and over her head. A twinge of pain nipped at her arm from the still-fresh cut, but she didn't lower her arms. He pulled the shirt the rest of the way off, and she was left standing there naked.

It made her feel horribly vulnerable. Unprotected.

She was cognizant of every scrape, every bruise, every bit of dried blood. Of the dirt and sweat and of her lithe, boyish figure.

She didn't have the curves other women had. Her hips barely made a mark outside her waistline, and her breasts were small, not plump and soft.

With shaking hands, she lowered her arms to cover herself, no longer able to bear what Eli was seeing.

He pried her hands away from her body then reached up to cup her face.

"You're beautiful, Tyana."

"You don't have to lie to me, Eli."

Anger flashed in his eyes. "I don't lie to women to get them into bed."

He didn't have to. The inference was there.

"You know what I see when I look at you, Tyana?"

"What?" she whispered, afraid of what he'd say and yet

eager. So eager.

"I see a warrior. A kickass, brave warrior of a woman. I see someone who is my equal. I see someone who is so breathtakingly beautiful that it hurts me to look at you without touching. I see someone who is complex, loyal, who isn't afraid of anything, and yet I see a fragility that makes me want to take you in my arms and shelter you from every bad thing that's ever happened to you and make sure nothing ever touches you again. That's what I see, Tyana. Don't ever fucking hide yourself from me. I won't let you."

She swallowed, let out a shaky breath and swallowed again. "I don't want to need you, Eli."

"I don't want to need you either, sugar, but as my granddaddy used to say, want in one hand and shit in the other and see which gets fuller faster."

Her shoulders shook with silent laughter. "We're a fucked-up pair."

"That we are. But I think we'd make one badass team."

She frowned. "I already have a team."

He put a finger over her lips. "Let's not ruin everything. That's just me getting carried away with wants and wishes."

He pulled her toward the bathroom and left her standing on the cool tile while he reached in to start the water. A few moments later, steam gathered and began fogging the doors.

He looked over and held out his hand for her. She stared at it for a moment and then slid her palm over his. His fingers curled over hers, and he tugged her into the shower.

For a few minutes they just stood there, letting the hot water pour over them. Then, finally, Eli squeezed shampoo into his hands and began washing her hair. He turned her around so that her back fit into his chest as his hands worked over her head, massaging, working the soap into her hair.

She closed her eyes and leaned further into him, enjoying the feel of his body, hard, muscular against her own.

Soon his hands moved down from her hair and over her body, lathering, touching, soaping every inch of her skin. He gently cleaned the cut on her arm and after he rinsed the soap away, he leaned down and pressed his lips to the wound just as he'd done earlier. Each touch sent her closer to madness as the ache grew between her legs and in her heart.

His fingertips found her nipples and worked them into hard points. He played awhile and then sent his hand seeking lower, down her belly to the apex at her legs. Her knees trembled as one finger slid between her folds. Lightning snaked up her spine when he touched her clit.

"There's definitely sweetness, sugar. I just have to dig for it," he murmured against her ear.

She twisted in his arms, her skin edgy and alive, crawling with need. She wanted to touch him and explore the planes of his body as he had done hers. Reaching for the soap, she squeezed the liquid into her hands and then pressed her palms to his chest.

Working in broad strokes, she traveled over his body, pausing over the scars, the tight muscles, the fine line of hair that worked down his midline.

His belly was taut, no softness to him. Her gaze drifted down to the dark hair at his groin, wet and flat against his skin from the shower. His cock suffered from no such malady. It was rigid, distended, as though it were reaching for her.

She wrapped her soapy hands around it and began a gentle massage. He groaned.

With one hand, she worked up and down, from base to tip. With the other, she cupped his balls, working his sac in her fingers as she stroked his cock harder.

He finally reached down and tore her hands away, pulling them up high, over her head and forcing her back against the shower wall. He kissed her hungrily as the water pelted his back. His cock bumped against her belly, burning into her skin. Then as if remembering her injured arm, he quickly lowered her hands and kissed the cut once again.

"I hope we're clean because I'm taking this show into the bedroom before it's all over with."

He reached behind him to shut off the water and then carefully pulled her against him as he backed out of the stall.

They dried quickly, their impatience showing as they rubbed themselves briskly with the towels. Eli reached over with his to give her hair an additional wipe as she dried the rest of her body.

"In the bedroom, sugar. Now."

They hurried out, and he caught up to her just as she reached the bed. He grabbed her arm and turned her around, her body colliding with his as his mouth met hers in a hungry advance.

He continued to walk her backward until she bumped against the mattress. Then he lowered her down. Her legs dangled over the side, and she started to hoist herself higher on the bed, but he stopped her with a hand.

"Don't move a muscle, sugar. You're just right."

She eyed him curiously as he parted her legs and knelt on the floor beside the bed. A shudder rolled over her body when she saw his mouth was level with her pussy.

Gentle fingers explored, tentative at first, light little touches that coaxed a response from her. They grew bolder, dipping into her wetness, spreading the layers of flesh and teasing the sensitive area beyond.

And then his tongue followed his fingers. He licked at her entrance, running a tight circle around it. Her thighs began to shake as every muscle contorted in response.

"You taste so sweet," he murmured, the words humming and vibrating against her pussy.

She closed her eyes and surrendered to his attentions. She let everything else fall away and gave herself to this one moment.

Never before had she given up so much control, power, to another person. But for now, she let go of her fear, her uncertainties, swallowed them back with fierce determination.

She wanted this. Craved it with a dangerous urgency.

His body slid up hers and his mouth blazed a trail over her belly, up to her breasts. He cupped her butt in his palms as she cradled his form. His tongue swirled around one nipple, teasing it into a tight point before he turned and did the same to the other.

She felt the hot shock of his erection between her legs. He spread her wider, still cupping her ass and suddenly he was inside her, deep, in one hard thrust.

Her eyes flew open, a gasp escaping her mouth. Hot. So

hot. Skin against skin. No latex barrier.

His mouth was against her neck and he nibbled his way up to her ear before he whispered, "Don't worry, sugar. I'll get the condom. I just couldn't resist one taste of you. I wanted to feel your heat surrounding my dick, just you, nothing else."

He slid back as he spoke, and her pussy rippled around his cock, tugging him. He stroked forward again, and her moan mixed with his growl of pleasure.

"Don't go. Not yet," she whispered.

He retreated and thrust again, and she sighed.

"You feel incredible," he said against her ear. He kissed the lobe, nibbled at it then slid his mouth down the curve of her neck. "I could stay awhile longer, until I get you off, sugar. Would you like that? Do you like the feel of us skin on skin?"

His words, like velvet, brushed over her, stroking soft.

"You told me I wouldn't have to do any of the work," she said with a smile. "Making decisions is work."

She felt him grin against her shoulder.

"Tell me what you like," he murmured. "Do you want me to touch your clit while I'm pounding into you? Do you want me to stroke your nipples? Do you want me deep when you come?"

She shivered uncontrollably. "Deep. I want you deep. I want your mouth on my breasts, your fingers on my clit."

He smiled again. "I love a woman who knows what she wants."

He ducked his head and sucked one nipple into his mouth, grazing it with his teeth while he moved a hand between them, sliding his fingers over her straining clit. He rocked his hips forward, thrusting deeply.

Only once had she ever experienced sex without a condom, and that time was long buried in painful memories. It wouldn't intrude here where it had no place. This was beautiful, not ugly, not hurtful.

Pleasure blossomed, growing and fanning out, building higher and higher as her body tightened around him. Tension grew, wonderful, edgy, almost painful in its intensity.

His fingers stroked as his mouth sucked at her breast. His cock worked deep, gliding through her wetness, rough and yet silken.

"Come for me, sugar. Give me your pleasure."

She wrapped her arms around his neck, yanked at the thong securing his hair. Black silk spilled over his shoulders. She threaded her fingers through the strands and pulled his head closer to her breast. As he turned his head to her other breast, his earring flashed in the light. She lowered one of her hands to finger the lobe of his ear.

He thrust again and strained against her body, burying himself to the hilt. His fingers expertly fluttered across her clit, light at first then harder.

"Come," he said again, a whisper across her nipple.

He pushed harder, driving her up to impossible heights. She buried both hands in his hair, arched upward as she split into a million pieces, each one hot, jagged, piercing and exquisitely pleasurable.

As she pulsed around his cock, he pulled out. She could feel his arm bumping against her and a moment later, hot liquid surged onto her belly. And then he collapsed against her, gathering her close, his mouth skating up her jaw to her lips.

"That wasn't very fair to you," she said hazily, her vision and speech still blurred by her orgasm.

He chuckled softly. "Oh no, sugar. We both got what we wanted. You got me deep, and I got to come all over you."

"I need another shower," she murmured. "We both do. And then I want sleep."

He kissed her forehead and smoothed her hair back. "I'll give us a quick rinse, sugar, and then we'll both get some rest."

Chapter Seventeen

Eli watched Tyana sleep. She hadn't stirred once when he'd slipped out of bed to dress. She was lying on her side, her knees drawn up protectively to her chest. Her bruised cheek and split lip faced outward.

He sat down on the edge of the bed and feathered one finger over the faint yellow and green discoloration on her face. She stirred and opened her eyes. For a long moment, she just stared at him, and then she reached down for the sheet, pulling it up over her chest as she sat up in bed.

"Good morning," he said.

She closed her eyes for a moment. "I did it again." She yanked the sheet down angrily and scooted past him to get out of bed. He put a hand on her arm.

"What did you do?"

She glanced sideways at him. "Lost perspective. Had sex with you when I should have been figuring out my next move. Damn it, Eli, I can't be around you. I can't keep doing this."

She balled her fists in frustration and started to shove herself off the bed. His hand tightened on her arm, and he pulled her back down.

"Cut yourself some slack, Tyana. You needed sleep. You're running on fumes. You aren't any good to your brother that way. You're rested now. We'll eat some breakfast, and then we'll figure out what has to be done."

She flinched. "We," she muttered. "There isn't a *we*, Eli."

He gripped her chin and turned it toward him, forcing her to face him. "Yes, Tyana. There is a we. You deny it all you want, but you came here for a reason, and it wasn't to kill anyone or hand-deliver me to Esteban."

Her eyes skittered sideways, breaking their gaze though he still held her chin in his hand. He leaned in and kissed the corner of her mouth.

"You go grab a shower and wake up. I'll fix something for breakfast. We need to talk. Come out when you're done."

She nodded and stood, then stalked toward the bathroom, her body back to its normal rigidity.

Eli sighed and shuffled to the kitchen. He found Ian and Braden already up, and he eyed them curiously, gauging their mood.

They looked tired and a little uneasy, but otherwise they seemed okay.

"So what happened last night?" Eli asked with no preamble.

Ian stopped what he was doing and put his hands on the countertop. Then he shoved off and turned around to stare at Eli.

"I wish to fuck I knew. I can't remember anything except knowing the shift was coming on. Next thing I know I was staring up at you from the ground and praying to God I hadn't just attacked my brother."

Braden looked up, his expression brooding. "Give yourself a break, man. Nothing happened."

"I saw you, Ian," Eli said quietly. "You were protecting him. From me. From Tyana. We wouldn't have been able to get close to him. Whether or not you retain any of yourself when you become the jaguar, your instincts obviously remain intact. You never made a move to hurt him."

Hope and relief flared in Ian's eyes and then he glanced sideways at Braden. "I'd thought I'd gotten better at controlling it and only letting go when I knew it was safe. Last night, though, it just came out of nowhere. I felt threatened. I remember feeling like Braden was threatened."

Eli rubbed his chin then dragged a hand through his hair. "My fault, I think. This shit with Tyana, drawing her here. You were probably reacting to the potential threat. It was a mistake," he admitted. "I didn't stop to think about what it would do to you two."

"So is she?" Braden broke in. "A threat?"

Eli shook his head. "We'll hash it out over breakfast. I'm asking you to trust me in this."

Ian nodded his acceptance as did Braden.

They were interrupted when Gabe ambled in, barefooted as usual, wearing a dingy T-shirt with a smartass saying on it and tattered jeans.

"You guys okay?" he asked. "I couldn't help but overhear that something went down last night."

"Yeah, we're good," Braden said.

Gabe looked uncomfortable and regret pooled in his eyes. "I'm sorry I wasn't here. I should have been. I was pissed at Eli and took off. It won't happen again."

"You're not our babysitter," Ian said sourly. "You can't be around us all the time. This is something we have to figure out and deal with on our own."

Gabe shrugged. "Yeah, I know. I hear you. But if something had happened...look, we've been together a long time. I owe you more than you got from me yesterday."

Eli held his hands up. "Let it go, man. We've got a situation to deal with here."

They all looked up when Tyana walked hesitantly into the kitchen. While her expression clearly said *don't fuck with me,* her demeanor was less certain.

Gabe folded his arms over his chest and watched her intently as she skated closer to Eli. Then her gaze went to Ian and Braden.

"Are you okay?" she asked, her voice tinged with concern.

They looked surprised by her question, but they both nodded.

She pulled out a small aerosol canister from her pocket, the same one she'd used on Eli in Singapore. She fiddled with it a little nervously then looked back up at the brothers.

"This might help. At first. It didn't work on Eli, and I assumed that you guys would all be stable like him."

Eli frowned. "What exactly is it?"

"It's an inhibitor created by the doctor we brought in for Damiano. At first it prevented his shifts when he felt them coming on. We also inject a stronger dosage when necessary."

"At first?" Ian asked with a frown.

Tyana gave him an unhappy look. "Over time he's built a resistance to it, so we're exploring other options."

"Try it out on me," Gabe volunteered.

Eli shot him a sharp glance.

Gabe shrugged. "I can control when I shift. It didn't work on you, but who's to say it won't work on me?"

"You're not going to be a fucking guinea pig for us," Braden growled. "How the hell do we know what's really in that thing?"

"You have no reason to trust me any more than I trust you," Tyana said simply. "I offered it because I've seen Damiano in the same place I saw you and Ian in last night. I wouldn't wish that on anyone."

Gabe spread his hands. "Eli says you're not a threat. So let's have it."

Shit. This wasn't something he wanted to happen. But Eli couldn't say a whole lot or he risked exposing his own secrets. He could only pray that it wouldn't work on Gabe either.

Gabe moved to stand in front of Tyana. He took in a deep breath. "You'll have to be quick. Once I start to shift, I'm pretty much gone. Now you see me, now you don't."

His body rippled once and then he started to fade from view. Tyana raised the canister and glanced at Eli, uncertainty flashing in her eyes. Then she sprayed it in Gabe's direction.

The result was instantaneous. He jerked back to form, swayed then looked at Tyana in astonishment. He closed his eyes in heavy concentration as he obviously tried to establish his invisibility. Nothing happened.

"Holy fuck," he whispered. "It worked. I can't shift."

Tyana's brow crinkled in consternation, and she looked at Eli. Everyone was looking at Eli.

"Why didn't it work on you, then?" she asked. "I don't understand."

"I don't know," he lied. "Why are Gabe and I stable and not the others? This shit doesn't seem to have a rhyme or reason."

Tyana turned her attention back to Gabe. "You can conjure clothing like Eli and yet Ian and Braden don't have that ability."

Gabe shook his head. "Not exactly."

"What do you mean *not exactly*?"

"The clothing stays. In fact anything touching me when I become invisible also becomes invisible. If I was naked when I shifted then I'd still be naked coming out of it."

Tyana frowned and once more looked over at Eli. "It doesn't make sense that the effects of the chemical are so random. You have such control, and yet even Gabe isn't immune to the inhibitor."

Eli shrugged and tried to act nonchalant, but his pulse was pounding through his veins. "I imagine it's a lot like trial studies for pharmaceuticals. Everyone has different reactions to different medications."

Ian walked over to where Tyana stood and extended his hand. "May I?"

She hesitated the briefest of seconds then placed the canister in Ian's hand. "I don't need it," she said softly. "It doesn't work on Damiano anymore. I wouldn't expect it to work on you forever."

"How long?" Ian demanded. "How long did it take for him to build up a resistance? How much time does this buy us?"

"Six months? We used it regularly and maybe that was part of the problem. We were so determined not to let him shift at all because he was so unpredictable. He's not like you...the others."

"How is he different?" Eli asked, his curiosity piqued.

She stared at him, her green eyes glittering with pain. "He can shift to anything. Well, I don't know if it can be *anything*, but he isn't limited to just one animal or one ability."

Silence greeted her announcement. Then Braden whistled.

"Shit."

"Yeah," Ian said in a low voice.

"Sit down, Tyana," Eli instructed. "You need to eat and we need to talk about a lot of things."

Ian backed away, still holding the canister. He walked over to Braden and handed it to him to examine. Tyana walked to the table and took a seat so that she faced the rest of them.

Slowly, Gabe, Ian and Braden joined her, sitting in awkward silence while Eli prepared breakfast. When he set their plates down in front of them, no one seemed eager to start eating. Eli sat and stared them all down. "Eat. Then we'll talk."

They ate in silence, only the clinking sounds of forks against plates echoing across the table. Several minutes later, Ian stood and started clearing the plates, most of which were still half full. When he returned, he sank into his chair and stared expectantly at Eli.

Eli in turn looked over at Tyana. "Ball's in your court, sugar. Talk."

Anger flashed in her eyes. "I've already told you. Esteban hired me to take out your buddies and bring you in alive. No mention of Gabe. I used Esteban for information because I didn't believe he had shit that could help Damiano. I didn't have time to track your asses down, and Esteban provided me with your location."

"Fuck," Ian snarled. "Who the fuck is Esteban, and how does he know shit about where we are?"

"Back up," Eli said in a deadly voice. "You told me that Esteban hired you, *not* that he provided you with our location."

"Does the entire goddamn world know where we are?" Braden asked.

"That's the reason I went to him," Tyana said. "Bastard sicced two of his cronies on me in Paris as a test. I knifed one of them, and the other took off. I wouldn't have fucked with the smarmy jerk at all if it weren't for the fact that he saved me time I didn't have to spare in looking for you."

"We can't stay here," Eli said.

Tyana nodded. "If Esteban doesn't present a problem, Falcon soon will."

Again, all four men turned their stares on her, and she shifted uncomfortably in her chair.

"Jonah won't be far behind. I got a good jump, but he'll catch up."

"I told you her ass was trouble," Gabe grumbled.

The beginnings of a full-blown headache were starting to

plague Eli. Realizing that the others hadn't been privy to the details Tyana had provided as to who Esteban was and what his role in this whole fiasco was, he brought them quickly up to speed.

By the time he was done, he had a table full of pissed-off men.

"I say we go take his ass out," Braden said. "Let's bring the fight to him."

Ian nodded. "I'm certainly for some payback."

Gabe grunted. "And what if he can help us?"

Heads turned in his direction.

"What are you suggesting, Gabe?" Eli asked.

He shrugged. "I don't know that I'm suggesting anything. I just wonder if killing him does more than remove a threat to us. What if he does have the means to help Ian and Braden?" He glanced over at Tyana. "And Damiano."

"Well, our first order of business has to be getting the hell out of here," Eli said. "We've got to move out and regroup then figure out what we do next."

The others nodded. Tyana met his gaze, her eyes questioning.

"You in, sugar?" he asked softly.

She looked at the others then back at Eli. "Yeah. I'm in."

Chapter Eighteen

They packed up, did a massive weapons check, got their technology in order and headed out, Gabe driving Ian and Braden in one four-wheel drive vehicle and Eli and Tyana in the other.

They set their rendezvous point at a hole-in-the-wall airstrip where they'd take a chopper, courtesy of Manuel Diego who ran a dubious charter service. They'd land in Puerto Santa Cruz and hop a boat to the Falkland Islands. Once there, they'd hole up in a safe house, plot their next move and wait for the jet.

Eli looked over at Tyana as they bounced and swayed along the shitty, narrow roads leading beyond the village at the base of the mountain.

"You go rogue on Falcon?"

She frowned and looked down. Her fingers curled into tight balls, and she avoided making eye contact with him.

"Jonah and I didn't see eye to eye on what needed to be done to help Damiano."

"So in other words, when he finds you, he's going to be one pissed-off man. With you and with me. Only he won't kill you. He won't have any compunction about killing me."

"Probably not," she admitted.

"I love how you show me affection, sugar. Glad I don't mind walking on the wild side, because fucking you is a serious risk to my health."

She turned then, her eyes flashing as she glared holes through him.

He chuckled. "Now that's what I prefer to see. All spit and vinegar. I prefer you pissed off to this meek and docile chick who's been posing as you for the last twenty-four hours."

"Asshole," she muttered.

"So what was your back-up plan?" he asked. He was genuinely curious, because she seemed too smart to put all her eggs in one basket.

"Back up to what?"

"Back up to me not providing the answers you needed for Damiano. You risk pissing off Esteban by double-crossing him. So if you get here and find I can't help you, what then?"

"I go after him," she said simply.

"Just like that?"

She nodded. "Just like that. He's made threats against D. As long as he lives and has the agenda of getting rid of the shifters, he's a danger to Damiano."

Eli shook his head. She was dead serious. No false bravado. Just calm and matter-of-fact, like she was talking about the weather or getting her nails done. The bad thing was, he totally believed her.

It made him damn uneasy. He didn't like the idea of her going after Esteban by herself. Hell, the thought of her going in with him and the others made him uneasy enough.

"I think I have a pretty good idea of how Jonah feels," Eli muttered.

She cocked an eyebrow and pinned him with a probing stare. "Tell me you're not getting soft on me, Eli. I gave you more credit than for you to get all manly-man on me and bust out with the *protect the poor girly-girl* mantra."

"You're hell on a man's ego, girl. Don't you understand us Neanderthal types love to swoop in and save the day? Carry the damsel in distress off and fuck her senseless while she swoons in gratitude?"

She cracked a grin. "You don't want them swooning because of your sexual prowess?"

"Well, that too."

"Sorry, but I've had to learn the hard way that the only person I can rely on is me. It saves a lot of grief."

She meant that as well. So serious. So young. Hell, she couldn't be much more than twenty-four? Maybe twenty-five?

"Someone sure did a number on you, sugar."

Her face darkened, and her lips pressed tightly together. Then she thrust her chin upward and stared challengingly at him. "I don't see you relying on other people. You're the typical loner. You have leader written all over you. Capable. Driven. Look out for your team, but you don't really rely on them. You expect them to rely on you. Am I right?"

Her assessment made him squirm. He glared back at her. "How about we stop with the armchair psychology."

She grinned innocently. "I will if you will."

"Deal."

He reached over, an unconscious gesture that he gave no prior thought to, and took her hand in his. She seemed as surprised as he felt by the tender action. He almost drew away, but she curled her fingers around his and relaxed.

"Eli, you there?"

The radio crackled as Gabe's voice echoed through the receiver.

Eli was forced to release her hand as he picked up the radio and held it to his mouth. "Yeah, go ahead."

"Problem, man. We need to reroute. The chopper is out."

"What the fuck is wrong with the chopper?"

There was a long pause. "Nothing's wrong with the chopper. It's Manuel. He's dead. Or at least I assume that's who I saw being toted out in a body bag. The place is swarming with the authorities."

Shit. "Okay then, Plan B. Haul your ass out of there and be careful. When all fails, do the one stupid thing your enemy wouldn't expect."

"Buenos Aires?"

"Yeah, we'll take the jet out of there."

"All right. I'll see you there in a few days, then. You and Tyana be careful."

He tossed the radio down and looked over at Tyana. "You up for a road trip, sugar?"

Chapter Nineteen

Their trip through rural Argentina was actually quite beautiful. It was country Tyana hadn't seen before despite how many times she'd trotted across the globe.

They'd stopped for petrol twice, small dingy little places that most people who weren't intimately familiar with the villages wouldn't dare to slow down for. It didn't seem to bother Eli, though. He even chatted amicably with one of the owners, an older man with sun-weathered skin and dusty, faded clothing. Eli's Spanish was impeccable.

When Eli climbed into the SUV and they started down the winding back roads, Tyana looked curiously over at him.

"Why here?"

"Why not?"

"I figured you and your team for true blue. Red, white and blue, that is. Solid patriots. All formerly employed by Uncle Sam. Yet as far as I can tell, none of you have set foot back in the States since the deal went down in Adharji."

He stared straight ahead, darkness falling over his face.

"We still don't know who set us up in Adharji. You say it was Esteban. First I've heard of that. And interestingly enough, after that incident, all our channels were cut off. All our contacts fizzled. No one was interested in giving us the time of day. A network we'd built for over five years was gone. We were forgotten. We no longer existed. According to the U.S. government, we all died in action."

"Ouch."

"So maybe you'll see why we're not exactly knocking ourselves out to get back to the good ole U.S. of A. It's my guess Uncle Sam will continue to ignore us as long as we stay dead. As much as we believed in what we did, I don't think any of us are kidding ourselves that we have a future."

"So you'll no longer recover hostages?"

He glanced sideways at her. "We're in a bit of a holding pattern, you know? It's hard to think about reorganizing our business when we have two guys who turn into pissed-off kitties at a moment's notice. Not to mention we have no resources, no contacts, no way to advertise when we're technically supposed to be dead. Right now our priority has to be finding a way to help Ian and Braden."

She nodded. She understood that motivation well. Falcon hadn't taken more than a handful of assignments since Damiano's condition deteriorated. They only accepted smaller ones that required two members of the Falcon team and any of their secondary network. Someone always stayed behind with D.

As though reading her mind, Eli reached over and took her hand again.

"I'm sorry about Damiano, Tyana. I wouldn't have left him behind. Things went to shit fast where we were being held, and we barely escaped with our lives. But if I had known he was still alive, I wouldn't have left without him."

She locked gazes with him and could see the sincerity reflected in his dark eyes.

"I believe you," she said softly.

"And," he added as he turned his attention back to the road, "if I had the means to help him—you—I would. But I don't have answers for you."

Disappointment made her chest ache. She'd been so sure Eli's stability was a sign that something could be done to help Damiano. That it was just another unexplained occurrence in a line of them heightened her despair.

She turned her gaze out her window, determined not to allow Eli to see the tears stinging her eyelids. His grip on her hand tightened as he squeezed comfortingly. But he didn't say anything further, and for that she was grateful.

"So what do we know about Esteban?" he asked several minutes later. "Apart from the fact that we were all his little experiment."

"He said he owns the largest pharmaceutical company in Europe and that for the last few years he's branched into other projects, namely human experimentation. He wanted warriors. My guess is he wanted an army of shifters. The instability was an unfortunate side effect. Which also explains why he wants you so badly."

He frowned and loosened his hold on her hand before slipping it away to grip the steering wheel. White showed around his knuckles as he navigated down the bumpy road.

"So he wants to know why I work, and the others are just collateral damage," he said quietly.

"Yeah, exactly. He offered to be benevolent and leave Damiano off his hit list, but again, I don't trust the piece of shit as far as I can throw him. It's obvious he doesn't want his failures floating around. Think of what it could do to him were it to get out that A. he was experimenting on humans, and B. that he unleashed a bunch of unstable shifters on the general populace."

Eli nodded. "We can't kill him. Not yet."

"What do you suggest then?"

He glanced over at her before returning his gaze to the road. "We hunt him down and extract information from him using any means necessary. If he created this bullshit, then he might well have an idea of how to fix it. If nothing else we might get the original formula of whatever the fuck chemical agent he used on us so we can break it down and have it analyzed."

Anticipation and, for the first time, a sense of hope crept over Tyana. She'd feel better if they had the resources of Falcon to back them, but Jonah wouldn't be doing her any special favors for a while. Tits on the other hand...

"I have a guy who can help us," she said.

"Thought you said Falcon was pissed at you."

She made a face then sighed. "My position with Falcon is probably tenuous at best. Jonah...well, he runs things and he gave me a direct order not to go after you. Besides, the guy who can help us lives to annoy the piss out of Jonah. He's the one who helped me get off the island and to Paris to my meeting with Esteban."

"I'm listening."

"His name is Tits. He does his own thing. Works for no one. Provides a lot of intel, backup, support, technology, you name it. Solo mercenary. Falcon's used him a lot."

"And what do you propose he do for us?"

She thought for a minute as she braced herself over a particularly rough patch of road. "He could gather intel on Esteban, monitor his movements so we know exactly where and what we're looking at. Do you and your team have passports? Alternate identities?"

Eli nodded. "Yeah, got all that covered."

"Okay then Tits could get us info on Esteban, and he could set us up a safe house somewhere close to Esteban so we can hit him when he least expects it."

"You're asking a lot, Tyana," Eli said softly. He turned to glance quickly at her, his eyes dark with indecision. "You're asking me to put not only my life but the lives of my team in your hands. You've made it quite clear you don't trust me, but you're asking me to trust you."

She understood his reluctance, even admired it. "When it comes to saving Damiano, I've done some stupid things. I've made bad decisions. I've taken responsibility for them all. There isn't a person I wouldn't lie to, step on, or kill to help him. The way I see it, if you can help me help him, then that loyalty extends to you. Once I give my word, I don't break it. And once you have my loyalty, that doesn't go away."

"And is that what you're doing, Tyana? Including me in your loyalty? Giving me your word that you're not going to knife me in the back when you no longer feel you need me?"

"What are you really asking, Eli? I'm sensing one hell of a loaded question here."

"Maybe I'm asking you to trust *me*. Maybe I'm saying that you and I have shared a lot more than a desire to help our respective teammates. Maybe I'm asking you where the hell I stand with you."

She shifted uncomfortably in her seat, the tight edge of panic swelling in her chest.

"Do *not* bring sex into this, Eli. Sex has nothing to do with trust. Sex is just sex. It doesn't *mean* anything."

"Uh huh. You keep telling yourself that, sugar. Well, here's the deal. I don't make it a habit of making love to a woman who doesn't trust me. So maybe you need to think about that the next time you want me to crawl inside you."

Making love. She had the sudden urge to clap her hands over her ears and childishly chant *no, no, no.* It didn't matter that she'd pondered the differences the night before, that she had allowed herself the fantasy of being made love to by this man as opposed to a quick fuck and a mediocre orgasm.

She couldn't have it both ways. She couldn't expect him to trust her, to, as he said, put his life and the lives of his team in her hands, when she couldn't offer him the same level of trust in return.

Did she trust him? She'd flatly denied the idea even when it had slipped out of her mouth. She didn't despise him. She didn't think he was a dishonorable man. Hell, who was she to judge someone's honor when she was willing to sacrifice her very soul to save her brother? Honor was bullshit. Idealistic bullshit fed to new military recruits. Honor didn't keep your ass safe. It didn't provide you with your next meal. It sure as hell didn't keep you from being knifed in the back by someone because you were stupid enough to trust them. Honor was for the weak.

And yet she felt safe with him. She didn't believe, deep down, that he had any intention of hurting her. Was that trust? She didn't know. She wasn't sure she wanted to know.

She trusted Damiano. She trusted Mad Dog and Jonah. She trusted herself. She didn't particularly see a need to widen that circle.

Silence fell between them, and Eli didn't make another attempt to touch her or alleviate the tension in the air. They drove steadily onward, and Tyana focused her attention on the landscape.

When darkness fell, they continued driving for a few hours before Eli turned off the road and onto an even smaller path leading into a densely wooded area.

Only the soft light from the dashboard illuminated the

interior, but she could feel him watching her as they pulled to a stop.

"Only one of us should sleep at a time. The other needs to keep watch. We can camp out in the truck. The seats recline. Won't be the most comfortable rest we've had, but it beats the ground."

She nodded, then realizing he couldn't see her, she muttered her assent.

"I'll take the first watch," she added. She wouldn't be able to sleep anyway, and she could take the longer shift, since she could always sleep while Eli drove the next day.

He didn't argue. He reached into the backseat and dragged out a heavier jacket and a blanket then shoved them toward her.

"It gets chilly out here at night."

She opened the door and stepped to the back where the weapons were secured. She already wore her knives on her, but she pulled out her rifle and her pistol and secured them before walking around to collect the coat and blanket from the front seat.

Eli reached across the seat and grabbed her wrist as she started to back away.

"If you hear anything, you wake me up."

"I can handle it," she said shortly. "Get some rest. I'll wake you later."

Chapter Twenty

Tyana sat, cloaked in darkness, fifty yards from where Eli had parked the SUV. She pulled the blanket further around her shoulders but was careful to keep her rifle in reach at all times.

There was a stillness to the air that unnerved her. No sound except the occasional breeze through the pines disturbed the night. No moon shone. The sky was black, the stars blanketed by heavy cloud cover.

For the first hour she kept her mind purposely blank, not wanting the distraction of letting her thoughts wander. The second hour she wondered how D was doing and if he was worried. Of course he was worried. But she hoped he kept his faith in her abilities.

The third hour she allowed herself to think about Jonah and just how pissed he was at her. Then she wondered if Jonah had taken off to overtake her, and had Mad Dog stayed behind with Damiano? Mad Dog would have wanted to go.

That was a kink in her plan she hadn't considered.

If both Jonah and Mad Dog pursued her, then that left D alone on the island with only the Falcon security team to help him.

She put her face in her hands and rubbed tiredly over her eyes.

Impulsive. Impetuous.

They were words that Jonah would hurl at her. He would accuse her of compromising Falcon for her own means, of putting her own priorities ahead of the team. And he'd be right on all counts.

But she wouldn't apologize. Not for putting D first. He came before her. Before Falcon.

At six hours she still stared broodingly into the dark, willing the dawn to come so she would no longer be alone.

A warm mist enveloped her, and she relaxed, the tension in her body dissipating as Eli wrapped himself around her, surrounding her in a light fog. He touched every part of her skin, light and seeking. A gentle sensation trailed down her cheek like the soft stroke of a painter's brush. Slowly, he came to form in front of her, his hands on her face.

"You should have woken me before now," he chided.

"I can sleep while you drive. You needed the rest more."

He tugged the blanket a little tighter around her and tucked the corners beneath her chin.

"Why don't you go back and get some sleep now?"

"I'm not tired yet," she murmured. That wasn't true. She was plenty tired, but she knew her brain wouldn't shut down enough for her to sleep.

"Then keep me company for a while," he said as he crawled up beside her.

He put an arm around her shoulders and drew her close into the shelter of his body. She relaxed and laid her head against his chest.

"Tell me about you," she said in a near whisper. "I only know what little I could dig up when I was looking for you and back when Falcon did background before accepting the guide job into Adharji."

"Not much to tell," he said. "No family. That was a requirement back when CHR was a spin-off to Special Forces. No ties. No life to speak of."

She frowned. "How did you get from being a specialized unit to leaving the military and going out on your own?"

Eli sighed. "Same reason most military teams get axed. Bureaucratic bullshit, cutbacks, changes in administration. Everyone comes in with their own agenda."

Tyana nodded. All reasons she loved being a part of Falcon. They didn't answer to anyone but themselves.

"Our team was formed with a take-no-prisoners attitude.

We were ruthless, and we did what we had to do in order to get the job done. We had a one hundred percent hostage recovery rate. Never lost a civilian. Bad guys? Didn't fare so well, and we didn't give a fuck.

"Then came changes in administration. They started making noises about dismantling us. We weren't exactly politically correct. Admin didn't want it to get out that the U.S. supported a military team that didn't adhere to political niceties.

"And then we had an assignment into a fuck hole in the Middle East. Several Americans were being held hostage by some fuck show who wanted the U.S. to surrender to His Royal Highness the King of Fuck-u-ban."

He turned his head toward Tyana. "You see the bright individuals we were working with here. Obviously with those kinds of demands there was going to be no negotiating, no reasoning with these brain children.

"So we went in to recover the hostages. Things were going well until one of the women, who'd evidently decided during her captivity that she sympathized with our poor misguided terrorists, decided to take a bullet for one of her captors.

"She stepped right in front of him. Took a round to the chest. The pisser was, she didn't even save the asshole. The bullet passed through her heart and took the guy behind her out anyway.

"We recovered the hostages and got the hell out. It was our first civilian casualty, and the guys in Washington jumped at the chance to wag a finger in our faces and disband us. There was no way I was going to let go of something I believe so strongly in.

"Ian, Braden, Gabe and I resigned and struck out on our own. The Army was more than willing to utilize our services as long as they didn't carry the ultimate responsibility. If a mission went to shit, they could throw their hands up and deny having any knowledge of a gun-for-hire hostage recovery group."

"Real nice," Tyana said dryly.

"It gets better," he said. "After what happened in Adharji, it was like we ceased to exist. We'd call needing intel, they'd pretend they didn't know who the fuck we were. All the contacts outside the military, mostly ex-military guys with ties to the government, wouldn't give us the time of day. I'm not convinced that the government and your Esteban weren't in it together."

She scowled. "He's not my Esteban."

He continued on, ignoring her protest. "Esteban might have been the brainchild behind the chemical that turned man into shifter, but what would he want with warriors? He planning to go to war? A pharmaceutical company?

"No, I'm thinking for him it was all about money. He'd create the freak of nature and let the U.S. government buy the product. Only it didn't turn out as well as Esteban hoped and no way Uncle Sam would pay a dime until Esteban could produce a working prototype. In this case, me. He wouldn't want Ian and Braden around as shining examples of his failure."

"That makes sense," she murmured. "It still doesn't explain why he has no interest in Gabe, in either killing him or having him brought in alive. When Esteban approached Falcon with the job, he was very fixated on you. Less so on Ian and Braden, but then he wanted them dead. But there was never a mention of Gabe then or later when he approached me outside of Falcon."

"No, it doesn't make sense unless he simply doesn't know about Gabe."

"So you're men without a country," she said, foregoing the subject of Gabe for the moment.

"Yeah, you could say that."

"I guess that's something we have in common," she said softly.

"So what about you?" he asked as he drew her a little closer to him. "How did you join up with Falcon?"

She stiffened and realized too late that by asking Eli for personal details she would be expected to reciprocate. Her skin itched just thinking about revealing parts of herself that she hadn't shared with anyone.

"Shouldn't we be going?" she asked as she checked the time. By the time they got back to the truck and on the road, it would be getting light.

Eli let out a small breath. "Yeah, I guess we should."

He stood and pulled Tyana up beside him. They started for the truck, and when they arrived, Eli opened the door to the backseat and handed her a small satellite transmitter.

"Think you can buzz your guy and have him find out what he can on Esteban's whereabouts?"

She nodded and took the equipment before climbing into the passenger seat. As Eli cautiously drove back out to the main road, she fitted the earpiece and entered a series of commands.

There was a long period, and the connection crackled and hummed in her ear. She adjusted the thin wire leading from her ear to her mouth. "Tits, if you're there, I could really use you right now."

She looked over at Eli in the darkness. "Is there a secure frequency I can upload to him?"

He reached over to the glove compartment and dug around, his arm pressed against her leg while he kept the other hand on the wheel. He dragged out a pen and a pad of paper, placed the pad on her knee and quickly jotted down a series of numbers.

"Tyana, long time no hear. You okay?"

"I'm fine, Tits. Look, I need you to switch to a secure frequency. I don't have my equipment on me."

"Yeah, I noticed it wasn't you flashing at me. Fire when ready."

She punched in the numbers. "I'm switching over. Holler when you're there."

She entered the numbers on the small keyboard and went through the complicated series of gateways. The static and interference in her earpiece died as crisp silence replaced it. A few seconds later, Tits' voice boomed over the connection.

"Now, what is it you need? I hope you're not wanting me to come pull your ass out of some shithole somewhere."

"You wish. I need intel on Esteban Morales. I need to know where he is, what he's doing and who he's doing it with. Once you figure that out, I need a safe house as close to him as you can manage."

"I don't like the sound of this, Ty."

"You don't have to like it. Just do it. It's important, Tits.

You know I wouldn't ask otherwise."

He grunted. "Yeah, I know."

"E me the info when you get it. I should have a decent enough signal to be able to read it by the time you collect it. I'd rather not do this live. Make sure it's encrypted."

Tits snorted. "I don't tell you how to do your job, baby girl."

"Yeah, yeah, do this for me and I'll give you another kiss."

"I want tongue this time."

"You got it last time, asshole."

He chuckled then broke the connection.

She pulled the receiver from her ear and pushed the unit off her lap and into the space between her and Eli.

"He should have the info we need by the time we reach Buenos Aires. At least then we'll know where we need to fly. Are you going to be able to get us out of Argentina?"

Eli smiled in the dim light. "Yeah, sugar. Just leave that part to me."

Chapter Twenty-One

Tyana dozed fitfully as they drove through small villages and a few larger towns. When Eli stopped for petrol, she dug around in one of the bags they'd packed for food.

They drove on, eating in silence, tension settling over them like a cloud.

She knew she hadn't been fair. But then it wasn't her job to be fair. If Eli wanted to unload on her, fine, but it didn't mean they had to have some mushy meeting of the minds and a therapy session starring her.

Still she could sense something in his attitude toward her. Disappointment? She slouched further down into her seat and turned so she couldn't see him or his occasional glances in her direction.

"I'm not going to stop tonight," he said, finally breaking the silence. "If I drive through, we can hit Buenos Aires by tomorrow afternoon."

She turned to look at him, his profile as he concentrated on the road in front of them. He pushed his hair back behind his ear and occasionally fidgeted with his earring.

"And what then?"

His gaze skittered sideways for a second. "Then we wait for your friend to tell us where we can find Esteban. I'll work on our flight details in the meantime."

"Do you have a place we can stay?"

He grinned. "Of course. Buenos Aires is a big place. Easy to lose yourself in the crowds. Though it would help if you got rid of the bloody jacket sometime between now and then."

She glanced down, realizing she hadn't even bothered to change since they'd left the compound.

"I'll change when we stop again," she murmured.

The hours dragged on. Even the scenery, which at first had offered an interesting diversion to Tyana, blurred in one unending line. She hated the silence but knew better than to try and draw Eli into conversation.

When darkness fell, she succumbed to sleep more out of desperation than fatigue.

When Eli shook her awake, though, bright sunlight streamed through the windshield, nearly blinding her. She blinked as she sought to get her bearings. She felt heavy and lethargic, like she was coming out of a coma.

"Where are we?" she mumbled.

"Reaching the outskirts of Buenos Aires," he replied.

She sat up straighter in her seat. "Shit. You should have woken me up."

"Why? You needed the rest. When was the last time you got more than a few hours of uninterrupted sleep?"

She didn't bother responding, because they both knew the answer to that one.

"Did the others make it yet?" she asked.

"Talked to them a while ago. They're a couple of hours behind. They'll meet us later."

She scrubbed the sleep from her eyes and focused on the direction they were heading. Sleek skyscrapers dotted the horizon and traffic around them increased as they drove further into the city.

It reminded her of European cities. Crowded. Similar architecture. It could be one of any of the major metropolises. It could swallow you whole. A person could be as obscure or as noticeable as they wanted.

But she was out of her element, and she knew she had to rely on Eli. This was his turf. Not hers. That dependence made her uneasy.

She absorbed the hectic pace around her as they continued to navigate the busy streets. Beyond the more stylish, modern buildings, they entered an older, more rundown part of the city where the shadows grew and the new and shiny faded.

Eli pulled into a three-story parking garage and parked on the top level. She eyed him curiously as he opened his door.

"Get your stuff. From here we walk."

She got out and hoisted her bag over her shoulder then walked around the back to get the bag containing their weapons. He took two duffel bags with clothes and electronics and headed toward the stairs.

They exited the garage into an alleyway, and he set off at a brisk pace. After four blocks of dodging trash bins and refuse thrown onto the streets from windows above, he stopped at a battered door and pulled out a key from his pocket.

She looked up to see there was no unit above this one and a glance to the side told her that this apartment adjoined a closed business. The windows of the business were busted out, and it looked as though no one had occupied the building in years.

Eli unlocked the door and ducked in, motioning for her to follow.

It was a simple one bedroom efficiency-style apartment with a small kitchen and a rag-tag couch straddling the space between the bedroom and the kitchen. A small television rested on a rickety stand by the window, but other than that, the apartment didn't boast much else.

"Home sweet home," he said as he dropped the bags onto the floor beside the couch. "At least until we hear from your friend."

And hopefully that would be soon. This place made her uneasy. Reminded her too much of things better forgotten. Even the smell was familiar. Dirt, poverty, pain...

She gripped her arms with her hands, rubbing up and down, trying desperately to make the fear go away.

"Hey, are you okay?" Eli asked softly.

She yanked her gaze to him. "Yes, I'm fine. What do we do now?"

"We wait," he said. "Are you hungry? There's a place a block or two away. We could grab something and bring it back here. It would give me a good chance to scope out the area."

She nodded. Even the unsavory reality of what lay out there on the streets was better than this place.

"Wait here. I'm going to shift and take a look around. I'll be back for you in a few minutes. Then we can go together if you like."

Again she nodded and tried to control the trembling of her hands.

He touched her briefly on the shoulder then moved away. She watched as he became a shadowy apparition and then disappeared altogether.

It was hard to curb her resentment. Why him and not Damiano? What roll of the dice came up with his lucky number? His ability was a gift, not the curse it was for D. Eli could use and exploit his ability to shift at will while Damiano struggled to prevent it from destroying him.

She dug through one of the bags and pulled out a clean pair of jeans and a shirt. She'd never gotten the chance to get out of her blood-spattered clothes. After a check of the bathroom, she turned on the small shower and waited for the water to heat. Realizing that lukewarm was the best it was going to get, she ducked in and quickly scrubbed the accumulated grime from her body.

A few minutes later, she stepped out and hurriedly dried off. Despite the heat and humidity, she shivered as she walked back into the living room to get her clothes.

She blocked out the smell, the sounds coming from outside, the awful memories of the dark holes in Prague as she quickly pulled off her clothes and stepped into her jeans. After she slipped the T-shirt on, she paced for a few moments then sat on the musty couch, hunched forward, her arms protectively around her midsection.

When Eli shimmered into view a half hour later, relief surged hot and forceful through her veins.

She rose from the couch and had to stop herself from going to him.

"Things are quiet, by Buenos Aires standards anyway," he said. "I took a look at the garage. Wanted to make sure we weren't followed."

She nodded.

"You want to go grab something to eat? I'd rather make it back here before dark."

"Yeah, okay."

He looked curiously at her, as though he were trying to see inside her. Her unease was tangible, she knew. He touched her lightly on the arm as he headed toward the door.

In an automatic gesture, she felt for her knives. Then she reached for her jacket. Though tattered and sporting a torn sleeve, it offered protection and hid the other knife. And she'd cleaned most of the blood off.

She followed Eli outside. The sun was sinking low in the sky as they walked down the street. It wasn't dark enough yet for the streetlights to pop on, so shadows began to yawn in the darkened corners.

She walked faster.

Two blocks up, they stopped at a street vendor where Eli ordered sausages and empanadas. As Tyana glanced down the streets at the intersection where they stood, she noticed that none of the restaurants seemed open.

She turned back to Eli as he collected the sack of food and paid for it.

"It doesn't seem very busy," she said as they began to walk back. "I would have thought it would be more crowded. More people out."

"They eat late here," he replied. "No one really goes out before nine which is why I wanted us to get our food and be back in our room before things got a lot busier. Much easier to tell if we're being followed this time of day."

She nodded but kept her eyes peeled as they crossed the street at the next intersection. As they walked past one of the alleyways, a childish cry of fright froze Tyana in her tracks.

She stared down the alley to see a young girl. Maybe twelve. Maybe thirteen. On the cusp of womanhood, yet so young. Too young. She was being shoved against the rough stone of the building wall by one man while another stood to the side leering.

Tyana's blood turned to ice. She felt those hands on her own body, ripping at her clothing, heard Damiano's hoarse protests as he fought to protect her.

Her hand was inside her coat even as she sprinted down the alleyway. She launched herself into the air, her foot connecting with the man holding the girl.

They went down in a tangle. The man bellowed in pain and rage as Tyana landed on top of him. She scrambled up, knife in hand and threw it at the other man before he could react to her attack.

It landed in his shoulder, embedded to the hilt. He staggered back, staring in disbelief as blood ran down his arm.

She turned to face the first attacker just as he lunged at her. He rammed into her like a freight train, and they both went down again. She hit the street with a bone-jarring thump. Pain speared through every muscle, and she gasped for breath.

She reared back to head butt him, but suddenly he was gone. Ripped from her body and thrown against the opposite wall. A snarl of rage echoed through the alley.

Tyana scrambled up in time to see Eli make quick work of the asshole. She turned to see about the girl, but she was gone. Tyana ran to the end of the alley and looked down the street only to see her disappear among the vendors.

"Are you all right?" Eli demanded beside her.

She nodded, still winded from her fall.

"What the fuck did you think you were doing, Tyana? Are you just trying to get yourself killed? Get us arrested? Jesus H. Christ, woman."

She whirled around, tears of rage nearly blinding her. "If you think I was going to stand by while those two animals raped her, you're crazy."

She yanked her jacket around her and hurried away from the alley, back toward the apartment. Eli kept pace with her, his hand touching her elbow. She jerked away from his touch as they reached the door of the apartment.

By the time they made it inside, she was shaking violently and she felt ill. So sick. She wanted to vomit.

"My knife," she said, and she didn't recognize her own voice. She fixated on the knife. "I lost the knife. Mad Dog gave it to me. I never go anywhere without it."

Eli touched her, tentative, testing. Concern was there in the light probing.

"You have other knives, Tyana," he said in a low voice.

She wrapped her arms as tight around her as she could, folding inward. She walked to the couch, her composure shattered. Like a leaf blowing in the wind, she wilted onto the sofa, her knees shaking, her limbs jittery, like a junkie in need of a fix.

Eli was there, in front of her, kneeling, his hands on the couch on either side of her hips. He made no effort to touch her, but worry was set like stone in his eyes.

"Tell me what the fuck happened back there, Tyana."

She closed her eyes and shook her head. God, she didn't want to remember. As long as she blocked those memories, she could go on, she could function, she could pretend it never happened, that those years before Jonah and Mad Dog didn't exist.

A gentle hand touched her cheek, cupped it in a warm, sweet grasp. "Tyana, listen to me. Nothing can hurt you here, sugar. It's only you and me. No one else."

To her horror, a tear rolled down her cheek, colliding with his hand. He brushed it away with his thumb, a tender gesture that proved to be her undoing. Another slipped down. And another. A low sob caught in her throat, and she swallowed fiercely, determined not to give in. Not to be weak.

She tried to turn away, but he wouldn't let her. He folded her in his arms and held her tightly as he rocked her gently back and forth. She pushed and he pulled. She tried to move away, to hide from him, but he kept those arms locked around her.

Emotion, raw and tearing, swelled in her throat. She fought against it, tried to keep it in, because once let loose, she would break.

And then he kissed her. One tiny, gentle brush of his lips against her forehead. Quite simply, she shattered. There in his arms. There was no defense against his quiet understanding.

She wrapped her arms around his neck and buried her face in his shoulder.

He held her. Soft. Comforting. His hands stroked repeatedly over her hair as her tears soaked into his shirt.

When there were no more tears to shed, she simply lay against him, limp, drained. He slid his hand over her damp cheek and pulled her away so that he could look at her.

"What happened, Tyana?" he asked. "What is it that you're so afraid to tell me...anyone?"

"That was me back there," she whispered. "It was me all over again. And no matter how hard I train, no matter how hard I become, it always comes back to me being a defenseless young girl fighting for survival on the streets. I can't forget her. I can't make her go away. I don't want to be her anymore."

His eyes softened. He carefully got off his knees and moved to sit on the couch beside her. She faced forward, her knees spread, her arms between her legs and her head bowed.

"Tyana, she'll always be there," Eli said softly. "She's an important part of who you are."

She shook her head.

"Tell me about her."

She turned her head to look at him, not sure she could get the words past her frozen lips. He reached out and tucked a strand of her hair behind her ear and let his hand linger there at her temple.

God. Where to start?

Chapter Twenty-Two

Tyana drew in several long, steadying breaths. Eli's fingers still touched lightly at her temple, drawing a line down her cheek and back up again.

"My earliest memory is of an orphanage in Prague. I remember being cold and hungry, and there were children crying. I don't know how I got there. Later I was scornfully told that my mother had dumped me on the doorstep and ran as fast as she could, but who knows if that's real or just the drummed up version of what they told every kid there.

"I used to hide in one of the corners, just hoping to escape notice. That's where Damiano found me. He was older, but skinny as I was and as dirty. I'll never forget how he took my hand and told me it would be okay, that he'd look out for me."

She bowed her head as another hot tear trailed down her cheek.

"He kept his promise," she whispered. "He took so much for me. Always put himself in front of me when the headmistress was angry or when the men came every month to select the orphans they wanted for the workhouses.

"As we got older, Damiano filled out more. He got bigger. I didn't develop the curves that the other girls did, and while I didn't understand then why that angered the headmistress, I realize now it was because she had every intention of selling me to the highest bidder.

"She ran a profitable business. Young virgins offered at premium prices. Damiano was so determined to protect me from that. When I did finally begin to have the semblance of breasts, he made me wrap them to keep my chest flat. We stayed as filthy as possible so no one would want us. Boys, especially good-looking boys like Damiano, were just as in demand as the girls."

Eli slid his hand up her back and palmed the back of her neck, massaging lightly, but he never said a word. He just listened.

"I think the headmistress caught on to us because one night she locked me in a room by myself. Later a man showed up. I was asleep. When I woke, he was there..." Her breath caught on a sob and she raised her hands to her throat in panic.

"It's all right, Tyana," Eli said soothingly. "I'm right here, sugar. Nothing can hurt you here."

"It hurt," she said in a small voice. "I couldn't fight him. I just lay there crying while he took his pleasure."

Eli pulled her into his arms, his fingers tight at her waist. She could feel the pounding of his heart and the tension in his big body.

"Damiano found me the next morning. I'll never forget the look in his eyes. He helped bathe me, and then he told me to wait for him, that we were getting out, but that first he had something to do."

She turned her head up to Eli. "He killed her," she whispered. "He killed the headmistress, and I wasn't sorry. I hated her. I *wanted* her to die."

There was no condemnation in Eli's eyes. Anger, sorrow, but no judgment. She lowered her head again.

"Damiano came back, took my hand and we fled into the streets. For months we existed hand to mouth, doing whatever we had to in order to survive. We stole, Damiano sold himself, just so we didn't starve. I hated myself for that. Hated that he sacrificed everything for me. I was at a point where I was willing to prostitute myself so that I could feed us both, and Damiano would have a warm place to sleep, where he'd be safe.

"He completely flipped out. I've never seen him so angry with me, never before then and never since."

Eli pressed a kiss to the top of her head and stroked her hair.

"One night I picked the pocket of a young man, only he was

on to me in two seconds flat. He chased me down and grabbed me by the scruff of the neck. He had a friend with him, and they laughed as I threatened to kill them. I don't think they believed me, but I would have.

"Damiano damn near killed himself trying to take them on, but they weren't even trying to hurt us. When we realized that, we took off as fast as we could."

"Jonah?" Eli asked.

She nodded. "And Mad Dog. They didn't catch us that night, but they tracked us down two days later. I still don't know why they did it. Maybe they felt sorry for us. But they took us in. Didn't offer us sympathy. Just asked if we wanted a better life. It took a long time for them to earn our trust but when they did, it never wavered. We owe them our lives. We would have never survived on the street."

"You would have," Eli murmured. "You're a survivor, Tyana." He levered away from her and framed her face in his hands. "You're one of the bravest and gutsiest people I know, man or woman. Damiano is lucky to have you."

She shook her head adamantly. "No, I'm the one who's lucky. I wouldn't have lasted a day in that orphanage if it weren't for him. He saved me."

Eli kissed her forehead tenderly then slid his lips down to kiss each eyelid as they fluttered underneath his mouth.

"I think you saved him as well," he said softly.

She closed her eyes and leaned until her forehead touched his. "I can't lose him, Eli."

"I know, sugar. And you won't. We'll find a way."

Such simple words, and yet they lifted her up, filled her with such comfort. She wasn't alone. Not anymore. Eli was helping her.

"You need to eat, and then I need to clean you up," he said. "I'm beginning to think you're using your face as a battering ram."

She smiled and to her surprise got teary-eyed again. He smudged the moisture with his thumb then kissed the spot just below her eye.

"You managed to salvage the food?" she asked.

"Uh huh. Not much gets between me and my food."

Relief, warm and liquid, pooled in her soul. He wasn't disgusted by her raw account of her childhood. He wasn't horrified by all she'd done and by all that had been done to her. For the first time in her life, she wondered if there was room for one more person in her heart.

Chapter Twenty-Three

Eli watched Tyana nibble at an empanada and was at a loss as to how to react to all she'd told him. He couldn't sit there and say it didn't matter, nor could he ignore the enormity of the fact that she'd shared such intimate details of her past with him.

What did he do? It didn't feel right to take her to bed and make long, sweet love to her, though it was precisely what he wanted. He wanted to make her forget, to let her know that it didn't matter to him, that only she mattered. But at the same time, how could he be sure that he wouldn't shatter her already fragile emotions? Wouldn't bring back those terrible memories of another man in another place?

And if he did ignore the urge, what kind of message was he sending? What would his reluctance to touch her say to her? That he was disgusted? That he no longer wanted her?

It was a hell of a hard spot to be in, and there weren't handbooks for this sort of thing. Make the wrong decision and he risked losing her completely.

That was the rub. Did he want to keep her? *Could* he keep her? She was his perfect match in a world where he never thought to find one. What woman could possibly understand his life, the things he'd done, the way he lived? Only a woman who shared those same experiences. Tyana.

He hadn't been honest with her, though. She clung to the hope that he could somehow provide help for Damiano, and he couldn't. His ability to shift wasn't something born of a freak science experiment gone bad. How could he tell her that and destroy her faith that somehow Damiano could be cured?

The small radio transmitter sitting on the floor beside the couch beeped, and he reached down to pick it up.

"Eli." Gabe's voice filtered through the static.

"Go ahead."

"We're in town. Number two house."

"Lay low. I'll be in touch when we move out again," Eli said before putting the radio aside.

He had calls to make, favors to call in, but until they knew where they were going, his only option was to sit tight and hope this Tits guy came through for Tyana.

Her haunted stare found his. "So we stay here?"

He nodded. "I'll make arrangements for us to fly out as soon as we have a location on Esteban."

She frowned, and lines of fatigue rippled across her forehead. "What then? What's our objective? Is it revenge or simply a fact-finding mission?"

He moved closer to her, wanting to be near yet so afraid she'd pull away. When she didn't, he settled beside her, their shoulders touching.

"Honestly? I want to kill the bastard. But that helps no one. I say we take him alive and make him talk. He doesn't want to die. He's too absorbed in his whole power trip. After we extract what information we can from him, we can decide whether he's worth more to us alive or if we kill him then."

She nodded. "I agree. If there is a way to help Damiano...and Ian and Braden..." She glanced up at him, questions burning in her eyes. "What about you, Eli? Are you happy with your abilities? You and Gabe aren't like the others. What if we find a way to make it all go away? Are you going to want that?"

He sat there frozen. It was only a matter of time, but he hadn't wanted it to be now. He didn't want to face her disappointment. He didn't want to hurt her.

"Eli? Did I say something wrong?"

He turned to face her, pulling one knee up on the couch. "Tyana, I'm not like the others."

She nodded. "I know. We just went over that."

He sighed. "No, I mean the chemical agent didn't do

anything to me."

Her eyebrows drew together in puzzlement, and she put the empanada down on her lap.

"You've been looking to the wrong guy for answers. I don't have them because I was able to shift long before the accident in Adharji. I was...born with the ability. Some freak accident of nature."

Her mouth fell open, and her pupils dilated in shock. "But...that's impossible. It's not logical. People aren't born that way."

He put his hand over hers, but she snatched it away. She stood abruptly and whirled around, her face a mass of confusion.

"You're serious, aren't you?"

"Yeah, Tyana. I'm serious. The whole reason we were able to get out of that damn prison camp before they started any experimenting was because I was able to shift. It's a secret I've carried since birth, but after the others...it became easier to hide. I mean, I no longer had to hide it. It could be explained by the chemical agent."

She closed her eyes and her shoulders slumped forward. "Then...then there really is no way to help Damiano, is there?"

He flinched at the grief in her voice, thick, so heavy it seemed to blanket the room. He'd expected anger, not resignation. But then he suspected she was at the end of her rope.

He stood and put his hands on her shoulders. When she wouldn't look at him, he moved a hand to her chin and gently prodded it upward.

"Listen to me, sugar. We'll find a way. Esteban started this and we're going to finish it. If he has information that can help us, we'll find it. I need you to believe that."

She leaned in close, laying her forehead against his chest. Her hands gripped his waist, balling the fabric of his shirt in her fists.

He put his arms around her and went with his instincts.

"Let me love you," he whispered. "Tonight is ours."

Her head came up, her eyes flashing a brilliant green. "You

said you wouldn't sleep with a woman who didn't trust you."

He cupped her chin and ducked his head. His lips hovered a mere inch over hers. "You trust me, sugar. You would've never told me everything you did if you didn't trust me."

Vulnerability shadowed her beautiful eyes. She swallowed then loosened her hold on his shirt. She let her hands fall to her sides.

"I do trust you," she whispered, and he realized how very hard those words had been for her to say.

He slid his hands down her lithe form, to the hem of her shirt, delved underneath then let his hands glide upward again, taking her shirt with them.

"This isn't sex, Tyana. I'm not going to fuck you."

Her breath escaped in a jerky wave.

"I'm going to make love to you."

Her lips parted in invitation, but he had to hear the words from those lips.

"Say it," he murmured. "I want to hear you say it."

She trembled against his fingers as he coaxed the shirt higher.

"Make love to me."

It was said so quiet he had to lean in to hear. Her breath blew softly against his cheek and sent a shiver down his spine.

"Kiss me," he said.

She wrapped her arms around his neck and slid her lips across his, soft as a butterfly's wings. He ran his hands under her arms, around to her back and pulled her close. Her shirt bunched between them as he deepened the kiss, as he explored her mouth.

He took a step forward, forcing her to take a step back. Slowly he moved them toward the bedroom, their lips fused tight. He tugged at her clothing, releasing her mouth long enough to yank the shirt over her head and toss it aside.

He lowered her to the bed, his mouth working down her jaw, to her neck and to the hollow at her throat. He kissed a line between her breasts as his fingers fumbled with her jeans.

The fly parted, and he pulled at the material, easing it over her hips and down her thighs. As the denim gathered at her knees, he bent and pressed a kiss to the soft cotton-covered vee.

When the jeans were removed, he stood staring down at her nearly naked body. Only her panties remained, a small scrap covering the softness of her womanhood.

He leaned down once more and spanned her small waist with his hands then dipped his fingers into the thin elastic band of her underwear. Tiny little goose bumps dotted her abdomen as he slowly started to lower the panties.

The silky, dark curls between her legs came into view, tempting him as he removed the last of her clothing. She lay naked in front of him, vulnerable, and yet there was such trust in her actions.

No tension, no wariness in her eyes. No suspicion.

He began to take off his own clothing, moving slow, wanting to prolong the moment. There was no rush, no race to orgasm this time. It wasn't about a quick fuck. It was about the delicious savoring of bodies, of their connection. It was about respecting the trust she'd offered him.

He lowered his body to hers, flesh on flesh, the warm sensation of skin sliding together.

"Are you on something, sugar?"

She stared up at him, their gazes colliding with hot intensity. Confusion flickered for a moment.

"I don't have a condom with me, and the last thing we need is to make a baby. I'm hoping you're on birth control."

She relaxed and wrapped her arms around his shoulders, pulling him further against her.

"I've been on birth control since Jonah dragged me to a clinic in Prague all those years ago."

"Are you okay with me not using a condom?"

She stared back at him, and he could see the same desire in her eyes. This was something they both wanted, but he wouldn't do anything that would put her at risk, that would destroy the fledgling trust between them.

"I don't..." She briefly looked away and when she looked back, the faint light of shame reflected in her eyes. "I don't have sex often. I've done things I'm not proud of. They were jobs...means of gaining information—" She broke off, her expression stricken.

"Like I was at first?"

She nodded and started to speak again, but he held a finger to her lips. "You don't have to explain yourself to me, sugar."

"What I'm trying to say is that I haven't had sex, before you, in a long time. Never unprotected, and routine physicals are mandatory for all Falcon members."

Relief tightened his chest. They were okay.

"What about you?" she asked quietly.

He kissed her, plucking at her bottom lip with his teeth. "Not in a while, sugar. A long while. And never without a condom. When you walked into that bar in Singapore, all thoughts of celibacy fled."

She smiled. "Then make love to me, Eli."

"You trust me?" he asked again. He wanted to make sure she believed him. A man would say damn near anything when it came to sex. He hadn't been above it in the past. But not when it mattered.

She hesitated only a fraction of a second before nodding.

"Do you trust me?" she asked. "I could be lying. You know of the things I've done..."

Again he silenced her with a finger. "I guess we'll have to trust each other, sugar. As we've stated many times before, we've had ample opportunity to kill each other. Now if this part of the conversation is over, I'd like to move on to other things."

His mouth closed around one pink-tipped breast. She arched into him, bowing her back off the bed with a moan. He loved how easily she fit against him. Neither of them were soft people and yet they cradled one another perfectly.

He traced the outline of a scar over her left breast, one he'd missed before, but then he'd been hurried, rushing to completion, lost in the pleasure she gave him.

He went exploring, looking for other battle scars. He found a crescent-shaped ridge on her right hip and a three-inch-long puckered line on the inside of her thigh. Even her feet weren't unscathed. He feathered over an old wound on the top of her right foot.

She jerked and laughed softly.

"Ticklish?" he asked.

"Very, and don't you dare use it against me."

He chuckled. "I bet you have a story for each of your scars. They'd probably stand my hair up on end, but I bet they're not dull."

"Maybe I'll tell you about them sometime," she said. "But right now I don't really feel like talking."

He slid back up her body, his sac rubbing against the inside of her leg. His cock was stiff and distended, and he ached to bury himself deep in her heat.

With one knee, he opened her wider. The soft hair of her pussy brushed his skin. He wanted his fingers there. He wanted his cock there. He wanted all of her all at once.

With tentative fingers, he touched the tuft of hair over her mound, delving between the warm folds of her femininity. He reached her damp core. Hot, so hot.

"Take me," she whispered.

His body shuddered at the erotic command. The words appealed to the primal male buried inside. It was a call to claim his woman, to mark her, to make her his. It was a call he couldn't ignore.

He reached down and grasped his cock. It was hard and pulsing in his hand. He stroked up and down, enjoying the sensation as he guided himself toward her opening.

He rubbed the head over her wetness before lodging himself just inside her velvet rim. He leaned forward, lowering himself over her body.

"Kiss me," he murmured.

She framed his face in her small hands and kissed him. Light at first, teasing, like she was exploring new territory. Then she grew bolder, licking over his lips with her tongue, coaxing him to open to her.

He inhaled her scent, her taste, as their tongues danced. He rolled his hips forward, sliding into her welcoming body. Pleasure. So much pleasure. He closed his eyes and rested his forehead against hers as he simply enjoyed the feeling of her flesh surrounding him.

"You scare me so much," she whispered. "But I can't stay away from you. I have this crazy, itchy, insane need when I'm around you, and I don't understand it."

He kissed the corner of her mouth then worked to her ear. He licked the shell then nibbled at the dainty lobe. "I don't want to scare you, sugar," he murmured against her ear as he rolled his hips again, sending him deeper inside her.

Her moan echoed close to his own ear.

"I want to make you feel good."

She twisted restlessly beneath him. She wrapped her slim legs around his hips and rose to meet his thrust.

"Take me," she murmured against his lips again. "Take me, Eli. Make me yours. I need you. God help me, I need you."

Her words were like a sweet balm. A cool, healing wind in a sun-scorched desert. He gathered her in his arms, as if he could protect her from the world, her past, anything that had the power to hurt her.

Again and again he buried himself deep, stroking through her wet flesh. Silken heat surrounded him. He was drowning in it.

Her hands tangled in his hair. Her fingers dug into his scalp as she gathered handfuls of the long strands. She held him to her, his mouth against her neck.

She convulsed around his cock, the delicate tissues swelling as her orgasm loomed. His balls tightened. Excruciating. The pressure started low in his cock and pushed outward, straining to be set free.

Faster, harder, he rocked against her. She dug her heels into his ass and cried out. Liquid heat exploded around his cock, and he lost what remaining hold he had on his control.

Flash fire. Electric sensation seared through his balls, up his cock then exploded outward as he jetted into her in jerky spurts.

She called his name. He kissed her. Devoured her mouth like a man starved. His frantic pace slowed, and his thrusts became slow and measured as he pulled them both back down to earth.

Finally he slipped free of her in a rush of warm fluid. He rested on top of her for a moment even though he knew he was too heavy. It just felt right. He didn't want to move.

She felt warm and soft beneath him where earlier he'd considered that neither of them were soft people. Yet now she was limber and pliant. Sated.

He rolled over and pulled her into his arms, resting his cheek on top of her head. Her chest rose and fell with his and deep contentment worked through him.

Her fingers slid up his side and to his shoulder as she snuggled closer to him.

"Tell me about you," she said in a lazy voice.

An uneasy sensation crawled across his skin. "What do you want to know?"

"What was it like to grow up so...different?"

Different. He almost laughed. Different implied something mild. Like maybe he liked knitting while other boys liked football. Being able to make yourself disappear in a cloud of mist? That was a little more extreme than just *different*.

"What about your parents?" she continued on, oblivious to the tension billowing through his chest. "Were they like you? Were there others in your family?"

He stiffened but forced himself to relax. He couldn't very well hold out on her now. Not after she'd trusted him with her deepest secrets. A sigh escaped him.

"No, they weren't like me. I don't know of anyone like me." It sounded utterly pathetic even to him. The hollow loneliness seemed to radiate from his voice. What was he supposed to tell her? That when his teammates had developed their freaky shifting abilities he didn't feel quite like a one man freak show?

"Then how?" She didn't even finish her question. She didn't have to.

"I don't have an answer for you," he said simply. "Some twist of the gene pool? Maybe my mother used too many cleaning supplies when she was pregnant with me or maybe she fell. I mean who the hell knows?"

He felt her frown against him. "What did they think about

your...abilities? Were they scared?"

Scared? He wasn't sure that was the appropriate way to describe his parents' reaction the day he'd run home, terrified, to tell them what had happened to him. He sighed again. This was going to be a long story.

"My parents were...religious." There wasn't an easy way to explain their fanaticism or the fact that he'd grown up in an isolated, wary world. "I didn't have many friends. In fact, most kids avoided me or made fun of my weirdness."

"You mean they knew?" she asked in surprise.

He laughed softly. "I was weird way before I learned of my abilities."

She pushed up from his chest and repositioned herself so that she could look into his eyes.

"My parents weren't exactly role models when it came to parental love and devotion. Not to say that they abused me. They made sure I had food and clothing, but they were far more concerned with their duties to the church. I say church. I'd classify it more as a cult. I've been to church, and they don't have much in common with the nutjob my parents followed.

"At any rate, I spent a lot of my childhood wishing I could disappear. I avoided any and all situations that would thrust me into the limelight. I was quiet and sullen."

It was her turn to laugh. "But you *could* disappear."

He rubbed his hand up and down her arm and ran his fingers over the curve of her elbow. "I didn't know I could until I was ten years old."

Her sound of shock was unmistakable.

"I broke my cardinal rule of never being noticed. Some dickheads were picking on a younger girl, and I knocked one of them on his ass. Then I ran like hell because there were four of them and only one of me, and I was a skinny, awkward son of a bitch. I hit a dead end in an alley and knew I was fucked. As I stood there waiting, knowing I was about to get the shit kicked out of me, all I could think was that I'd give anything to be able to disappear. And then the weirdest thing happened. I felt lighter. My vision changed, and I looked down and couldn't see myself anymore.

"It scared me worse than the bullies I was facing down. But

then they ran into the alley. I was so sure I was busted, but they couldn't see me. They looked right through me and then ran back out."

"Bet you didn't think it was so scary then," she teased.

He grimaced. "I was still scared shitless. I was in total panic thinking I'd never materialize again. And then suddenly I was back. Just like that. I ran the entire way home just seconds away from crapping in my pants."

She laughed and rubbed her cheek over his chest, burrowing a little deeper into his embrace.

"When I got home, I burst into my parents' Bible study. They were pretty pissed because no one interrupts the word of the Lord. Then I spilled my story, and all they did was stare at me like I'd lost my mind. Then my mother started muttering about the evils of television and how they needed to start a prayer session for little boys who told tales.

"I knew they weren't going to listen to me so I shut my eyes and willed myself to disappear. This time I became smoke. It was the freakiest thing. I could see them, and I could see the wisps of smoke. I can still remember the looks of horror on their faces. I couldn't hold onto it long, and I materialized again."

He broke off and fell silent for a long moment.

She sat up again and touched his cheek as if she could sense his discomfort. Discomfort. What a word. He was reliving the day his parents had disowned him, and all he could drum up to describe the feeling was *discomfort*.

"What happened then?" she asked softly.

"They, uh, wigged out."

"That bad, huh."

He nodded. "Yeah. They packed up and left with the church. It's kinda funny now. They thought I was the Antichrist."

Her eyes were wide with shock. "They left you?"

He shrugged. "Yeah."

"Oh, Eli, I'm so sorry," she said in dismay. "What did you do?"

He cracked a rueful smile. "Well, I can tell you what I didn't do. I didn't go around broadcasting the fact that I could do neat little smoke tricks. I was on my own until the local cops figured out my parents had split. They made a half-hearted effort to locate them, and I ended up in foster care."

"Foster care?"

"Yeah, it's sorta like an orphanage, I guess."

She frowned.

"Not like yours, I don't imagine," he murmured. "Foster care is when a family agrees to take in a child who either doesn't have parents or has been taken from them. Anyway, I was in and out of homes until I graduated high school. Then I joined the military, and the rest, as they say, is history."

"And your parents?" she asked. "Did you ever see them again?"

He cleared his throat. "Not exactly. I went to their funeral when I was eighteen."

"What happened?"

"Mass suicide," he said with a grimace. "Freaking cult they ran around with decided to pull another Jim Jones and kill themselves. The thing is, all during the funeral, all I could think was that they'd done me a huge favor by ditching me. If I'd stayed with them, I'd probably be brainwashed and dead alongside them."

"Wow," she breathed. "That doesn't make my childhood sound so bad now."

He wrapped his arms tighter around her. "I was okay, Tyana. No one ever abused me like they did you."

"We're both survivors," she said simply.

He kissed the top of her head. "That we are, sugar. That we are."

She wrapped her body sensuously around his, her legs twining like silken threads with his.

"Make love to me again," she whispered.

She turned her face up to his and their lips brushed and held.

"I thought you'd never ask."

Chapter Twenty-Four

Somewhere between the haziness of her dream world and the pleasurable aftermath of their lovemaking, Tyana heard the beep of her communicator. She struggled out from the layers of fog surrounding her like a comforting cloak and quietly extricated herself from Eli's arms and legs.

"You all right, sugar?"

Eli's sleepy voice brushed over her ears, the sound giving her a warm buzz.

"I think I just heard from Tits," she said as she got up and walked naked toward the couch.

She dug into the backpack and pulled out the slim mobile unit. Eli came in behind her and sat down on the couch next to her as she opened the case and entered a series of passcodes.

In a few moments, the message flashed on the screen. She scanned rapidly over it. Classic Tits, no beating around the bush. Just the necessary information.

She glanced up at Eli who had leaned forward. "Esteban is currently holed up in Germany. Neu Ulm. Breeding ground for radical terrorists. Coincidence, huh."

"Yeah, I doubt it," Eli muttered.

"It's not going to be easy to go in after Esteban," she murmured. "That area is already under so much scrutiny. Security is tight. Tits arranged a house as well as a cover. We're a team of photo journalists traveling through Germany. Still, it's going to be risky."

"Every mission is," Eli said. "Esteban's desire to stay alive will help us. He's a rich son of a bitch, and I bet he's lining some local pockets there. He probably funds half the terrorist activity."

"Still think he's working with the U.S. government?" she asked.

Eli's face darkened. "I don't know, sugar. I wish I did. I'm not naïve enough to discount the notion. Until it's proven otherwise, I have to assume the worst. I've had to work at building a network for my team from the ground up again. It's slow going. No idea who I can trust. After Adharji, my U.S. contacts dropped me like a whore with the clap. It's why you're going to be more help than I would be in locating and capturing Esteban. Falcon hasn't been compromised the way CHR has."

"I'm sure Jonah would disagree," she murmured. "He'll say that I've single-handedly brought down the entire team."

"Not an optimist, is he."

She laughed. "No. Not Jonah. Brooding bastard. That's him to a tee."

"Well, you've done your part. Now I have to get us to Germany."

"Going to have a problem with that?" she asked.

Eli shook his head. "My pilot is here in Buenos Aires. He's very well connected. But then I pay him a lot to be. He can get us into most airports under no scrutiny or cargo checks. If he can't get us directly into Neu Ulm, he can get us close and we can hoof it the rest of the way. Either way, in a few days time, we'll have Esteban."

Tyana nodded. "Tits is going to make sure we have what we need at the house he snagged for us. He has a man at one of the Army bases."

"All right, sugar. You get dressed, and let me make a few calls. I'll need to round up the rest of my team and make sure they're present and accounted for when we hit the airport. We won't want to be hanging around for long."

She leaned over and put her hand on his cheek then kissed him long and hard. "Thank you. I know you're doing this as much for you and your team, but thank you."

He kissed her back, sliding one hand behind her neck and holding her possessively. "Don't thank me, sugar. I might get us killed yet."

ꕤ

It was still dark when they assembled at the small airstrip on the outskirts of Buenos Aires. Gabe, Ian and Braden were waiting inside the plane when Tyana and Eli boarded.

She glanced at the three men, gauging their mood, their demeanor. They were silent, alert and wary.

No one spoke until they were in the air, and then they gathered in the small lounging area in the middle of the plane. Eli relayed the information they'd received from Tits.

"It's a risky job," Eli said. "We have no back-up. We're a five man team going into a relatively unknown situation with only sparse intel."

Gabe snorted. "Like that's anything new? It'll be like old times, only this time we'll expect to have no support instead of expecting it and not getting it when things go to shit."

Ian nodded. "It won't be anything we haven't done before." His gaze found Tyana. "The chemical you gave us. It works."

She smiled faintly. "I'm glad. I hope it works longer for you than it did for Damiano."

"Can we get more?" Braden spoke up.

"Assuming we don't die and that Marcus is someone I'll still have access to when this is all over with, I'll ask him to examine you and Ian if you want. He's the doctor who created the formula for Damiano. I don't know a lot about it. Marcus explained that it was an inhibitor that reacts with and paralyzes the chemical receptors in the brain that apparently control the urge to shift."

Braden nodded.

"That's also assuming we haven't become members of a newly formed Falcon hit list," Eli said dryly. "I don't imagine I'm very popular with them right now."

Guilt crept over Tyana. Not only did she have to deal with the fact that she'd compromised Falcon and gone against a direct order from Jonah, but she'd put Eli's team at risk by doing so. Jonah didn't tolerate any threat to Falcon's security. He'd definitely see Eli as a big one.

"Well if they kick you out, I'm sure Eli here will be more than happy to offer you a spot on CHR," Gabe said slyly.

Eli shot him a quelling stare.

"Why isn't Esteban on Falcon's hit list?" Ian asked. "Why are we the ones going after this guy? Seems to me Jonah would want some payback for what he did to Damiano."

Tyana shook her head. "Because Jonah doesn't believe Esteban can help Damiano. And Jonah doesn't know that Esteban was behind the chemical attack in Adharji. I didn't know until I met Esteban in Paris, and if I had gone to Jonah with that information, he would have still shut me down."

"Is Damiano that bad?" Braden asked. There was a hint of dread in his voice, as if he could see into his own future and knew that whatever Damiano had degraded to would eventually come to him.

"Marcus doesn't think there is a cure," she said softly. "He believes that if Damiano is going to survive he has to learn to cope and control his powers. His DNA has been altered. This isn't some disease or sickness that can be cured by medicine."

Ian stared at Gabe and Eli. "And maybe it's sort of a sick twist on evolution. The strong adapt and the weak die off. Gabe and Eli seemed to readily adapt to their 'powers'."

Tyana stole a glance at Eli, who stiffened at Ian's words. He hadn't told them that his shifting ability came with birth—a freak aberration in his DNA at conception. And maybe now she understood why. They looked at Eli and Gabe as hope that they too would adapt and survive.

She turned her gaze to Gabe. He was the wildcard. The only one of the entire group who had actually been able to harness his abilities. Why?

He returned her stare with bland indifference.

But the inhibitor worked on him while it hadn't on Eli. So he wasn't completely invulnerable.

"Our objective has to be to take Esteban and make him talk," Eli said, bringing the conversation back to the heart of the matter. "We don't have room for emotion, rage or revenge." He looked at Tyana pointedly, and she had an eerie sense of déjà vu, as if Jonah was standing in front of her lecturing her about going off half-cocked. "This is a job. Cut and dried. We go in, extract Esteban from his hidey hole, and then we can address the other issues that concern us and our wellbeing as a team. Understood?"

The others slowly nodded their agreement. Tyana dipped her head in acknowledgement.

Chapter Twenty-Five

It was nearing dusk when they drove into Neu Ulm. Two vehicles drove down the small street toward the house Tits had arranged, lots of useless camera equipment in the back. The more useful equipment like guns and ammo were carefully tucked underneath.

They entered the driveway through a weathered archway covered with ivy. Tyana's brow rose as she caught sight of the house. She was expecting a cottage. Not a big-ass mini mansion.

It was a two-story stone house covered in the same ivy as the archway. Square and boxy, but more importantly, there was a high fence around the perimeter offering privacy.

Eli parked in the semicircle drive in front of the door, and Gabe pulled in behind him. They all got out, and Tyana reached for her bag after checking to make sure her remaining knives were securely fastened to her person.

She waited for Gabe, Ian and Braden to catch up while Eli headed for the door. They each carried cases or bags.

"Nice digs you got for us, Tyana girl," Gabe offered with a grin.

She started after Eli with the others trailing behind. Eli opened the door and pulled his pistol. Taking her cue from him, she gripped one of her knives in one hand and reached for her Glock with the other.

Behind her, there was a slight rustle as the others prepared to go in.

They walked into the darkened foyer.

Eli motioned toward the large living room to the right. Tyana stayed close behind him, and when they entered the living room, she flipped her backpack off and dropped it onto one of the chairs.

Eli turned as the others came in behind him. "We need to fan out and make sure the house is secure," he murmured. "Meet back here in five minutes and we'll figure out our next move."

There was no warning for what happened next. Tyana heard Eli grunt, felt Gabe stumble beside her, heard Ian curse and Braden gasp. She whirled, her eyes widening in horror when she saw the multiple darts protruding from the men.

Then she saw Esteban step from the shadows of the dining room, three men with dart guns surrounding him. She yanked up her pistol and prepared to launch her knife with her other hand.

"Nicely done, Miss Berezovsky," Esteban said as he walked further into the living room.

Beside her, Eli had crumpled to the floor, and he seemed almost paralyzed. But his accusing stare found her. God, he couldn't think she'd set them up.

And when things couldn't get any weirder, the front door burst open behind her. She jumped to the side to assess the new threat but froze when she looked into the very angry eyes of Jonah.

Jonah, Mad Dog and Damiano swarmed into the room, assault rifles up. Tyana yanked her pistol back to Esteban.

"What did you do to them?" she demanded.

Jonah stepped in front of her, his gun pointed at Esteban. "You have what you want, Morales. Now we have what we want. I'd say it's in our best interests to stand down. Or we can shoot each other and shed a lot of blood. Your choice."

"Take her. She served her purpose," Esteban said.

Mad Dog grabbed her wrist and Tyana yanked it away. "No! Goddamn it, Jonah, no! You can't do this!"

Mad Dog yanked Tyana to him and applied enough pressure to her other wrist to make her drop her gun. He knocked her knife out of her hand with the butt of his rifle and then simply threw her over his shoulder and barreled out the front door.

Tyana looked back to see Eli and his men still helpless on the floor, but Eli's gaze followed her the entire way. Cold rage burned in his dark eyes. Betrayal. Dear God.

Tyana exploded in fury, kicking and flailing at Mad Dog. Jonah backed from the house, his gun still trained on Esteban while Damiano hurried toward the truck that Eli and Tyana had driven to the house.

Mad Dog tried to stuff her into the SUV, and she fought like a deranged woman. She executed a kick to his midsection, knocking him back a foot.

"Damn it, D, hurry up with that shit," Mad Dog barked out.

Tyana launched herself from the truck, her intention to go in after Eli and the others. Jonah caught her, and she punched him full in the face. His neck snapped back, but he retained his grip on her arm.

In the end, it took the combined efforts of both Mad Dog and Jonah to force her to the ground. Through tears of rage, she saw Damiano approach and then felt the prick of a needle in her arm.

She stared accusingly up at Damiano. "How could you?" she whispered.

"How could I not?" he asked.

The world swayed and blurred around her. She felt herself being lifted and then tossed into the backseat of the SUV. A hot tear slipped down her cheek as her eyes fluttered closed and everything went black.

ꟼ

Eli lay there, helpless fury blowing through his veins. He couldn't move. He couldn't shift. He just lay there like a fucking vegetable as Esteban's men swarmed around his team.

She'd played him. Played him in the worst way. She'd made him care, and then she'd knifed him in the back.

Because of him and his stupid decision to trust Tyana, his team would likely die. He couldn't save them this time. He couldn't even save himself.

A hard boot rammed into his ribs, and he grunted in pain. He felt himself lifted by three men. He was thrown onto the couch, his arms twisted behind him and tied. His feet were bound next.

Gabe, Ian and Braden were receiving similar treatment as they were restrained.

Eli closed his eyes. He hoped to hell it was worth it to Tyana. He hoped whatever she got out of this deal would enable her to sleep at night. If he managed to escape with his life, though, he'd make damn sure she never had another night's peace.

Chapter Twenty-Six

Tyana climbed back to consciousness, her head aching vilely, and her tongue felt like it was three sizes too big. She blinked to try and bring the room into focus, but she wasn't having much success.

She heard voices. Jonah. Mad Dog. Damiano. And then she remembered.

"How much of that shit did you give her, D? She's been out like a fucking light for hours."

She surged upward and immediately regretted it. The room swam around her, and she had the sudden urge to vomit.

"Whoa, not so fast," Damiano said as he gripped her shoulder to steady her.

She put a shaky hand to her head. God, it hurt. It pounded as she tried to put together what had gone down.

"How long?" she rasped.

"How long what?" D asked.

"How long have I been out?" How long had Eli and his team been in Esteban's clutches? Nausea rose in her stomach again.

"Exactly six hours and twenty minutes," came Jonah's stony reply.

She rocketed to her feet, shrugging off Damiano's hand. She weaved, and her knees threatened to buckle, but she remained upright by sheer willpower.

"Where are we?" she demanded. She looked around, her vision clearer now, and answered her own question. "Paris."

She locked gazes with Jonah. "Why? Why did you do it? Goddamn it, Jonah, how could you do that?"

"Now hold on a minute, baby girl," Mad Dog began.

"Stand down, Mad Dog," Jonah said in a controlled voice. "Let her say her piece. Then I'll say mine." His eyes glittered with anger, and she knew he was simmering beneath his deceptive calm.

"How could you set me up that way? How could you set up Eli and his team? Do you have any idea what you've done?"

Jonah walked forward, his features locked in stone. "One, we didn't set you up. Two, I don't give a damn about Eli and his team. Three, you brought this on yourself when you blatantly disregarded a direct order from me to stay your ass on the island.

"What the fuck were you going to do, Ty? What were you thinking confronting Esteban like that? What would have happened if we didn't show up? I'll tell you what. He would have killed you."

She shook her head. "Esteban wouldn't have known we were there if you hadn't told him. How did you know?" And then it hit her. "Tits. That son of a bitch."

"Tits doesn't owe you any loyalty," Jonah said coldly. "And we didn't say jack to Esteban. I don't even know why the fuck you're so hot to trot for this guy. Why were you there with Eli and his team? Last I heard you were going after Eli, not changing your loyalties, Ty."

The pounding in her head was vicious. She closed her eyes and swallowed back the rising nausea.

"Jonah, we don't need to do this now." Damiano's concerned voice filtered through the fog surrounding her. "She's not well."

Her eyes flew open again. "No, D, now is precisely when we have to do this. We're losing time." She turned her attention back to Jonah. "You know why I went after Eli. What you don't know is why Esteban wanted him too. He's the bastard who unleashed the chemical agent on Eli and his team. On Damiano. He's the reason Damiano is the way he is. It was a goddamn experiment. One that didn't work out too well. I thought Eli might have answers. He's stable. I thought his team would be stable like him. I was wrong."

Jonah held up his hand. "I don't give a damn about Eli and

his team. What I care about is the fact that you could have been killed. You don't get that. I won't trade your life for some half-assed scheme to try and save D's ass."

"You're not listening to me," she said in frustration. "You stood there and handed Eli and his men over to Esteban. I went to Germany with Eli and his men because we were going after Esteban. We were going to take him down and make him talk. He created the chemical that turned them into shifters. If nothing else, we could have gained access to the chemical, had it broken down and analyzed, and maybe we could have come up with a way to help them and D. But you sold us out to Esteban. Goddamn it, Jonah, why?"

"I had nothing to do with why Esteban was there," Jonah said icily. "Tits told me where you were going to be and when. We went there to extract you and to remove Eli as a threat to you. I wasn't about to have a goddamn showdown with Esteban and risk the lives of *my* team for Eli Chance."

She rubbed her eyes wearily. "Then how did he know? God, how could he have known?" She let out a shaky breath. "They think I betrayed them. They think I sold them out to Esteban. They trusted me."

"Why should you care?" Jonah asked with a raised brow.

"You didn't see them," she said softly. "The brothers, Ian and Braden? They're not stable like Eli and Gabe. They're like D. They can't control their shifts. Eli and Gabe, their stability is unexplained." She wouldn't betray Eli's secret. Not even now.

She glanced back into Jonah's eyes and saw the resolve simmering there. No way she'd ever budge him. And she knew what she had to do.

"I quit," she said.

"What?" Mad Dog's outburst rang out over the room.

"Care to repeat that?" Jonah said.

"I quit Falcon. You're right. I compromised the team, and I've obviously lost all objectivity. I'm out effective immediately."

"Ty, no," Damiano said as he walked up behind her and put his hands over her shoulders.

She turned and wrapped her arms around him, holding him tight. "I love you, D," she whispered. "But this is something I have to do."

She pulled back and started to walk away but Jonah caught her arm in his strong grip. Then he reached out with his other hand to cup her chin. He forced her to meet his gaze.

"Why?"

She looked away.

"Look at me. For once be straight with me, goddamn it. You tell me why you're quitting, and you tell me what the fuck you're planning even now. Because if you think I'm just going to let you walk out like that, you've lost what little of your mind you have left. We're *family*, Ty. And you don't quit family."

"I'm going after Eli and the others. I have to try and save them."

Curses blistered her ears from three sides.

"I can understand why you'd go against me for D," Jonah said. "I do not understand why you'd quit Falcon and leave this family for Eli and his team."

Tears shimmered like glass, and she bit the inside of her cheek, drawing blood, to staunch her reaction to Jonah's words.

"Jesus H. Christ. You're in love with him," Mad Dog said, an edge of horror to his voice.

She whipped around to glare at Mad Dog. "This has nothing to do with love and everything to do with keeping my word. With not betraying men who tried to help me. Love has no place in this conversation. This is about doing what's right. I won't let that bastard experiment on them. I won't let him torture them before he decides he no longer has a use for them and kills them."

Jonah turned her to face him, gently this time, his thumb brushing against the moisture at the rim of her eye.

"Look at me, Ty," he said softly. "Eli has been different from the beginning. Everyone here knows it. It's why we've worried about you so damn much. We could see how much he affected you. I didn't want him anywhere near you. Now you look at me. Straight in the eye. And you tell me that love has nothing to do with you being willing to turn your back on your family and walk out of Falcon."

A tear trickled down, butting into Jonah's hand.

"I don't know," she whispered. "I only know I can't live with myself if he dies. He hates me now anyway. He thinks I betrayed him. I saw the look in his eyes. I can live with that as long as I can save him now."

Damiano moved to stand beside Tyana. He slid a hand over her shoulder and squeezed. "If you love him, Ty, then that's enough for me. I'll help you. You don't have to do this alone."

"You can't," she protested.

"Shut up," Jonah bit out. "You don't get to make the rules. I'm still the leader of Falcon and of this family. You're not going in to save Eli alone. We go as a team or no one goes. Understand? Are you going to listen this time or do I have to sedate your ass again and tie you to the bed?"

She threw her arms around Jonah, who stumbled back in surprise.

"Good grief," he muttered. "Can't you fall in love without getting so goddamn mushy?"

But his arms came around her tight and hugged her close to his much larger body. She could feel the racing of his heart, the jerky intake of his breath. He'd been afraid for her.

"I love you," she whispered so only he could hear. "And I'm sorry."

He squeezed her then released her, stepping away as he regained his composure.

She bumped into Mad Dog who put a hand at her back.

"Don't ever pull a dumbass stunt like saying you quit," he said gruffly.

She turned and looked into his eyes. There was love there. Yeah, she knew without a doubt both he and Jonah had been pissed enough to wring her neck, but they loved her. They were right. They were family.

She reached out and took his hand and pulled it up to her chest.

"Don't even say it," Mad Dog said with a shake of his head. "We've got a rescue to plan, and we don't need a freaking eye watering contest."

"I love you," she said sincerely.

He rolled his eyes and yanked her into his arms. "Don't ever scare me like that again, Ty. We're a team. We're a family.

We work together. Always."

She nodded against his chest. "Yeah, I get it." And she did.

She pulled away and smiled over at D who was watching the mush fest with an amused expression. "How are you?" she asked. "Really."

He shrugged. "I'm making it. If I keep a light dose of the sedative in my system all the time and take a larger dose when I go to bed, it seems to keep me calm, and I don't have the urge to shift like I did before."

She glanced over at Jonah. "I gave Ian and Braden the inhibitor. It works on them. For now. I promised if you guys didn't toss me out of Falcon I'd have Marcus examine them and see if he could offer any help."

"They have to be alive for that, and the longer we sit here yapping and getting in touch with our feelings, the less likely it will be that they stay that way. If they aren't already dead."

She shuddered. "They have to be. I won't let them down."

"Stop taking the goddamn world on your shoulders, Ty," Mad Dog growled.

"Enough already," Jonah said, holding his hand up to stop the bickering that was about to ensue. "I've got to gather our secondary. D, you need to get me intel on the most likely location of Esteban and then verify it. Mad Dog, you're in charge of weapons."

Then he turned to Tyana. "I don't want you to take this the wrong way, but you look like shit. Get some rest. We'll figure this out. If you aren't up to snuff by go time, then your ass will stay here, so bear that in mind as you argue with me about resting."

She laughed. Relief made her lightheaded. This was her team. Her family. She had complete faith in their ability to find Eli. And rest sounded pretty good to her aching head.

Chapter Twenty-Seven

Tyana slept fitfully and woke to find Damiano sitting on the end of her bed watching her. He seemed thinner, and it reminded her too much of the boy he'd been instead of the bulky man he'd grown up to be.

"Hey," she said in a husky voice as she sat up and drew her legs to her chest.

"Hey yourself. Feel any better?"

She craned her neck back and forth to work out the kinks, and to her satisfaction, the headache was gone.

"Yeah, I do."

He studied her, his eyes holding a multitude of questions. And finally he asked one.

"Was Mad Dog right? Do you love him?"

Tyana sighed. "You don't ask the easy ones, do you?" She reached over and took his hand, twining her fingers with his and squeezing. Just being able to touch him made her feel better. It seemed they'd been separated for too long.

"You were the first person in my life that I loved," she said honestly. "Jonah and Mad Dog were the second and third. Beyond that, I've never loved another human being. Love is...scary. What scares me more than the thought of...loving—" she nearly choked on the word, "—of loving him, is the fact that I need him." She looked up at Damiano. "I *need* him, D."

"Then I'm glad to help you save him," Damiano said. "You deserve to be happy, Ty. If he can make you happy, then I want that for you."

She turned her legs over the side of the bed and scooted down against him. She leaned her head on his shoulder, and he wrapped an arm around her.

"Did they find him yet?" she asked anxiously. "You're in here and not pecking away on your computer so I can only assume you've done your part and Jonah and Mad Dog are off drawing up the tactical plans?"

He nodded.

"Where?" She held her breath.

"My computer skills weren't really that necessary. Yet. Tits actually came through on this one. He tagged Esteban after the deal went down in Germany. Monitored his movements. He hoofed it into Switzerland immediately. His pharmaceutical company owns a large research facility in a remote region of the Alps. We believe he took Eli and his men there."

He stroked her hair soothingly as he spoke.

"If he's there, Ty, we'll get him. You know when Jonah sets his mind to something, he simply won't accept any other alternative but success."

She pulled away from Damiano and looked him in the eye. "Are you angry with me, D?"

His cheeks puffed as he blew out his breath. "No, Ty, I'm not angry. Well, I guess I am in a way. I'm pissed that you'd risk your life for me. You have to know that I could never accept that my recovery came because of your death."

"And yet you'd do the same for me," she said softly.

He gave a half laugh. "Yeah, I would. In a heartbeat."

"Hey you two," Mad Dog said from the door. He leaned in, bracing one hand on the frame. "Jonah's called a meeting. We're almost ready to roll."

Tyana surged up and hurried to the door. Mad Dog didn't move right away to let her pass.

"It's good to have you back, Ty," he said in a serious tone.

She punched him in the gut. He grunted and doubled over.

"It's good to be back," she said as she walked by.

His chuckle carried after her as she headed toward the living room.

ꕥ

Armed with satellite imagery of the medical facility, Falcon moved in. They knew where guards were posted, where security cameras scanned the perimeter and how many men were on the outside.

Damiano stayed behind in the high-tech military vehicle Tits had provided to monitor communications between the team members and to direct Falcon's movements once they were inside.

Jonah ordered the secondary to move in and disable the guard towers. They worked quickly and efficiently while Damiano hacked into the surveillance system so he could see inside the facility.

"All systems go," Damiano said.

Tyana, Mad Dog and Jonah checked to make sure their earpieces were secure.

"Falcon one ready," Jonah said.

"Falcon two ready," Mad Dog spoke up.

"Falcon three ready," Tyana added.

The three stood outside the wall surrounding the facility, heavily armed, awaiting Damiano's next instructions.

"Guard towers are down. Outside surveillance is down," Damiano reported. "You're cleared for go."

Jonah pointed at Mad Dog and Tyana. "As we discussed. This is an in and out operation. Mad Dog, you take the south entrance, I'll take the north. Ty, you enter through the west wing. If D's intel is correct, they're being held in the innermost sanctum. This isn't a time to get soft. Shoot first, ask questions later, and if things go bad, get your asses back to the rendezvous point."

Mad Dog and Tyana both nodded.

"Then let's do this," Jonah said grimly.

Adrenaline surged through Tyana's veins, rushing like a river. She had every confidence in Falcon's abilities. Jonah hired and trained the best. With the outside guard taken out and the Falcon secondary already working through the building to secure the exits, getting in to recover Eli and the others should be just another day on the job.

They split up, Jonah and Mad Dog heading in opposite directions. Tyana detached the rope and hook from her vest and slung the hook over the wall. She yanked to make sure it would hold and then she began to pull herself up and over the wall.

She dropped down on the other side and pulled the strap on her gun until the stock slid over her shoulder and into her hand. She moved quickly to the west entrance, and to her satisfaction, saw two fallen guards at the door. Falcon secondary had done their jobs.

When she entered the building, two things struck her. The god-awful chill and the deafening silence.

"Talk to me, D," she murmured. "Where am I going?"

The three of them wore tracking devices, and D had the schematics of the building uploaded to his computer so he could monitor their location and guide them on the most expedient path to the center. And thank God, because there was a veritable maze of hallways and corridors. Someone could wander for hours and never find their way in or out.

"Keep moving forward, Ty. Pass two more hallways and take a right. I'm not picking up shit on the infrared. Are you hearing anything down there?"

That would explain the chill. Was it to cloak body heat? Still, he should be able to pick up something.

"Now take a left three hallways down. Once you make that left, you're going to make an immediate right then an immediate left again."

"You're making me dizzy," she muttered.

D paused then spoke again, this time to Jonah and then to Mad Dog as he gave them instructions. All communications went through D. Less distracting than having them all talking over each other.

"Okay, Ty, you're doing fine. Take your next left. You'll land in a circular corridor. There are three of those. One in each wing. Jonah and Mad Dog are closing in on their locations. If your guys are being held here, they should be in one of those inner rooms."

God, let them be here. Don't let me be too late.

"Okay, I'm here."

She entered the hallway and saw a door right in front of her. She reached into her vest and pulled out the small explosive device and stuck it on the security panel.

"I'm blowing the first door," she said. "Tell Mad Dog and Jonah heads up because if they don't know we're here already, they'll know in a few seconds."

"Be careful, Ty."

"Always."

She set the timer then raced around the bend to the next door where she set her next explosive.

"How many doors am I looking for?" she murmured as she set the timer.

"Three more," D replied.

She crouched next to the current door and waited for the first to blow. The explosion rocked the hallway, and she put her hand out to balance herself. She shot up and ran around, her rifle up.

Two men in lab coats staggered out of the room, waving their hands in big, exaggerated motions. She fired two rounds and they both dropped in their tracks.

She stepped over their bodies and went into the room. *Fuck.* It was empty. Just a bunch of lab and computer equipment.

"Room one clear," she reported back. Then she hauled ass back into the hallway to see if the noise had startled any of the other rooms into action. As thick as the damn walls were, though, it wouldn't surprise her if the explosion hadn't even been heard inside the other rooms.

Big advantage to her if that was the case.

She sprinted back to room two and hit the start button as she skidded by en route to room three. She slapped the explosive on the panel and entered the time again.

Again, the explosion sounded, and she backtracked to the room. This time, no one hit the hallway so she slowed and raised her rifle. Back to the wall, she eased around the doorway then bolted in, ready to shoot the first person who moved.

Her heart fell to her feet when she saw Eli, caged in a clear, plexiglass square that looked to be airtight. A long tube ran from the ceiling and was attached to the top. Was it to pump in oxygen? Was this how they prevented him from escaping if he shifted?

Rage made her tremble, but she forced herself to calm down and move quickly to the box. He opened his eyes when she approached, but his vision was unfocused. He looked to be heavily drugged. *Fuck.*

She couldn't blow it without risking injury to Eli. She could shoot it but it could send pieces of the plexiglass into his body.

"Goddamn it, D, I need you," she said in desperation. "I found Eli. They've got him in some kind of a damn box. It looks like it's linked to their computer system. Can you figure out how to open it?"

"Give me a minute, Ty. I've locked on to your location. Let me see what I can do."

A few seconds later, the security pad on the face of the box lit up and then the top popped up with a whoosh as the airlock was broken. She ran over and looked down over the edge.

Eli stared up at her, anger glinting in his dark eyes. She didn't have time to hash it out.

"Get your ass up," she hissed.

She reached down to tug at his arms. He was heavy and lethargic. He struggled to get to his knees, hanging on to the edge with white-knuckled hands.

She tossed one of his arms over her shoulders, careful to keep her gun up with her free hand.

"Step over, I've got you," she said.

She staggered under his weight but refused to let go. She held him up by sheer force of will.

"Why are you here?" he rasped, his voice hoarse and pain-filled.

"I don't have time to get into it with you, Eli," she said as she hauled him toward the door. "I'm more concerned with saving your ass, so shut the fuck up and help me out here."

Damiano chuckled in her ear. "Rock on, girl."

Damn. She'd forgotten D could hear everything she said.

They ducked into the hallway, and she looked both ways.

"I need you, D. Help me get him out of here."

She listened intently and navigated while dragging Eli along. What the hell had they done to him? Fear clogged her throat.

As they veered into another hallway, Tyana looked up to see an armed guard pointing his rifle right at her and Eli. Reacting quickly, she shoved Eli to the floor and shot at the same time the guard did.

Pain slammed into her leg, and her knees buckled. The guard went down with a thump. Her aim had been truer than his.

Jesus, it hurt. She looked down to see blood pouring from a hole in her upper leg. Another few inches and it would have hit her femoral artery, and she'd be on the floor bleeding out.

"Ty, talk to me, goddamn it. I heard gunfire. What the fuck is going on?"

"I took a hit," she said faintly.

D swore viciously in her ear. "Get the hell out, do you hear me, Ty?"

"D, I'm okay. Took a round in the leg. I can make it. I'm coming with Eli."

She staggered over to the guard and used her knife to cut his shirt off. She quickly fashioned a long bandage and wrapped it tightly around her leg several times to apply pressure and slow the bleeding.

The adrenaline buzz was fast wearing off, and her entire leg felt like someone had tossed her in petrol and lit a match.

She made it back to Eli who was trying to pull himself off the floor.

"That...was...stupid," he growled. "Leave me, Tyana. You can't make it out with me."

"Listen to him, Ty," Damiano urged. "I'll send Jonah and Mad Dog to get Eli."

"Fuck that," she snarled. "I'm almost there. If Eli will shut the fuck up and get moving."

She looped his arm back over her shoulders, and ignoring the searing agony each time she moved her leg, she started forward again. Eli was gaining strength. He seemed to be helping her along more.

"Can you shift?" she asked. Damn sure would make it easier to get him out if he could.

"No. Too drugged. They used a paralytic. Only reason I can move at all right now is I was due for another injection and the last one is wearing off. You showed up before they did."

"Lucky you."

They burst out of the exit, and she did a quick survey to make sure they weren't walking into more trouble. She hobbled to the wall where she'd climbed over. No way was she going to get Eli over that wall. Fuck.

She eased him behind a hedge of greenery and laid him on the ground. "Talk to me, Eli. Where are the others? Do you know?"

"Ty, forget the others," D barked in her ear. "You get your ass out of there and let Jonah and Mad Dog find them."

"Shut it, D, or I swear I'll turn your ass off." She grabbed Eli by the shirt and shook him. "Think, Eli. Tell me where the others are."

"They couldn't have been far," he said. "I heard them once when my door was opened."

"You stay here," she said as she shoved him back down on the ground. "D, I've stashed Eli where I went over the wall. Make damn sure someone comes for him. I'm going back in after the others."

Damiano's curses fell on deaf ears as she walked back to the entrance, half dragging her leg. She gritted her teeth against the jarring pain that snaked up her body with each step.

Suck it up. It wasn't the first time she'd taken a bullet, and it probably wouldn't be the last.

"I'm working on memory here, D. Tell me if I'm going wrong."

"You're fine." D's voice was firm, and she needed that strength. Grasped onto it with both hands.

She made it back to the door where her explosive was set and ready to go. Then, she thought better of having such a short timeframe and added another three seconds to give her more time to move out.

She forced herself up, put the stock of her gun down on the floor to act as a crutch and hauled her ass as fast as she could in the opposite direction.

"Jonah and Mad Dog are taking fire, but they'll be there to back you up as soon as they can," D said in her ear.

She gritted her teeth and rounded the bend just as the explosion rocked the hallway.

Gun up, she hurried back, her rifle sight trained on the doorway. When no one was forthcoming, she ducked in.

"Shit."

"What is it?" Damiano demanded.

"Cats," she replied. "I wasn't counting on them being in fucking jaguar and panther form."

D was uncharacteristically silent.

The two cats were caged separately. Iron bars and a simple padlock were her only obstacles, so this was something she wouldn't need D for. Well, that and the keys were lying on the table three feet from the cages.

Taking a deep breath to ward off her pain and fear, she collected the keys and edged over to the first cage. The panther. This was Braden if she remembered correctly.

"Nice kitty," she murmured as she fumbled with the lock. God help her, this might be the dumbest thing she'd ever done.

She threw open the cage with one arm and tightened her grip on her rifle as she backed cautiously away to unlock the other cage.

The panther jumped from the cage and crouched warily in front of her. Her hands shook as she managed to get the lock off the second cage while her eyes never left the panther.

The jaguar hissed and bared his teeth as she started to crack open the cage. Oh hell, it was now or never. She threw the lid open and backed away, tripping when her leg gave out. She let out a cry of pain as she hit the floor.

The cats circled her, intermittent growls spilling from their throats. The jaguar came closer, and Tyana closed her eyes, prepared for death.

He sniffed cautiously at her shoulder then lowered his head

and nuzzled the wound on her leg. The panther stalked in on her other side and bumped her side with his head.

She stared dumbly as they continued to nudge at her. Good God, they wanted her to get up and go. She pushed herself up.

"I don't know if you understand a word I'm saying, but we've got to get the hell out of here," she said as she struggled toward the door. "Eli is out already. All that's left is Gabe."

The cats flanked her as she made it out into the hallway. Her leg was growing more numb with each passing minute. She hoped to hell Jonah and Mad Dog had made it over by now but she wouldn't ask Damiano, because he'd worry that she was fading. And she was.

Footsteps, several of them, echoed in the hallway. She flattened herself against the wall with her gun at the ready. This was going to suck.

Three men rounded the corner at a fast clip. She shot the first before they even realized she was there. She managed to squeeze off another round before the third shot back.

She slammed against the wall as the bullet tore into her shoulder. The cats launched themselves at the men. "D," she gasped. "I'm hit again."

The sounds of the cats' screams mingled with those of the men. Her breaths came hard and sporadic. It hurt. Fuck, it hurt. She glanced down, trying to assess the damage but all she could see was blood, red, pouring onto the floor.

Chapter Twenty-Eight

Through hazy vision, Tyana saw two sets of cats' eyes close to her face. She felt a warm tongue on her cheek and soft fur rub against her nose.

"Go," she whispered. "You have to get out. They'll kill you."

She pushed at the jaguar with her uninjured arm and was stunned at the weakness of the gesture, how much of her strength it sapped to make such a small movement.

"Ty, Ty, speak to me." D's frantic voice shot through her ear, and she winced.

She tried to push herself away from the wall, tried to get herself up off the floor.

"*Go*," she told the cats as she fell back, her strength spent.

To her relief, they loped off.

"D, the cats are out. If the Falcon secondary is moving in, make damn sure no one shoots them."

"I don't give a damn about the fucking cats," Damiano bit out. "Can you move? Can you get the hell out?"

Shit. She couldn't even lie to him because he'd see she was still stationary.

"No," she said quietly. "I'm down."

More sounds echoed through the hallway. Loud footsteps. More than one person. A lot of them.

"D, is the Falcon secondary moving in?" she asked, unable to keep the fear from her voice.

Before he could respond, she looked up and saw four men round the corner. Not Falcon. Her heart sank. Her rifle dangled uselessly from her hand. She couldn't even lift it.

ꕥ

Eli shoved himself off the ground, trying to shake off the effects of the paralytic. His mind was clearing now. Fear replaced the fog.

Two men, guns up, sprinted toward him. He recognized them as members of Falcon. The ones who'd shown up in Germany. Neither was Damiano which only left Jonah and Mad Dog. The man in front clearly had to be Jonah.

As he rose to meet the potential threat, two cats burst from the exit he and Tyana had come through.

Falcon halted, their guns up and trained on the cats. But they didn't immediately shoot.

The cats collapsed on the ground and began their excruciating shift. Eli stumbled over to their naked bodies.

"Tyana. Where is Tyana?" he demanded.

Ian stared at him in confusion. "I don't know," he said in a weak voice.

The two men from Falcon knelt over Ian and Braden. They dug fatigues out of their packs and thrust them at the naked men.

"Get them on," Jonah barked. "Then tell me where the fuck Tyana is."

"She went back in after you," Eli explained to the men as they dressed. "You came out. She didn't."

Jonah cupped a hand to his ear then cursed. Mad Dog paled.

"She's taken another round. She's down," Jonah reported.

He dug into his pocket then thrust a small ear piece at Eli. "Put this on. You won't have voice, but you'll be able to hear. We're going in after Ty."

Eli pushed the receiver into his ear and immediately heard the voice of another man urgently asking for Tyana to report her condition.

"We're going too," Ian said. "If she went down saving us,

we're not leaving her."

Jonah didn't argue. He and Mad Dog tossed the two men extra guns.

"Jonah, she's on the move." The voice crackled in Eli's ear. Damiano. "Not under her own power. They're Esteban's men. They're moving her."

There was another moment of silence. "Lower level. They said lower level and goddamn it, Jonah, I've lost her location. She's not showing up anymore. You need to move."

"All right, we're going in," Jonah said to the four men. "Fan out. Damiano has lost her location. He mentioned a lower level so we have to find our way down. We don't have time to waste."

"Jonah, Falcon secondary has secured the south wing," Damiano reported.

"Have them close in on our location from the opposite direction," Jonah said. "I want no stone unturned."

As he turned to go into the building, Eli reached out and grabbed his arm.

"I can shift. The drug has worn off enough. I can go into places you guys can't. I need voice, though."

Without hesitation, Jonah reached over and tore Mad Dog's receiver from the front of his vest and slapped it on Eli's chest. "Go," he ordered.

Eli summoned every bit of his mental energy and evaporated into a fine mist. He streaked into the building and disappeared into the ventilation system. Behind him, he heard the steady footsteps of the others as they ran inside.

ℵ

Damiano was about to go mad. He itched from the inside out. It took every ounce of his strength not to give in to the urge to shift. To become a predator and go after the ones who held Ty.

Only the fact that he knew he was her only voice, her only comfort, prevented his complete loss of control.

The men who'd taken her were angry. They argued among

themselves, cursing the fact that Esteban had disappeared when the compound was attacked. Damiano flinched when he heard Ty cry out in pain.

God, what were they doing to her? He needed to see. He needed her location. He felt so goddamn helpless.

"Bitch won't live long enough for us to use her as a bargaining tool," one of them complained.

She cried out again, and one of them laughed cruelly.

Damiano summoned every bit of control. He had to help her. Just like he had in Prague. He wouldn't let her suffer like this.

Tears streamed down his cheeks as he drew in a shaky breath. "Ty, listen to me." He purposely made his voice soft and low, soothing. "I want you to go to our place. You remember it, don't you? Remember back at the orphanage, we'd go to our special place where no one could touch us. No one could hurt us. It was just you and me in the most wonderful place we could imagine. Go there now, Ty. Do it for me."

"I love you, D," she whispered in a choked voice. Was she choking on her own blood? Had she taken a hit to the chest? "Tell Jonah I'm sorry."

Jonah and Mad Dog paused for just a second as Damiano's haunted voice filled their ears. And then Tyana's apology. Grief, thick and relentless grabbed hold of Jonah. For the first time in two decades, he faced losing someone important to him. He'd sworn after Adharji that he'd never let anyone close again. Would never allow himself to bleed over anyone. But Falcon was his family and Tyana, Mad Dog and Damiano had, despite his best efforts, become all-important. He wouldn't lose them. Not now. Not ever.

"We won't lose her," Jonah vowed. "Do you hear me, D? We won't lose her. You tell her that. Tell her we're coming for her and goddamn it, she's not allowed to die."

Eli streaked downward, to the lower level of the building. He'd found the single elevator shaft in the center of the facility. There was blood in the shuttle. Tyana's blood.

Through more vents he floated until finally he heard voices. He moved silent as a whisper down into the room. Tyana lay on the floor, her leg bent at an odd angle, one arm bloodied, the other carelessly thrown aside. Her eyes were open but glassy and fixed on some distant object.

Four men stood to the side arguing. Eli did a quick survey of the room. A lone assault rifle, one the men had laid against the wall, was a few feet away. He would have to be fast. Shift and shoot.

Ignoring the rage that consumed him, and the worry over Tyana's so-still form, he wrapped around the rifle, a single thin plume of smoke.

With a jolt, he commanded himself back to form, holding the image of the transmitter in his mind. Screw the clothes. If they came, they came, but he needed that transmitter.

His hands gripped the gun just as the shocked stares of the men found him. He laid down a round of fire into their midst. Three fell while the fourth rolled away. He came up firing.

Heat singed Eli's arm, but he ignored it and pumped three rounds into the fourth man's chest. He sagged like a deflated balloon.

"Damiano, can you hear me?"

"Yeah, I read you. What the fuck is going on in there?"

"I'm with Tyana. I've taken a hit. It's not bad. I need cover getting out of here."

"Is Tyana alive?" Damiano demanded.

Eli knelt, afraid to touch his fingers to her neck. He felt the faintest flutter, slow and unsteady. "She's alive. For now. But fading fast. Get a chopper in here as fast as you can. She needs to get to the hospital yesterday."

He quickly relayed the information on his location to Damiano, and then he gathered Tyana in his arms. He hoisted her up, and she sagged limply, her head dangling over his injured arm.

He adjusted his hold on her so that her head sagged against his chest instead, and he rested his chin on top to keep her in place.

God, there was so much blood.

"Don't die," he whispered. "Don't die, Tyana. Not for me."

ഊ

Ian and Braden gained more strength as determination fueled their movements. Whatever the reason for Tyana saving them, she had, and they wouldn't let her go down for that.

They sprinted down the hallways, glancing right and left, looking for any movement, any sign of blood. As they rounded one of the corridors, Ian stopped cold. Braden collided with him, nearly knocking him off balance.

Esteban stood in their path holding an assault rifle trained on Ian. Rage billowed over Ian, lighting fire to every one of his nerve endings. This was the fucker responsible for his and Braden's condition. The bastard had kept them caged, taunting them endlessly until they'd shifted. There was no telling what he'd done to them while they were in shifted form. It was probably a blessing that they had no memory of being cats.

"You'll never live," Ian taunted.

Esteban smiled, an eerie, empty expression that suggested he wasn't all there. There was a bloody gash on his neck that looked remarkably like it had been inflicted with claws. It wasn't a new wound. The blood had congealed and dried, dark red, on his skin.

"Which one of us got you, Esteban?" Ian asked. "Looks like you pissed the cat off one too many times."

"I don't need you," Esteban spat. "It's never been about you. You're both expendable." He raised his gun. Braden shouldered his rifle in response and Ian gripped his tighter.

"Which is it going to be?" Ian asked quietly. "You don't have to die. Put the gun down."

Esteban laughed. "Nice try. You won't get any information from me."

He fired the rifle, and Ian jerked, expecting the pain to lash over him. To his horror, Gabe's body materialized in front of him, his face a mask of agony. Blood trickled from the corner of his mouth as he stared into Ian's eyes. Like a puppet being cut free of his strings, Gabe sagged to the floor.

"No!" Esteban screamed. "What have you done? You stupid fool! You were stable."

Esteban fired his weapon again as he began to run. The shot went wild as Esteban dove into one of the rooms.

Ian didn't even bother pursuing him. His attention was focused on Gabe's fallen body. He sank to his knees and pressed his hands over the gaping wound in Gabe's chest. Braden hit the floor beside him. "Ian. Braden." It came out as a trickle, as if the names barely managed to escape.

Shit. Shit! They were stuck in here with no means of communication. Panic settled hard into Ian's stomach as more blood ran through his fingers.

"Don't talk, man. We'll get you out of here," Braden said.

"No. Listen to me. I have to tell you something. I need you to listen closely."

Gabe's hands curled into Ian's shirt, and he pulled him nearer with flagging strength.

"Tyana didn't betray us. I did."

"What?" Ian demanded. "Gabe, you're not making any sense. Shut up and let us get you out."

Gabe shook his head and moaned. He coughed and more blood spilled over his lips.

"I have a sister. Katie. On my laptop. Information about her. What you'll need to find her. They threatened her."

"Sister?" Ian exchanged confused glances with his brother. Gabe didn't have a sister. None of them had family. It was a prerequisite to join the team when they were still in the military.

"Promise me," Gabe said, his grip tightening around Ian's shirt. "I don't deserve anything from you guys but Katie is innocent. They want her. I'm stable..."

Ian pressed harder on the wound, despair tightening his throat as he realized nothing he was doing was staunching the blood flow. "We'll find her, Gabe."

"I'm sorry," he murmured. "Tell Eli...so sorry. They said they'd kill her if I didn't give you guys up. Realized too late. They wouldn't kill her...they want her...like me...she's all I had."

His eyes seemed to fix on a spot beyond Ian and Braden, and then they slowly closed and his head fell to the side.

"Son of a bitch," Braden hissed. "Goddamn it, no!"

Ian moved his bloody hands to Gabe's neck, desperately feeling for a pulse. Grief and anger ricocheted through him when he got no response. No flutter to tell him Gabe was still alive.

Chapter Twenty-Nine

Jonah and Mad Dog rounded a corridor and immediately fell back as shots were fired in their direction. They flattened themselves against the wall.

"Goddamn it, we don't have time for this," Mad Dog snarled.

Jonah stared at him. "Ty needs us. Let's do this. She doesn't have much time."

Mad Dog held up three fingers and did a silent countdown. Jonah ducked low and Mad Dog hurled himself around the corner, rolling and firing.

The staccato of gunshots filled the hallway as he and Jonah laid down fire. Bullets tore into the wall above Jonah's head. The two men in the front went down. Three behind began a hasty retreat and ran right into three members of the Falcon secondary.

"You're with me," Jonah barked to his men as he bolted up and raced down the corridor to the heart of the complex.

A few seconds later, they swarmed into an inner room. Small, circular in shape. It housed a glass tube that looked like an elevator shaft. Bingo. Their way down.

He and his men fell back as a low whir sounded, indicating the elevator was in use. Jonah pointed to two of his men to position themselves to the right and motioned to Mad Dog and the remaining man to go left. Jonah took position in front and waited.

When the glass pane slid upward, the door of the elevator revolved sideways and Eli stumbled out carrying Ty. Jonah froze for an infinitesimal moment. He saw the blood dripping from Ty's leg and arm, saw how still she lay in Eli's arms. Fear whispered through his veins.

"I want a perimeter around her." Mad Dog intervened when Jonah remained silent for that one moment. "We move out, now. D, we're coming out. Make damn sure there's a chopper waiting in the vicinity. I don't care how you make it happen."

"ETA is two minutes," Damiano returned.

Jonah recovered and rushed toward Eli. He moved to take Ty from Eli's arms, but Eli fixed him with a cold stare. It was the stare of a man who feared losing everything. Of a man who wasn't going to let anyone take her from him.

"I'll take your front," Jonah said.

Eli nodded, tightened his grip around Ty's limp body and fell in behind Jonah.

Mad Dog and the three secondaries closed ranks around Eli, and they rushed toward the exit.

"Perimeter and facility is secure," Damiano reported. "Falcon secondary awaits your next orders."

"Tell them to maintain their position. I want a complete sweep of the facility," Jonah said even as he charged forward. "I want computers, disks, surveillance. I want every piece of information they can find. Nothing gets left behind."

Eli held his precious burden closer as he followed behind Jonah. His chest was tight with emotion, with fear. Paralyzing, agonizing fear. He couldn't breathe. Through the panic, he remembered his own men.

"Damiano, do you have a location on Ian and Braden? Has anyone reported seeing Gabe?" He couldn't damn well leave them behind, but he wouldn't leave Tyana either.

"Negative. They aren't wired. Wait a minute. I'm getting a report from Falcon secondary. They're removing Gabe's body. Ian and Braden are with them." There was a long pause. "I'm sorry, Eli."

Eli stumbled for a moment, recovered his footing and pressed on, his chest encased in ice. Gabe was gone. Tyana was dying in his arms. He'd been helpless to stop any of it.

They burst out of the west entrance, and Jonah held up a hand. "Everyone back and take cover. I'm going to blow the wall."

Beat the hell out of going over.

Eli backed into the building with the three Falcon secondaries hovering protectively around him. He turned, shielding Tyana's body with his.

She was so deathly pale. The dark red blood contrasted starkly against the white of her skin. He kissed her forehead.

"Don't die, sugar," he whispered. "You and I have way too much to work out."

The explosion rocked the entire building. Plaster and light fixtures rained down from the ceiling. Eli closed more tightly around Tyana as one of the florescent tubes bounced off his shoulder.

"Let's go," Jonah ordered from the entrance.

Eli hurried out to see a gaping hole in the stone wall. They ran through it and up the rocky terrain surrounding the complex.

"Chopper is landing a quarter mile away," Jonah said close to Eli's ear. "We've got to move."

Gathering strength he didn't have, mustering the energy from reserves he hadn't drawn on since his escape from Adharji, Eli broke into a run.

As they topped the next hill, they saw a chopper touch down in the small valley and a medic hop out with a backboard.

Jonah didn't waste any time climbing into the helicopter as Eli gently laid her down on the backboard.

"Load and go," the medic said, and Eli recognized his accent as American. Was he military?

They hustled Tyana into the helicopter, and Eli didn't ask. He piled in behind them, leaving Mad Dog with the Falcon secondary.

Eli and Jonah exchanged a long look before Jonah finally nodded his acceptance.

The helicopter rose as the two medics worked in unison, one intubating her while the other started dual IVs.

ഇ

Eli paced the confines of the waiting room of the private hospital. He'd refused treatment himself, and one of the medics who'd brought Tyana in slapped a bandage on the bloody crease on his arm, but Eli didn't give it a second glance.

He wanted answers. A lot of them. Gabe was dead. Ian and Braden were being examined by the Falcon doctor, Marcus, so he couldn't even ask them what went down with Gabe.

And Tyana. He closed his eyes. She was still in surgery. Her prognosis had been grim with the amount of blood loss. Jonah and Mad Dog stood at the far window, their faces locked in stone. Damiano sat with his face in his hands, alone, away from the others.

Several hours into their vigil, Ian and Braden walked into the waiting room accompanied by Marcus. Faint hope glimmered in their eyes. He wanted to ask about Gabe but forced himself to first ask what Marcus had been able to determine.

"He thinks daily injections will work for a while and the inhibitor will work for sudden and uncontrolled shifts," Ian said as they gathered close to Eli.

"But as I told your men, it could only be temporary. If they become acclimated to the drug, the effectiveness is lost. It could very well be that what has happened with Damiano will happen to them," Marcus added.

Eli nodded grimly.

"Jonah is in the process of getting me all the data and computer files from the research facility. If there is a way I can find the original chemical composition used in the attack in Adharji, then maybe I can offer a more suitable alternative. Until then, as clichéd as it may sound, you can only take it one day at a time."

Marcus turned and walked over to sit by Damiano. Eli could hear him ask if Damiano was okay and if he needed another injection. Eli turned his focus on the two brothers.

"What happened to Gabe?"

A mixture of anger and sorrow crossed their features.

"Tyana didn't betray us, Eli," Ian said. "Gabe did."

Eli's brow twisted, and he leaned in closer. "What?"

"He admitted it right before he died," Braden said. "We got to him too late to get him out. He has a sister. A *sister* for God's sake. He said that Esteban was threatening her, using her to make him sell us out."

Eli dragged a hand through his hair, caught the strands in a bunch and clenched his fist. "I don't understand."

"He pleaded with us to save her," Ian said quietly. "He said Esteban wants her. Rambled on about how he was stable. It didn't make a lot of sense. Told us there was information in his laptop on how to find his sister. Said she was all he had."

Eli swore. Then he closed his eyes. Gabe had betrayed them? It certainly made more sense now. How else would Esteban have known they were in Argentina?

"Why have Tyana go after us, then? It makes no sense."

Braden shrugged. "Maybe she was insurance in case Gabe flaked. He had to know she had some serious motivation to want to bring us in if it meant helping Damiano."

"I hate to break up the reunion, but you and I need to talk," Jonah broke in. His eyes glittered, and behind him, Mad Dog stood, arms crossed, obviously planning to be a party to whatever conversation ensued.

Eli turned to Ian. "Find Gabe's laptop. Figure out what the hell this stuff is about his sister. We'll figure out what to do about it later."

He stepped away from the brothers and eyed Jonah and Mad Dog cautiously.

"Sorry about your man," Mad Dog said gruffly.

Eli nodded and wondered if they'd overheard Ian's statement that Gabe had been the one who betrayed them.

"I'm in a huge quandary about what to do about you," Jonah said. "I should take you out."

Eli stared levelly at him. "You can try."

"I'd love to be able to blame you. Place all the blame on you," Jonah continued, ignoring Eli's challenge. "But I'm afraid Ty shoulders most of the blame for the situation she got herself into. Personally, I think you're bad news. If I had my way, you wouldn't be within a country of Ty."

"Let's skip the chitchat, okay?" Eli snapped. "If you want to take this outside, let's go. But to be perfectly honest, when Tyana wakes up, I don't want to have to explain to her that I killed her freaking team."

"You seem awfully confident that she's going to wake up. She took two bullets for you, Chance."

"She'll live," Eli gritted out. He wouldn't entertain any alternative. She had to live.

"You better hope she does because if she dies, your life isn't going to be worth a damn thing."

"You're right about that," Eli said quietly. "If she dies, my life *won't* be worth a damn thing."

Mad Dog's eyes flickered, and his expression eased slightly.

"Why did you come for us?" Eli asked. "Why bother? It's obvious you'd prefer I wasn't breathing."

Jonah stared coldly at him. "Because Ty would have come after you by herself. She was willing to quit Falcon for you. Tell me, Chance, are you worth it? Did she choose wrong?"

Eli let out a long, pent-up breath. Tyana had been willing to give up her team for him? He shook his head to clear the cobwebs.

Then he stared back at Jonah and hardened his gaze. "If you think I'm going to spill my guts to you, fuck off."

Jonah pressed in close, their noses just an inch apart. "If you think I'm going to hand over my sister to you, you fuck off. She stays with Falcon. With her family. If you want any part of her then you'll have to come on her terms."

Eli didn't back down. "What the fuck is this, a job offer?"

Jonah relaxed the tiniest bit. "Falcon could use you. Your men need Marcus. We aren't going to let Ty go. So you figure it out."

"Your human relations skills suck ass."

Mad Dog broke into laughter again. "Yeah, well get used to it. It doesn't improve. Trust me."

Eli slid his gaze over to Mad Dog.

"She was ours first," Mad Dog said softly. "We look out for her. Always. If you have an interest in being part of her life you need to know that. It's a package deal. We aren't going away."

"Jesus Christ," Eli muttered. "Do we at least get our own bedroom?"

Jonah scowled again. "It wouldn't be a good time to remind me of just how close you got to Ty. Now do we have an understanding?"

Eli nodded. And hell, what else could he do? His team had gone to shit. Gabe was dead and now they had his sister to contend with. He needed Falcon, as much as it pissed him off to admit. But more than that, he needed Tyana. If having her with him meant putting up with her surly-ass legion of brothers, then oh well.

Chapter Thirty

Tyana opened her eyes and stared up at a pristine white ceiling. Her entire body felt stiff, and she quickly discovered that moving wasn't much of an option. Panic set in. The last thing she remembered was being hauled down to a lower level by Esteban's henchmen. Had she survived only to be held prisoner?

"Hey, there she is."

Relief, sweet and cooling, washed over her as she heard Mad Dog's voice. His face came into view along with Jonah's. A warm hand closed over hers, and she slowly managed to move her head enough so that she could see Damiano sitting next to her.

She was in a hospital. Alive. And there was a reason moving was so difficult. She glanced down to see her left arm and shoulder swathed in bandages and her left leg encased in stiff plaster.

"What the hell did they do to me?" she grumbled.

Relief sparked in Jonah's dark eyes. Amusement lit Mad Dog's. Then she saw him. Eli. Standing in the background.

Their gazes locked as she looked hungrily at him. He was alive. He was safe. She went weak with the knowledge.

Mad Dog bent over, temporarily obscuring her view of Eli. He kissed her forehead. "You scared the shit out of us, baby girl."

"The only reason I'm not kicking your ass is because it wouldn't be a fair fight," Jonah growled. "You look pitiful in all those bandages."

She laughed and promptly regretted it as pain wracked through her chest. Mother of God, she hurt. D squeezed her hand, and she turned her gaze to him. "You okay?" she asked softly.

His eyes looked suspiciously wet. Then he shook his head. "Only you would wake up after three days in the hospital and ask if *I'm* okay."

Her eyes widened. "Three days? Was it that bad?"

Jonah nodded, his expression grim. "We thought we were going to lose you, Ty."

"I'm not going anywhere. Too much fun being a pain in your ass."

He finally cracked a smile. And then he bent and touched her cheek in a gentle gesture. "I love you too, little sister."

He stood and glanced back at Eli who was still in the background, standing there, hands shoved into his jeans pockets. Jonah directed a quick glance at Mad Dog and Damiano, and they started for the door.

"We'll be back later to check on you," Damiano said.

A few seconds later, she and Eli were alone. He walked slowly to the side of her bed and sat down in the chair vacated by D. He reached tentatively over and curled his hand around hers. His fingers trembled against her palm.

"Ian and Braden?" she asked fearfully.

"They're fine," he said.

"Gabe?"

Eli looked down and shook his head. "He didn't make it."

"I'm sorry."

His eyes flashed back up to hers. "Don't be sorry. Gabe was the one who betrayed us. I let you walk into a trap. I let my men walk into a trap. You should have left us, Tyana. You never should have come back for us."

He broke off and looked to be struggling to compose himself.

"How could I not?" she whispered.

"You took a bullet for me. You took a bullet for my men. You owed us nothing, Tyana. I'm so goddamn mad at you for putting yourself in front of me. It should have been me."

His thumb stroked over her hand, gentle where his words were harsh.

"I need you," she said simply, and this time, it was easy to say. Light amidst the pain. Relief.

"And I need you," he said hoarsely. "Where does this leave us, sugar?"

She pushed the pain and her blurry vision aside so she could focus. Sleep was calling to her, but this was important. Maybe the most important thing she'd ever do. Besides, laying your heart out wasn't supposed to be easy.

"I don't know what you want...what you expect from me, Eli. But I can't change. I'm a part of Falcon. My job is dangerous. Falcon is my family, though."

The corner of his mouth lifted into a crooked smile. "Jonah has already laid down the law in that regard. I think he was afraid I'd haul you away over my shoulder."

"I still have to find a way to help D. That priority hasn't changed. I'm just going to try to be smarter about how I do it."

"That's good, sugar, because between you and me, I don't want you chasing some other guy down and seducing him."

She smiled and groaned.

"We can do this later," he said as he tenderly smoothed a hand over her brow. "You're hurting. I can see it in those gorgeous eyes of yours. You need rest."

"No. Not yet." She shook off his interruption and went back to the heart of the matter. "Can you accept that, Eli? Do we have any sort of future together?"

He leaned over and took her free hand in both of his. He brought it to his lips and kissed each finger. "Jonah and I had a little talk. Seems he isn't opposed to me joining Falcon, and he's made it clear that's the only way you and I will be together." He laughed. "Protective, that one is. I imagine we'll butt heads because we're both used to being the boss, but I can deal with it." His expression grew serious again. "What I can't deal with is being without you."

She sighed, part in contentment and part in bone-deep weariness. "That would be perfect. Then I can look out for your ass."

He shook his head. "Life with you is going to be interesting to say the least, sugar."

"Eli? What about your team?"

He sobered. "They've got some long days ahead. Marcus has examined them and has them on the same regimen he started Damiano on before he grew immune to it. We've got some loose ends to tie up with Gabe. A sister we didn't know he had. I think your team just grew by three men. Think you can handle that?"

She touched his mouth with her hand as his grip around her fingers loosened. "I think you and I will make a great team, Eli. I won't lie to you and say it doesn't scare me to death. I've never relied on anyone but myself and Falcon. I don't know how good I'll be at this, but I want to try."

"We'll work it out, sugar. I'm not going anywhere. Now I want you to get some rest, okay? You've got a long recovery ahead of you."

She made a face, but her eyes were already closing. Try as she might, she couldn't keep them open.

She felt Eli's lips on hers, light, loving. "I'll get the nurse to give you something for pain, sugar. Sleep. I'll be here when you wake up."

Chapter Thirty-One

Tyana's room resembled an army training camp. Six men, well, seven, if you counted the mild-mannered Marcus, stood in various poses, from slouching against the wall to being draped across too-small chairs. And Eli was parked on the bed next to her, his body pressed against her side.

Black shirts, camo pants and combat boots. They looked like they were ready to go to war. While they'd refrained from carrying their rifles into the hospital, Tyana knew that Mad Dog would be sporting his knives.

This was verified when he laid a sheathed knife on the bed next to her. It was identical to the one he'd given her before. The one she'd lost in Buenos Aires.

She trailed her fingers over the polished hilt and smiled up at him. "Thanks, Mad Dog."

"Don't lose this one, okay?"

"She's grown way too fond of those damn things," Jonah grumbled.

"I taught her well," Mad Dog said.

"So what's the plan?" she asked pointedly. "Doc says I can get out of here tomorrow, and after three weeks in here, I'm ready to crawl out if I have to."

Beside her, Eli stiffened. "Just cool your jets, sugar. You're in no shape to do anything but what we tell you."

"Uh oh," Mad Dog mumbled.

Damiano cracked a grin while Ian and Braden glanced warily at Tyana.

"When I get out of this cast, I'm going to kick your ass for that," she said darkly, and elbowed him in the ribs with her good arm.

"Well until then, I'd say you're as helpless as a one-legged man in an ass kicking contest," Eli said smugly.

She sighed. "I ask again. What's the plan?"

Jonah's lips worked as he suppressed a smile. What was the world coming to when the brooding bastard was actually lightening up?

"We go back to the island," Jonah said. "We're flying you home."

She glanced up at Eli a little anxiously.

"Don't worry, sugar, I'm coming too. Jonah even promised me a place at the dinner table if I mind my manners."

She laughed then looked over at Ian and Braden. Jonah also looked questioningly at them.

"Braden and I are flying back to the States. We dug out the information on Gabe's sister. If Gabe was telling the truth, then she's probably in a lot of danger. I don't know how much contact Gabe had with her so I don't know how much, if anything, she knows, but we aim to find out."

"Need back-up?" Jonah asked.

"No, it's better if we do this alone. We want to attract as little attention as possible, and the last we heard, Falcon wasn't exactly welcome in the U.S.," Ian added with a grin.

"That's what happens when you blow shit up in Uncle Sam's backyard," Mad Dog murmured.

"Will you be okay?" Jonah asked, and to Tyana's surprise, he actually sounded concerned. Maybe her weeks in the hospital had resulted in a little male bonding.

Braden nodded. "Marcus has been monitoring our progress. We've only had one uncontrolled shift in the last three weeks. The injections seem to be working well, and we have the inhibitor as back-up, and in a worst case scenario, we have tranquilizers that would knock an elephant on its ass."

"All right. If you need help, you know how to reach us."

Tyana's gaze found Damiano, who had been quiet throughout the entire conversation. "How are you doing?" she asked softly.

Marcus slid his hand over Damiano's shoulder and squeezed in a gesture of support.

"Better," D replied. "I won't say great, but I'm working on it."

"We'll have plenty of time to work on it while you babysit me on the island," she consoled.

"I thought that was my job," Eli said as he slid his arm around her neck. He landed a kiss on her temple, and she scowled.

"Cut that shit out," she grumbled. It was embarrassing in front of all the guys.

He chuckled softly in her ear then leaned in closer. "If that makes you uncomfortable, I probably shouldn't tell you that Jonah has moved you and me to our own wing. I'll leave you to figure that one out."

Her cheeks warmed, and she fought the blush as it crept up her neck.

The entire room burst out laughing. She watched them in awe, her heart lighting up as the people she loved most in the world smiled and joked.

This...*this* was family. Her family. And that felt pretty damn good.

About the Author

Maya Banks is the pen name for Sharon Long, who writes for Samhain under both names. She lives in Texas with her husband, three children and assortment of cats. When she's not writing, she can be found hunting, fishing or playing poker. A southern girl born and bred, Maya loves life below the Mason Dixon, and more importantly, loves bringing southern characters and settings to life in her stories.

To learn more about Maya, please visit www.mayabanks.com. Send an email to Maya at maya@mayabanks.com or join her Yahoo! group to join in the fun with other readers as well as Maya: http://groups.yahoo.com/group/writeminded_readers.